MARIMBA

MARIMBA

RICHARD HOYT

A TOM DOHERTY ASSOCIATES BOOK
NEW YORK

MARIMBA

This book has been printed on acid-free paper.

A Tor Book
Published by Tom Doherty Associates, Inc.
175 Fifth Avenue
New York, N.Y. 10010

Tor ® is a registered trademark of Tom Doherty Associates, Inc.

Library of Congress Cataloging-in-Publication Data

Hoyt, Richard, 1941–
    Marimba / Richard Hoyt.
        p.   cm.
    ISBN 0–312–85193–6
    I. Title.
    PS3558.O975M33   1992
    813'.54—dc20   92–233
                                                  CIP

First Edition: July 1992

Printed in the United States of America

0 9 8 7 6 5 4 3 2 1

For Frank and Luis

Ogun kills on the right and destroys on the right.
Ogun kills on the left and destroys on the left.
Ogun kills suddenly in the house and suddenly in the field.
Ogun kills the child with the iron with which it plays.
Ogun kills in silence.

—reported by Ulli Beier in *Yoruba Poetry*

Pronounced *Aw-goon*

ONE

TO PLAY THE INSTRUMENT

Topper MacRae had an idea that sweet little Lourdes Martinez had something sweet to offer him on the 45-minute run back to the berth at King's Bay in Biscayne Bay, and his hands trembled as he turned to close the hatch door.

The 45-foot-long Striker hit a swell, and MacRae had to grab for the rail to keep from tumbling down the metal stairs.

From below, Lourdes said, "I take it you've got them all taken care of, Topper. They're on board and everything." By "they" she meant the 25-man crew of the American-owned, Liberian-registered, 5,000-ton freighter, fresh in from Venezuela—now floating serenely 15 miles offshore.

"They're all on board and coffeeing up. They're anxious to get drunk and laid when they get ashore, not necessarily in that order. Blondes. They all want blondes."

"And you got those things down there and marked? They're not going to get fouled up by seawater or anything?"

"Got 'em both. Watertight. Two hundred fifty keys each. Nobody but me and thee and a few fish have any idea where they are." He heard a musical instrument, a kazoo, competing with the churning 800-horsepower turbo-charged diesels and stepped into the engine room to find Lourdes naked. That is, most of her. In a conventional sense.

He said, "Whoa!"

Lourdes played another refrain on the kazoo. She sat spraddle-legged on the deck, knees wide. Her right side—that is, her right leg, exactly half of her torso, her right shoulder, and her right arm—was covered with motor oil. She had carefully done her face in the same manner: the right half of her forehead, nose, and upper lip; half her chin and throat.

A plastic oilcan with a capped snout lay empty on the deck.

"You didn't do that with one hand."

"Nope. Took two. Got rid of the mess on my left hand with that grease cleaner you've got in there."

Lourdes played a riff on the kazoo again, then sang:

I got a dog, and his fur is black
Pet him on the head, and you won't go back
Black, black, black
Pet him on the head, and you won't go back

Then she said, "You like kazoos, Topper?"

"Sure, I like kazoos."

"Do you like the oil, Topper? Exactly half of me. Wasn't easy."

"Sexy." She was showing pink down there. He could hardly take his eyes off her crotch.

She put the kazoo back in her mouth and played a different refrain while MacRae admired her half-and-half body. She removed the kazoo and sang:

My old black dog loves chewin' on a bone
Chewin' on a bone, chewin' on a bone
Bone, bone, bone
Loves chewin' on a bone

"Christ, do you ever look fuckable," he said. "You got a dog?"

"Everybody's got a dog, don't they?"

"And what's his name?"

She shook her head. "Marimba."

"Oh?" MacRae grinned. In Miami, marimba meant the

drug trade. Drug dealers were marimbeiros, marimba players.

"That's it. That's his name."

"Marimba? Really?"

"Yep."

"Is he a hound, or a chihuahua, or what?"

Lourdes shook her head. "A Doberman. Big old friendly thing. As nice a dog as you'd ever want to meet. Would you like to finish my back? I wanted to do a neat job, but I can't get my hands back there."

"Oh, hell yes." He grabbed for support as the boat plunged into another swell.

"Then why don't you grab another quart of 10–40 out of that box."

MacRae did as he was told.

Lourdes turned, knees wide, and leaned up against the wall with the palms of her hand. Her right leg was oiled, and one extraordinary bun. This was a Cuban butt, sensuously outsized, and exquisitely shaped. She had oiled the back of her arm and shoulder and neck too, but the oil line stopped short of her spine.

She flipped her mane of gleaming black hair. She looked back at him. "You like the back side too, Topper?"

"It's wonderful."

"A girl needs help sometimes. Run it right up my spine."

"Exactly half and half."

"That's it."

MacRae dropped to his knees. He poured some oil on his right fingers and finished the job, running a neat line up her spine and over the inside of her shoulder. The muscles of her back felt warm and delicate.

She turned around and resumed her original position, knees wide. She grabbed his crotch with her clean hand and begin kneading the nipple of her oily breast with her right. She squeezed him. "Does that feel good, Topper?"

"Yes, it does." Even with the racket of the storm he could hear her breathing.

She dropped her oily hand to her crotch, still gripping him viselike.

She liked it hard and fast. She pumped her hand with a frenzy.

She stiffened with a tremor. She gave him a hard squeeze. "Why don't you take that thing out of there?"

Oblivious to the oil on one hand, MacRae unzipped his jeans and did as he was told. He sucked in his breath at the warmth of her hand.

Lourdes Martinez surprised him. She pushed him back and grabbed his balls. She was upon his cock with her mouth, sucking with abandon.

He looked down on the sprawl of black hair and her back and rump, divided by the oil that ended exactly at her spine. One half of her was a deep purple, the other a gorgeous, pale *café au lait*. It was dramatic as hell. And sexy. Ooooohhhh!

The mistress of Marimba was good and evil, yin and yang, beautiful and . . .

Topper MacRae popped his nuts.

Lourdes Martinez's mother, Carmela Maria, was born on August 10, 1947 to Pablo Augosto and Josefina Maria Baerga in Matanzas, 60 miles east of Havana. Carmela Maria was the youngest of five daughters. To their dismay, Pablo and Josefina had no sons.

Pablo was a sergeant in Fulgencio Batista's secret police. Josefina and her mother and her grandmother were all priestesses, santeras, of Santería—the way of the saints.

It went without saying that Carmela Maria and her children would one day become initiates as well.

Captain Donald Fowler's armpits were great swamps of fetid sweat. He was in a crappy mood as he crawled into the passenger's side of the squad car. More gnawed-upon human bones.

This time a bag lady had plucked what she recognized as a human hand out of a garbage can.

A human hand. Dog bones!

Bones were biodegradable, dammit. If the lazy pervert had pitched them into the water, bacteria and bugs would have taken care of everything. As it stood, the fucked-PR manure was going to hit the fan on the evening news.

Sergeant Garcia eyed the rearview mirror as he backed the Chevrolet sedan out of Fowler's reserved slot.

Fowler sucked air between his teeth, a sound of resignation.

Garcia said, "They're gonna torch us tonight."

Fowler grunted. A noncommittal grunt.

Garcia opened his mouth to say something more, then thought better of it.

It occurred to Fowler that the light was yellow in south Florida. He remembered briefly the cool, blue light and the crisp, exhilarating air back in Colorado where he had grown up. On a day like this, the air that smothered Miami smelled like the locker room of a high-school gym.

Fowler turned down the volume of the squawk box so he could think a little. The Dade Metro Police Department had 73 cops on suspension, suspected of playing the marimba; Jah Ben Jah's followers were restless; and now this.

Seventy-three cops, 80 percent of the vice squad. Ten percent of the entire force. On the take to drug dealers! Reporters from the *New York Times* and the *Washington Post* were down to find out why. What was going on in Miami, they wanted to know. Naturally, the first person they turned to for the answer to everything was Captain Donald Fowler, aka Captain Drug Buster.

Well, no. Fowler was not the first. The first was Chief George Dersham, who was hip deep in the political quicksand of crooked cops, restless blacks, and gnawed-upon bones.

In the matter of scandals, Fowler had deduced that the public imagination worked in rhythmic trilogies: one, two, three, and you were out. Fowler didn't know if this had to do with the Holy Trinity, baseball, or ready-set-go, but one thing was certain: one of these cookers had to be snuffed *pronto*.

In recent years, blacks had cost Miami millions in lost tourist dollars because city officials had not kissed the ass of the Reverend Tutu when he came calling. As a form of contrition for snubbing Tutu, the mayor had gone so far as to proclaim a Jah Ben Jah day.

And the powers that be in the police department, Fowler among them, had backed off and watched as the politicians kissed the asses of Jah Ben Jah's white-robed followers. Jah Ben Jah. God, son of God. No modesty there. All the while, Jah had been casually ordering people murdered.

Now, with Jah on trial, his followers were bitching because the number of blacks in prison was out of proportion to the black population. Fowler didn't understand what they wanted.

No, the truth was he just didn't want to think about it. Let somebody else deal with it. He had a new find of bones on his mind—a human hand that had been chewed bare by canine teeth.

Sid Khartoum's Spanish was not good enough to keep up with the fast-talking Latins, and he did not speak their Indian dialects, but he was amused to hear, clearly, the name "Einstein" used in reference to his hair. They were calling him Einstein.

Khartoum was aware that he was quite a sight, a tall, quiet, solo gringo with wild—if not outright crazed—silver hair that cascaded across his shoulders in a tangle of wild curls and with an outsized mustache to go with it.

On top of the snarl and tangle of hair, Khartoum wore a light khaki desert hat of the kind associated with Brits in old war movies; floppy, with a flat, vented top and a brim to provide shade for neck, ears, and beak. His pilot's eyeglasses had thin black rims, at once sleek and efficient.

Khartoum wore a "Darryl's Horse's Ass Bar, Manzanita, Oregon" cotton T-shirt and a small backpack that was empty save for a Swiss army knife. His tattered Reeboks had seen miles. His blue jeans were slightly frayed at the cuffs.

In the Third World, neatness was at a premium. When you lived in a hovel, you wanted to look good. Judging by the movies, the gringos had everything. They lived forever in antiseptic cleanliness, and so could afford to be casual.

Despite his hair—evidence that he was too cheap or too lazy to get a haircut—Khartoum was no hippie traveler; the locals sensed that intuitively. He was utilitarian. A contrarian. Antifashion. He might have a Bohemian imagination, but he was no drifter or Peace Corps volunteer. He was there for a purpose.

He was either a spy or a smuggler. If he was a spy, he was there because of power and politics. If he was a smuggler, he was there because of cocaine. There were those among them who had helped the visiting Bolivians chop an airstrip out of the underbrush, so they knew his business. Sid Khartoum was a pilot. He played the marimba.

The West African beginnings of Santería, brought to Cuba by enslaved Yorubas, were organized around the vital path of the moral *ashe*, the blood of cosmic life. The divine current of *ashe* radiates the power of Olodumare, the unique king. Olodumare's *ashe* is refracted into the *ashe* of many *orishas*, or spirits.

The mystery and power of an *orisha* underlie all important activities in Yoruba life. There are some 1,400 *orishas* of the home and 1,200 of the marketplace.

As personifications of *ashe*, the *orishas* can be put at the disposal of human brings who honor them properly—these are *omo-orishas*, children of the saints.

Sid Khartoum took a walk down by the river where tiny women did laundry in shallow water that rippled and burbled and murmured over round stones on its way to the Caribbean. They looked up at him with large brown eyes as they beat their clothes against the rocks.

In the wretched poverty of this place and in the fears and dreams behind those brown eyes and others like them, Khartoum knew, lay the first faint notes of the marimba's disheartening music. But one had to listen carefully.

Khartoum checked the time. In a couple of hours, the Bolivians would be coming to drive him and his payload to the airstrip.

Khartoum knelt and stuck his hand in the warm water, then yanked it back immediately. Eight or 10 minnows less than an inch long had swarmed around his fingers, attempting to chew at his skin. Mostly they'd nuzzled the hair on the back of his hand; their ineffectual nibbling had startled rather than hurt him. Fish had to eat too; everybody had to eat. This was what everything came down to in the end, he supposed.

He walked up to the market at the edge of the village where the locals, many of them Indians, had gathered earlier in the day to sell produce from the backs of battered pickup trucks and carts pulled by donkeys and small, skinny horses.

Khartoum browsed among heads of white cabbage of a type that held up for weeks without refrigeration; a kind of purple-skinned sweet potato, board-hard when raw, but delicious when cooked; pale-green chayotes, a delicately flavored and abundant squash; small purple peppers that were said to be the hottest in the world; tomatoes hardly larger than golf balls; and light-skinned potatoes the size of marbles.

The little potatoes looked sweet and tender, and Khartoum had a momentary longing for the creamed peas and new potatoes his mother used to fix in the springtime. There were handsome watermelons in the market, but no lettuce; lettuce did not grow well in tropical heat, and there were no refrigerators.

It seemed to Khartoum that everything was small in that part of Nicaragua: the people; the fish; the vegetables; the donkeys and horses. It was the same at the places he had flown out of in Guatemala and Honduras.

As the sun fell lower over the jungle to the west and the market began breaking up, Khartoum bought a small watermelon that barely fit into his backpack and a handful of ripe tomatoes that he ate like apples as he returned to the lethargic village and his hotel, if it could be called that.

The tomatoes, however small, were delicious, unlike the pallid pretend-tomatoes, flavorless and hard as hockey pucks, that were picked green and ripened with gas before reaching American supermarkets. In Khartoum's opinion it was possible to throw a curve ball with one of those tomatoes, but they were hardly something anybody in his right mind would want to consume.

He went up to his room and stripped out of his sweaty clothes. The single chair had such rickety legs that he didn't chance sitting on it. He scooted the small wooden table over by his bed.

Other than the bed and the table, and the rickety chair that he couldn't use, the room contained a shard of mirror held in place by bent nails, and a chest of drawers with varnished veneer on top that curled up like dried mud; one drawer was missing, and a second was without knobs. The chest of drawers was base for the room's single small fan.

Strawlike material leaked out of one side of the lumpy mattress that was marred by pecker tracks and amoeba-shaped stains from sweaty bodies of sleepers past. The pillow, so thin it could hardly qualify as such, was likewise filthy, but Khartoum was no stranger to the Third World and over the years had learned to make do.

In fact, Khartoum preferred such a room to the sterile barrenness of a Holiday Inn or Best Western, which to him had all the soul of Moonbase Alpha. He sat squat-legged on the bed, his back to the window for light. He tightened a knob to prevent the fan from sweeping to and fro, and aimed it directly on his sweaty torso.

He got out his reading glasses and the copy of the *New York Times Book Review* that he had brought with him from Miami. He was interested in this particular issue because it featured reviews of three books dealing with drug traffic and the war on drugs.

He put the watermelon on the table, split it, and cut the heart into manageable chunks. Squatting there on the filthy bed in the languorous heat, air beating against him, he read the book reviews.

Khartoum speared and ate sweet chunks of watermelon as he read, savoring the taste. Surely it was the best watermelon he'd ever eaten. He wiped his mouth with the back of his hand.

He still had some time left. He got out his Macintosh laptop and began working on his report for Sheridan Harnar. Well, "report" or even "journal" didn't quite cover his assignment. What Harnar had in mind was something more than that—more on the order of a literary letter from the marimba. Harnar wanted facts, yes, but also texture. Primary rather than secondary sources.

This was a challenge that especially appealed to Khartoum, although Harnar had had no way of knowing that when he hired him. Khartoum often fancied that if he had it to do all over again, he would have become an anthropologist rather than a spook or soldier of fortune. But fate had decided otherwise. In Khartoum's opinion, the best anthropologists, those who were remembered and therefore made a difference, did their damnedest to grip and hold their readers with an affecting narrative. Margaret Mead came to mind, although many of her judgments were later challenged.

Khartoum was determined, as much as possible, to live among marimba players from Latin America to Miami. He would watch, not judge, although a recommendation was part of his contract with Harnar.

Khartoum dug at a bug bite with his fingernails and smiled, remembering a poem from his youth:

> *Rooty, toot, toot!*
> *We're the girls from the institute.*
> *We don't smoke, and we don't chew.*
> *And we don't go with boys that do.*

Khartoum supposed that most of the authors of the books on the marimba reviewed in the *Times* almost surely lived in that tidy, righteous, if possibly uptight, institute. They were not to be blamed for that especially; they did not have Khartoum's experience or the backing of Sheridan Harnar.

Of course Sid Khartoum was not his real name at all. His real name was James Burlane, long since sacked from the Central Intelligence Agency by DCI William Casey. Burlane now worked the field for Mixed Enterprises, an imaginative firm comprised solely of himself and Ara Schott, a former director of counter-intelligence at Langley.

James Burlane tapped the button on the plastic mouse with his forefinger and opened a file. The cursor went *blink, blink, blink,* waiting for his next command.

Luis Fernandez cut the 50-horsepower Johnson outboard to an idle. He was studying the lovely aqua water for a likely spot for yellowtail snappers, although just what made one place better than another five miles offshore was bewildering to James Burlane.

Although they were officially after yellowtails, Burlane and Roberto Guzmán would have been satisfied with anything Fernandez found. They got out their pipes and lit up a pinch of sticky green—wonderful pot—leaving the decision of where they should fish to Fernandez, whose boat it was and who knew what he was doing.

Burlane had always thought chumming was the practice of scattering bait on the water to attract the fish to a general area. But chumming for the elusive and wary yellowtail was different.

Fernandez opened three plastic buckets, one with ground-up fish entrails and heads; one with a sort of horse feed—kernels of corn, oats, and wheat—and one with sand. He took several handfuls of ground-up fish and flopped them in a fourth, empty bucket, then added equal amounts of grain and sand. These he kneaded like bread dough.

"What is this?" Burlane was impressed by Fernandez's alchemy. Guts, grain, and sand.

Fernandez looked amused. "You never chummed like this, Khartoum? You never fished before? Where'd you say you were from?"

Burlane said, "Oregon, originally. Asia lately."

"Oregon? Where in Oregon?"

"Portland, most recently."

"Ah, Portland. Lots of rain, eh?"

"West of the Cascades, but that's only a third of the state."

"The Cascades?"

"Mountains. We've got mountains and ocean. Desert too."

Fernandez said, "I don't know what you call chumming in Oregon, Khartoum, but here, when you want to catch yellow-tails, this is what you do." He took a scoop of goo and formed it into a ball, patting it smooth. He stuck his thumb in the ball and inserted the hooked piece of squid with a lead weight just above the hook, then packed the ball tightly again. "First, you wrap this sucker."

He began wrapping his line around the ball: six times, he changed directions; six times, he changed directions; six times, he changed directions. Finally, he was finished; the ball and its hidden hook and weight were wrapped with fishing line.

He dumped the wrapped ball overboard and kept the bail of his spinning reel open. The line peeled away as the chum ball was swept to the northeast by the current. A cloud of melting sand followed its descent.

He said, "Yellowtail are almost impossible to catch any way but this. They'll see that stream of sand melting away and get curious. They follow the chum ball as it disintegrates. They get right up there on it. They watch all those edible goodies peeling away, and maybe they grab a kernel of corn and a bit of fish guts or whatever. No problem. No harm done. But when they see that beautiful bit of succulent squid, they can't resist. Then, at the last second, they figure why not? See that?"

Burlane certainly did.

Fernandez's line began peeling off the bail extra fast.

"Watch." He popped the bail closed and yanked on the rod. He grinned. "Got one on. See what I mean? This is chumming."

Guzmán, eyeing Burlane from the corner of his eye, said, "It's the same reason the drug war is so stupid."

"Oh? How's that?" Burlane watched Fernandez reel in his fish.

Fernandez, grinning, swung the wriggling yellowtail aboard. The fish was close to a foot long. "What do you think, a keeper?"

"Looks good to me," Burlane said.

Guzmán said, "Nice fish, Luis!"

Fernandez removed the wriggling yellowtail from his hook and pitched it in the ice chest.

Guzmán said, "You figure the squid for coke, Khartoum. An edict has been sent forth: no more eating squid because once you start eating it, you don't want to eat anything else. In order to catch the offending squid eaters, the cops are out there pretending to be yellowtails. Only yellowtails with no appetite."

"But no such fish exists."

"Exactly. But the public has been led to believe that day after day the cops're able to swim around and ignore the grain that's peeling off the chum ball without ever once taking a sample."

"The grain is prohibited as well, I take it."

"Prohibited, but not as bad as squid. You know how appetite works."

"Everybody has to eat."

Guzmán said, "Everybody eats, yes, but rules that apply to ordinary yellowtail don't apply to police fish. You have to remember that. Right, Luis?"

"They're above the rules," Fernandez said. "Unaccountable." He started forming another chum ball.

Guzmán said, "So eventually they say why not? What the hell? It's in their nature. They can't help themselves."

"They go for the squid," Burlane said.

"That's why seventy-three Dade Metro cops are being investigated for taking marimba money. The psychology of temptation is simple enough. It's at the heart of a sting. The cops flash a few goodies in front of the fish. They throw out a little bait at first, then bigger and juicier goodies. It's chum they're offering. They chum for marimbeiros. You have to be careful if you play the marimba."

The stocky, muscular Guzmán, with a great mane of curly brown hair and a solid nose, had a Mediterranean look about him. His eyes were arresting because they were an unexpected pale blue-gray. He had six gold chains roped around his neck and a diamond stickpin earring in his left ear, high drag for an undercover agent of the FBI's Organized Crime Unit.

The slender, brown-eyed Luis Fernandez at six feet was tallish for a Cuban, and was not fond of gold chains and stickpin earrings. Serviceable sneakers, blue jeans, a striped T-shirt, and a Los Angeles Dodgers baseball cap were good enough for him. Fernandez was undercover for the Drug Enforcement Administration.

Fernandez dumped his new chum ball into the water and watched it sink, trailing sand and grain and guts.

Burlane was aware that Guzmán and Fernandez were both watching him carefully—judging his reaction to their chumming story.

Thus fisherman very likely watched fisherman.

Fishermen certainly watched fish.

Fish kept his eye on the chum.

The *orishas*, or spirits, have the ability to teach properly trained priests, *santeros*, and priestesses, *santeras*, the way things were in Ile-Ife, the original world that radiated outward from a single palm tree. When a *santero* faces a problem in the here and now, he consults his *orisha* to find how the spirits in Ile-Ife once resolved a similar situation.

One's relationship to an *orisha* is deepened through sacrifice, *ebo*. When an *orisha* is given a gift of plants or animals, he or she is disposed to offer gifts in return. Without the *ashe* of the *orishas*, humans would destroy one another. Without *ebo*, the *orishas* would die.

Vida para vida.

Life for life.

4

It was buckeroo time. Yahoo time. The DEA's Luis Fernandez had made it past the last Coast Guard checkpoint, and was now cruising safely across Biscayne Bay.

Miami was two miles dead ahead.

Fernandez kept the fuel-injected, turbo-charged eight-cylinder Mercury engine on 5,500 RPMs, which turned about 90 miles an hour, and the cigarette boat slammed *ka-ba-ba-ba bump, bump, bump, ka-ba-ba-ba bump, bump, bump,* over the water.

The Anglo pilot Sid Khartoum had gotten a kick out of the 30 miles an hour that Fernandez had coaxed from the 50-horsepower Johnson on his fishing boat. He'd have to show Khartoum what real speed was all about. Get him in the right frame of mind, and maybe Fernandez would learn something.

The pale-yellow Caribbean moon reflected off the cherry-red, 36-foot-long fiberglass hood of the cigarette boat.

Beside him the incredible Marta Martinez, glistening black hair streaming in the wind, was all teeth and brown eyes, and warmth.

Fernandez thought *coño*, what a sexy little bitch! Was he ever going to get laid when he got to Miami! That is, assuming

Marta didn't find out that most of his alleged cargo of 1,500 keys of *perla blanca* cocaine was bogus.

He held the bucking boat under control with his left hand and slipped his right hand under her shoulder and over her breast. A rock-solid little number. No bra. Her nipple was hard.

Marta pretended to be shocked. "What on earth are you doing?"

The boat zoomed *ka-ba-ba-ba bump, bump, bump.* Fernandez massaged the tight nipple with the palm of his hand. "You like fast cars too?" He bet she did. He bet her sister Lourdes did too, not to mention her brother Eduardo and Mima Martinez, the matriarch of the clan.

Marta turned to free her nipple, then snuggled closer. She said, "Two can play that game." Her hand strayed to his crotch.

Her body felt wonderful. But the hand! Oooo! He grinned. "Ay! What're you doing there?"

"You don't like that?"

"Good girls don't do that. And what if I should run into something?"

"I don't have to be a good girl all the time, do I? And we're not in any parking lot. Nobody to run into out here." She gave his crotch a peremptory squeeze.

"I'll give you six weeks to stop that, you little witch."

"You said something about fast cars. What kind of fast cars?"

"Oh, I don't know. Jaguars, say."

She squeezed again, harder. "Jaguars?"

"Ay, *cojónes*! Sure, Jaguars. Would you like a Jaguar?" He figured what the hell; it was a government Jaguar, not his. If the Martinez family was doing what he suspected . . . ay, *Dios*!

That hand! That hand!

Marta smiled. She had beautiful teeth, did Marta. Would she ever like a Jaguar! Jaguar was the magic word. Or one of them, at least.

The mention of the car had really turned her on.

A wave pitched her on her side.

She got up, giggling. She was determined to finish the job. She grabbed his belt buckle again.

He could hardly believe it. He said, "*Quieres singar aguí afuera?*"

Marta began unfastening the buckle.

* * *

Roman Catholic priests assigned the task of bringing New World slaves into the Vatican's far-flung flock were practical as well as pious clerics. They assigned Biblical saints to this or that *orisha*, although they couldn't match the hundreds of spirits of Yoruba lore.

With the addition of Christian saints to the religion, Hispanic Cubans became increasingly attracted to Santería, and by the late nineteenth century there were both white santeros and large, growing communities of white believers on the island.

A hundred years later, it was not unusual to see Cuban-Americans of Spanish ancestry wearing large, wooden Santería beads in fashionable shops and restaurants or coming and going from the Miami airport.

5

Señora Josefina Baerga, trying in vain to bear her husband a son, made Carmela Maria wait until she was 19 before she assigned her an *orisha*. When she did, she shocked everyone by giving her Ogun, the hunter and protector, a temperamental *orisha* traditionally assigned to a male.

Tradition called for a santero, not a santera, and it was widely concluded that poor Josefina had let her desire for a son get in the way of common sense.

For her part, Carmela was thrilled to have Ogun as her *orisha*. She loved the passionate Santería rituals, especially on those occasions, such as *ebo*, or the giving of sacrifice, when she opened her mind and cleared her heart, and Ogun descended upon her.

She loved the Spanish term *"la santa montada."* The saint mounted.

She was as a horse.

Ogun the rider.

Then the rider went further.

He entered her.

Ay!

And they were as one.

On these occasions, Carmela's possession by Ogun was so

very exquisite, so sweet and wonderful there was no expressing it in any language understood by humans. She did not just walk with him or talk with him as the Christians did with Jesus.

No. She *was* Ogun. *Became* him.

She traveled as one with Ogun on the *ashe* to Ile-Ife, and learned the ways of the *ara orun*—the people of heaven.

In January 1960, three months after Carmela Maria finished her nine-month apprenticeship to become a full-fledged santera, Pablo Baerga—fleeing the certain retaliation of Fidel Castro on those who had done Batista's bidding—packed himself and his family off to Miami, and settled in Hialeah.

Carmela was too much in love with Ogun to settle for a boring flesh-and-blood husband, and for the next six years devoted herself almost entirely to the ecstasies of serving Ogun and other *orishas*. But she was lonely still, and Ogun advised her to marry Marine Gunnery Sergeant José Martinez, whom she met at a *mesa blanca*, a form of seance in which believers breach the world of the *orishas*.

She gave birth to a son, Eduardo, in 1969, and a daughter, Lourdes, in 1972; she was pregnant with her second daughter, Marta, when her husband was killed in El Salvador in 1974.

Following José's death, the widow Carmela Martinez, struggling to support her family, plunged herself into Santería with renewed passion, and in due time became one of the most famous and powerful santeras in the Miami area. There were her detractors, who said her fierce love of Ogun was bound to cause trouble for her, but Carmela attributed this to envy by small people.

When Mima was around believers, she ordinarily referred to her main *orisha* as Ogun. When she was with Cuban Catholics, she called him Santiago. When she was with Catholics and Protestants who did not know the way of the saints, or when she as joking with her family, she sought the cooperation of St. Peter, the name given Ogun by the Catholic priests.

It was Ogun who originally encouraged the impoverished widow to enter the drug trade and live comfortably for a change. Ogun was riveted by the startling white of the cocaine. White was ordinarily the color of the animal to be offered in *ebo*. Sacrificial white. White doves. White roosters. White goats.

To protect the Martinezes from harm in their new venture, Ogun told Mima to buy a Doberman, which she should name Marimba. He should be black as ebony, but with handsome white teeth.

And when it was time for *ebo*, Ogun descended unto Marimba and mounted him, entered the dog as he entered Mima.

Ogun *became* Marimba. *Was* Marimba.

Mima knew what Marimba wanted.

What Marimba wanted, Marimba got.

Vida para vida.

As the matriarch of the Martinez clan turned 40—by then called Mima, for mama, by those who knew her—she was prosperous from the marimba, being protected from the law by Ogun's special dog.

Having all the pocket money she might require, Mima looked into the mirror one day, and, seeing a younger version of her mother, began to worry that the passing years would curse her with her mother's *párpados*—sagging, baggy, eyes—and so consulted the *orishas*.

The *orishas* were practical-minded, as she knew they would be. They told her to find a plastic surgeon.

"*Contra!*" she told her daughters. "If you're fat, you diet. If you've got crooked teeth, you get 'em straightened. If you've got bags, get rid of the things. Teeth or bags, what's the difference?"

Mima passed on the surgeons for people with budgets, going directly to the best. She said she wanted to look more like the actress Natalie Wood, to whom she had been told she bore a superficial resemblance, and requested a butt like the actress Sissy Spacek's.

In the end, although Mimi would not admit it, she fell short of being Natalie Wood's double. She did resemble the actress in a vague sort of way, but the warmth and vulnerability and fragility of Ms. Wood's face was somehow lacking.

Even so, when Mima Martinez went strolling down Miami Beach in a thong bikini, smooth-skinned Sissy Spacek behind twitching this way and that, there were few males in sight with a standard dose of hormones who did not covertly scope her form.

Lourdes said the retooled Mima was so sexy maybe mother and two daughters should rotate parts. "*Carajo!* Marta and I wouldn't mind having a turn sitting around all day watching soap operas and counting hundred-dollar bills."

Eduardo gave his mother a sexy whack on the rump. "You know what they say, Mima. Vice is nice, but incest is best."

Mima slapped him playfully and laughed. "A happy home is the blessing of St. Peter."

6

Mima Martinez didn't like it that Marta had breached the rules of the family's established business practice on her date with the marimbeiro Luis Fernandez.

Marta knew better, and Mima didn't like it one damn bit. She said, "If he was running fifteen hundred keys you should have told us. We take the opportunity when it presents itself. As it stands now, we have no idea if he was running *perla blanca* or not."

"Mima, he opened a key. It was good stuff."

Mima rolled her eyes. "Opened a key! One key? Who picked the key to sample, you or him?"

Marta said nothing.

"What if he was a cop? Answer me."

"Oh, Mima."

"Don't 'Oh, Mima' me. You let him buy you off with a stupid car. What's one car compared to fifteen hundred keys? Besides, you already have a Ferrari. What do you need with a Jaguar? We have a system. It works, and we have to stick with it."

"I was thinking Eduardo could do his thing the next run."

"The next run! Ay! The next run we could all be in jail. I

don't care if that car does sell for forty thousand dollars. There's no telling who's owned it before. We all have a part to play. We know our parts."

"Yes, Mima."

"We follow the score to the note. We are not jazzmen. We do not improvise. If we improvise we get into trouble. And this marimbeiro. What's his name again?"

"Luis Fernandez."

"Fernandez. I don't want you making any more runs with him. In fact, I don't want him making any more runs at all. Period. I want you to bring him home to meet your mother whether he makes another run or not. You're a proper young lady. It's about time I saw him for myself."

"Yes, Mima. I'll bring him home."

Lourdes said, "Marta knows she shouldn't have done it, Mima. Eduardo says he can get rid of the car with no problem. Right, Eduardo?"

"*Sí*," Eduardo said. He used a toothpick to dig at a bit of roast pork stuck in his molars. "I can move the Jag in a couple of weeks. I know a guy in Seattle. Maybe I won't get forty thou, but it'll be a clean piece of change."

Mima said, "We do not go our separate ways, Marta."

"*Sí*, Mima."

"A few simple precautions is all I ask. You and Lourdes are supposed to be college students. When you drive your Mercedes or Ferrari, use a parking garage. If you're going to the beach or somewhere where the garages are likely to be full, take the Yugo, that's what it's for."

Lourdes made a *yuch!* face.

"It's cute, Lourdes."

"Tinny little thing."

"Nobody's asking you to use it all the time. Which reminds me, I want you to keep the top up on your Mercedes when you're tooling around Miami. What's the point of tinted windshields if you drive with the top down? Use your air-conditioning."

"Mima!"

"You can lower the top when you drive to the Keys or to Fort Lauderdale or Palm Beach. Is that asking too much? Really!" Mima was finished with the subject of automobiles. "Now model your dress for us, Marta."

Marta turned before the wall mirror, looking at her profile.

She wore what looked like a translucent blue tube; her breasts threatened to spill over the top, and the bottom ended just below her buns.

Eduardo reached over and pulled the top of her dress out a couple of inches and let it go, snapping her *whap!* on the breast.

"Ay! *Come mierda!*" Marta massaged her boob with her hand.

Lourdes said, *"Tu eres bobo!"*

"It stretches. I thought so," Eduardo said.

"Of course it stretches. How else would it stay on? Let me try snapping you on the tit."

"How does that work? Do you sort of roll it on and off like a stocking? Do you have underwear on under there? What do you do, just pull it up and bend over? You can do it in a closet, I bet. Knock off the preliminaries."

"Come mierda!"

Eduardo lit a Marlboro and took a drag, exhaling the smoke slowly. "I'd still like to know whether or not you're wearing underwear."

Marta, laughing, grabbed her purse and threw it at her leering, grinning brother. "How do you like the dress, Mima?"

Mima studied her daughter's provocative backside. *Mmmmmm.* "I think it's a cute outfit, Marta. And very, very sexy. Turn around again. Show it off a little."

"Show off a *little?*" Eduardo whooped.

Marta, glaring at her brother, turned around again.

Mima laughed. "Well, I suppose as long as you aren't breaking any law."

Eduardo, turning serious, said, "I don't think we'll have any problem with Marta getting arrested for her dress, Mima. But I do think we have a real problem with Marimba's appetite. How long can we keep this up?"

Mima bunched her almost-Natalie Wood face. This was not a subject she wanted to talk about any more than Marta had wanted to talk about her date with Luis Fernandez.

"We can't keep it up, Mima. We just can't. He'll just have to be satisfied with something else."

Mima said, "He must be fed, Eduardo, so we'll feed him. And please don't talk to me about changing his habits. Cravings can be hard to kick."

"But Mima . . ."

"I don't want to talk about it, Eduardo. I mean it. We have to have him, and that's that. We know what he likes. He requires it. We will get it for him."

"Mima, are you sure we have to have him? Really sure?"

"The *orishas* teach us *vida para vida*, Eduardo. It is what *ebos* are all about. We give Ogun fresh blood. In return, Ogun gives us life. Through Marimba, he protects us."

"Mima!"

Mima raised her chin slightly, a signal she was finished with the subject.

7

Sergeant Garcia turned right on the ramp at Eighth Street and drove west on Route 41, which followed the Tamiami Canal. This route from Miami through the Everglades to the Gulf Coast of Florida was known as the Tamiami Trail.

"They'll be asking what kind of a place is this when a couple of kids can't go for a bike ride without running into the bones of drug dealers."

Donald Fowler said, "Oh, yeah. They'll love it."

"We got half the force working on it. What do they expect?"

Fowler sighed. What they expected was everything, right now. To make matters worse, the hand found by the bag lady, identified by a fracture line on the left little finger, had once belonged to Topper MacRae, a Dade Metro cop working undercover in Biscayne Bay. This was something the department was attempting to keep under its collective Stetson.

In a couple of minutes Fowler and Garcia spotted four squad cars parked on the shoulder of the highway, along with a car Fowler recognized: it belonged to a *Miami Herald* police reporter. No tube people yet, thank God. Three cops were at the highway keeping gawkers from jamming up traffic.

The cops were all waiting for Fowler. They needed his permission to move the bones. Garcia parked behind one of the squad cars.

Donald Fowler walked leisurely along the shoulder, then squatted on the gravel beside Bill Sanderson, a potbellied police reporter from the *Miami Herald*, and looked down at the water's edge.

In the deep grass, he could see part of a skull and the end of a smallish bone. A rib? And the rounded curve of a joint or large knuckle. Some of the previous bones had been hacked or sawed; they all had been gnawed upon by the teeth of a large canine.

Since the police had bones and not skeletons, they had no precise way of knowing how many victims were involved in the six finds, although the forensics people said there were seven. This would be find seven, victim eight. Or victims eight and nine. By estimating the rate of deterioration of the bones, the medical examiner said the seven prior killings had taken place over a two-year period.

Detective Hodge, a first-rate tech man, was on one knee, examining the bones. Hodge looked up and saw Fowler with Sanderson. "If you'll give me a second, Captain. We've got just about everything we're going to get."

"Take your time."

Sanderson finished scribbling notes in a spiral notebook. He said, "Well, Captain Drug Buster. Too bad the dogfood killer hadn't struck before "60 Minutes" did their piece on you. Morley Safer would have run with it. Did the killer eat his victims and give his dog the bones, or was this strictly a dog-food operation? Was the killer any good at cutting meat, or an amateur hacker?"

Sanderson took a drag on the Marlboro that never left his lips, squinting as the smoke curled past his eyes. He said, "Maybe the bodies had so much cocaine in their blood, the dog got addicted to that? It isn't the meat so much as the wonderful seasoning." He laughed soundlessly. "I remember a television ad when I was kid. 'Dr. Ross dogfood tastes doggone good. Woof! Woof!'"

Fowler wondered how long it would take for the tube people to join the circus. "Tell me something, Sanderson. Just why in the hell is it you guys always write about drugs? Drugs this. Drugs that. Never the specific kind of drug. Wouldn't it be more accurate to say cocaine, if cocaine was at issue? Or marijuana, if we were dealing with pot? To be honest, I've never understood that."

Sanderson looked surprised. "Same reason we use ''Canes' instead of 'Hurricanes.'"

"And what reason would that be?"

"'Canes' counts four and a half in a headline. 'Hurricanes' runs to ten. Not good at all. Too wide. Not impossible, but not good. Can't say anything if one word hogs all the space."

"What?"

Sanderson grinned. "Short words fit more easily into headlines. Some letters are wider than others. In the lingo, *jflits* are skinny. *Whammies* are fat."

"And a jflit is?"

"The letters *j*, *f*, *l*, *i*, and *t*. They each take a halfcount of space, so they're skinny. The letters *w* and *m* count one and a half. They're fat. All others letters are one each. You add a half count for capitals."

"Ahhh."

"Thus heroin with a lower-case *h* counts five and a half points. One point each for the *e*, *r*, *o*, and *n*. Half a point for the *i*. Alcohol runs six. Tobacco and cocaine each run six and a half."

"Shit!"

"Marijuana requires an impossible eight counts, hardly space left to say anything else. Drug with a lower-case *d* is a tidy four."

"Hence the word of choice. Fuck accuracy."

"I'd make book that the length of the word is the chief enemy of people who want to legalize marijuana," Sanderson said, lighting a new cigarette. "Drugs and 'Canes. An apostrophe is a half count, by the way. A space between words counts one."

"What about 'minorities'? Wouldn't 'black' be shorter and more specific than 'minorities'?"

"Shorter than 'minorities,' yep." Sanderson furrowed his brow. "Problem is we can't do it. Can't call blacks blacks all the time because they want to maintain the fiction that they don't have shit because of blanket prejudice by whites against all nonwhites. Blacks fucking up doesn't have anything to do with it. So we're stuck with 'minorities.' 'African-American' is flat-out impossible."

"Jesus!"

"Jesus counts five, Captain. Short words go far. 'God,' dog spelled backwards, counts just three and a half. No fucking wonder He's had such a run. Note that we don't call Him Jehovah or Yahweh—six and six and a half respectively. The devil's a tidy four and a half. Beats Lucifer, six counts, or Satan, at five. Now then, what can you tell me about the dog-food killer?"

Fowler gave Sanderson a sardonic grin. "Not a bunch."

"Another drug dealer?"

"The others were."

"So you think this will be too?"

"Maybe. Probably, even. But we don't know now. We'll have to check 'em out."

"Maybe a crooked cop killed them. Plenty of suspects there."

Fowler snorted.

Hodge looked up at Fowler. "You can come on down now, Captain."

Fowler hesitated, wondering where to step.

"It's okay, we've checked the slope. Nothing but the kids' prints."

Sanderson called down to Hodge. "What'd he do, throw 'em off the shoulder?"

Hodge didn't answer. He studied the bones, massaging his chin with his hand.

Fowler started to pick his way down the bank to where the bones lay: a human skull, four human ribs, one human femur. A skull with teeth offered the possibility of identifying the current victim through dental records.

Hodge said, "Uh, Captain! I think we better keep the public out of here for the moment. It's always possible we could still come up with a footprint."

Fowler, annoyed, turned to find Sanderson just behind him. "You want to wait up here until we finish? Jesus Christ!"

"Hey!" Sanderson stopped, looking offended.

"We're trying to conduct an investigation. Do you mind?"

Sanderson minded, but he retreated to the edge of the shoulder and scribbled another note.

Fowler reached the bones.

He looked at the tooth marks on the skull. The animal that

had done that was one hungry son of a bitch. "Fuck!" Fowler muttered.

Sanderson laughed. He called down, "Fuck is direct and to the point and only runs three and a half—that's why it's a classic—but we can't use it on account of the Christians."

Fowler shook his head. "Where the hell they come up with clowns like you, Sanderson?"

"Corpus Christi, Texas. Covering Texas cops. Cops're the same everywhere. Editors know that."

Fowler heard a car door slam and looked up. The first of the tube people had arrived.

Roberta Warren, a pretty young woman with auburn hair, called down, "Captain Fowler! Can we come down, Captain Fowler?"

Fowler wanted to correct her and say "may we" but didn't. It was asking too much that a television reporter be literate. Literacy was not required for these petty ringmasters charged with keeping the action moving. They would report the facts with serious faces, but behind the mask of gravity lay their real delivery, which Fowler mentally translated as:

Yowza! Yowza! Yowza! Look at this, everybody. This is one for the books. The asshole who's been butchering human beings and feeding them to his dog has done it again. Two teenagers found a skull this time. With incredible, deep teeth marks all over it. Isn't this wild? Can you believe it? Look at this. Over here in this ring. Yowza! Yowza! Yowza!

Behind the yowzas, in the dark recesses of the public psyche, lay the insidious, subliminal fear that made this a real story, and Fowler knew it. This was the region of the limbic, and the reporters, reckless, played it to the limit:

It could have been you, couldn't it, TV watcher? Maybe it will be. Maybe you'll be next. Maybe you'll step into some shadows on your way to buy a quart of Dairy Maid milk or a jar of Hellman's mayonnaise, and this giant canine with chiseled fangs will leap GRRRRROWWWWWWWWWWW! *from the darkness and* CHOMP!

Fowler said, "We'll be up in a minute." He knew she wanted a nice tight shot of the skull, teeth marks and all. If he could prevent her from getting it, and if he was lucky, the restless Jah Ben Jah followers would take up most of the time on the evening news. They were Chief Dersham's responsibility, not his.

"Is there any reason why not?" she asked.

"I just don't want you down here. This is a simple matter of decency. These bones are the mutilated remains of human beings. I can't imagine their families would want them displayed on the six o'clock news for the entertainment of the public."

"Human beings in the plural?"

Fowler sighed. "I have no way of knowing yet. Maybe just one, I don't know."

"How is anybody going to recognize those bones? You have to find out who they are before any relatives can have their feelings hurt. These are bones, Captain. It isn't like they're complete bodies."

"They're human bones. No."

"Think, for heaven's sake."

"I said no, and I mean it." Fowler didn't want those teeth marks on the tube.

Warren, cameraman at her side, strode determinedly along the edge of the highway in her high heels. She stopped and looked back him, her mouth tight. She continued, long legs scissoring.

Watching her, Fowler's mouth turned dry. A truly pissed-off woman was not to be trifled with. Now what was the silly bitch up to?

She stopped again. She looked back. Her eyes narrowed. She called, "The canal belongs to the public, Captain Fowler," and plunged down the bank, high heels and all, her cameraman close behind.

Fowler knelt quickly by the bones, blocking the cameraman's new angle.

, She gestured with her hands as she told the cameraman what she wanted.

"Now what?" Fowler said. He kept his face toward the bones and away from the camera.

Hodge shrugged. "Beats me."

Hodge watched the cameraman pan from the squad cars to the ditch. He said, "He got squad cars in the picture. Big deal."

With a twist of his wrist, the cameraman moved in on the kneeling Fowler.

Softly, Hodge said, "Stay put, Don. You've got the fucker blocked."

Fowler held his ground, pretending to examine the bones.

Warren yelled. "Hey, Chief! Chief Fowler!"

Forgetting the bones, Fowler turned.

The cameraman, grinning, held tight on the tooth-scarred skull.

Warren held her fist high. "Got that action with sound..All right!"

The dismayed Fowler hadn't been able to help it; there had been media speculation that Mayor Paul Hernandez would soon replace the besieged Chief George Dersham with Fowler.

Sanderson, who had watched the action, laughed lustily, another Marlboro lodged between his lips. He removed the cigarette. "The wonderful world of television. They make you, and they break you, eh, Captain Drug Buster?" He broke into a falsetto. "And reporting live from human doggie bones found along the Tamiami Trail, here is Roberta Warren."

Hodge narrowed his eyes. "Shut the fuck up, Sanderson."

Sanderson looked hurt and gave them a flagrant limp wrist. "Swearing at a reporter is like slapping an enlisted man. Didn't you know that? Oh, my, yes. You know what happened to General Patton in Sicily. You brutes!" He giggled. "Sadists."

8

Ever since he'd snubbed Bishop Tutu, the black community in Miami had made life rough on Mayor Paul Hernandez. Now, with the Dade Metro Police under siege on charges of corruption, and with Jah Ben Jah's followers still demonstrating in front of the courthouse, two undercover cops—one Dade Metro, the other DEA—had been found with their bones gnawed on by some son-of-a-bitch's dog.

The cops on the take were Chief Dersham's responsibility, and there was nothing Hernandez could do about the bones except wait for Dersham's man Captain Fowler to somehow deliver.

In response to black discontent, Hernandez's media man, Ron Torberg, had advised him to give Jah Ben Jah some public strokes. He said blacks loved public gestures and attention as much as they did overpriced basketball shoes and ghetto blasters, and nearly as much as they liked raping and killing one another. Torberg was a bigoted scumbag, but he knew the media.

Give Jah a day, Torberg had said. Present him with a fancy scroll at City Hall. Let the blacks get dressed up in their colorful outfits and parade and make passionate speeches; indulge their love of hyperbole. This infantile but necessary game was transparent to everybody but the blacks, poor sons of bitches.

Torberg said Hernandez had to understand that the media were his friends, not his enemies. The local stations would see to it that the blacks got to be on TV. It was the function of television, not the cops, to calm racial unrest.

Torberg recommended that Hernandez act according to an Arab proverb that holds that while all truths are good, not all truths are good to say. Such a taboo was logical; if you can't change something, then shut your mouth. Tell them what they want to hear.

Hernandez thereupon announced a Jah Ben Jah Day, in which the Great Man was to be honored for his wit and wisdom, benevolence, and service to community. The mayor issued this decree without taking the simple precaution of first checking with the cops to make sure everything was on the up-and-up.

At the time, Hernandez actually believed the horseshit he had been told about Jah. He had actually fallen for the politically correct, that is, ass-kissing profile of Jah in the *Miami Herald*.

Jah Ben Jah told his flock, and anybody else who would listen, that the African culture they had been screwed out of was based on a solid family: mom, dad, kids. He admonished his followers to lay off drugs; they needed to learn the values of thrift and hard work. What a wonderful man was Jah Ben Jah!

The cops, it turned out, were *at that very moment* gathering information for a grand jury indictment of Jah and 16 of his aids and assistants on charges ranging from peddling drugs to extortion and murder. It was like City Hall was located in Miami and the police department—with a communication link of Dixie cups and string—was on the fucking moon.

Police chief to mayor.

Mayor to police chief.

Do you read me? Do you read me?

Mierda!

If Hernandez had had any brains, he would have figured it out.

Now, too late, the prosecutors were telling him that crack cocaine, rather than thrift and hard work, had paid for Jah Ben Jah's six Rolls-Royces. The prophet's henchmen, on his instruction, had murdered 13 people. A lawyer had told the judge that Jah's 11 common-law wives, none over the age of 16, were the

Great Man's due as a Christian prophet. As proof, he provided the court with a list of ambiguous quotes from the Bible.

As Hernandez saw it, there were two basic strategies for political survival:

One was to dig in at the local level, a big frog in a small pond, and stay there, using IOUs and favors to guarantee reelection.

The second was to hop quickly from one office to the next before news of your ordinariness caught up with you. You aimed for a quick strike at the U.S. House or Senate. There, unless you had public sex with a dog or took the wrong position on abortion or gun control, the rules written by Congressional incumbents all but guaranteed reelection for as long as you wanted. This was universally acknowledged as the best deal in all politics.

Voters loved to watch the blossoming of public images, but once the petals were blown away by the hard wind of truth, they turned to other, more enchanting flowers.

Mayor Hernandez opted for the quick-rise gambit, knowing all the while that one biggie screw-up could scuttle his career.

He couldn't help but feel a bit sorry for Chief Dersham, but was careful to quash useless sentiment. Public sympathy for someone on his way out was dangerous. Dersham's snug position on the political sled, what the Russians called a *droshka*, was not automatic. It had to be justified. Hernandez called this position phenomenon The *Droshka* Effect.

If the wolves got too close, they had to be placated and the *droshka* lightened for more speed. As the man in charge and so responsible for the entire sled, Hernandez would have no choice but to push Dersham off the back. The psychology of changing baseball managers applied to police chiefs. Dersham was associated with the old. The public, easily bored and ever craving drama, had appetite for the new.

The offering of political meat had to be exquisitely timed. Hernandez had to judge the strength and determination of the pursuing wolves. Only when a sacrifice was absolutely necessary, and not before, should he offer a victim. This required a delicate balance between the need to maintain public and department morale and common sense.

To push Dersham too soon was to risk public backlash.

To push too late was to risk being consumed by the wolves himself.

9

Chief George Dersham's blood sugared and his mouth turned dry when he got Mayor Hernandez's lengthy note outlining the possible consequences of letting the dog-food killer remain at large.

Dersham had the same gaunt, hollow-eyed, slightly distracted look that General William Westmoreland had developed after years of futile pursuit of the Vietcong, and for much the same reason. In the absence of a possible clear-cut military victory, Dersham was asked to pursue limited objectives in the war on drugs. Instead of supporting him and his troops wholeheartedly, a large, vocal portion of the public believed the entire exercise was costly bullshit that had robbed them of their civil rights.

When he was younger and had vision and ideals—plus a touch of swagger to his walk—the media had been in love with him. Then, it had paid to be on Dersham's side.

Now, many of his most passionate allies were having second thoughts—including Hernandez. Dersham was in danger of being tarred by those two awful, ugly words: old and loser.

Dersham's colleagues once openly envied him for having a

hot-looking, big-titted redhead for a mistress. And he had secretly relished their jealousy. The comfort of Charmain's tits and the feeling of her powerful thighs wrapped around him had been such joy.

Now, Dersham had to be careful Charmain wasn't used against him. When the moralists were turned loose, he knew he was doomed. The public would forgive him for dipping into petty cash or allowing cops to take legal shortcuts to obtain evidence. But his getting to play with his lady's wonderful tits was a perk that was unforgivable to people who were unwilling to publicly admit that playing with a redhead's tits was fun.

The balding Dersham, lately given to girth, knew of Captain Fowler's ambition to replace him, but could never admit it publicly without exposing weakness.

The same was true of the tiny red lines that mapped Dersham's face. Was he perhaps a touch fond of the bottle? Dersham complained about his skin. The tropics really weren't the place for someone with skin like his. Never were.

If investigation of corruption in the department had in any way eroded his reputation, Chief Dersham was determined to appear oblivious. His strategy, always, was to push forcefully onward as though he was ensconced at the front of what Hernandez called the political *droshka. He* would decide the timing of his departure, not some flashy, angle-playing Cuban like Paul Hernandez.

But it was true, Dersham had to admit, that the media wolves were closing fast on the Mayor's overloaded, under-powered *droshka.*

Hernandez's note gave him fair warning. If Dersham didn't stop the madman who was feeding people to a dog, he himself would wind up food for canines.

Dersham knew there were all kinds of phobias: fear of spiders; fear of snakes; fear of heights; fear of enclosed places. There was *cynophobia*, fear of dogs; *hemophobia*, fear of blood; and *necrophobia*, fear of death.

Dersham was convinced he had a touch of all three.

Was there a special Latin word for fear of being eaten?

A fear of teeth.

Razor-sharp incisors ripping flesh.

Whiiiiiite teeeeeeettthhh!

10

James Burlane had postponed rearranging his cramped balls for several minutes when he felt a peremptory itch. This was no time for scratching.

The ram's horn in front of Burlane controlled the altitude of the aircraft, much like a joystick in a video game. He kept the airspeed at a steady 90 knots an hour, just above stalling.

Burlane stared at the instrument panel, keeping his eye steady on the altimeter and airspeed indicator and on the radar that gave the plane's position.

When you were 50 feet above the Caribbean, you had to keep your eyes on the altitude and airspeed. And Burlane didn't want to get his leg caught in the throw line that tied the duffel bags together or have the autopilot malfunction and put him in the drink.

Fifty feet was well below the Coast Guard radar. They had improved it, but still there were limits. If you had good equipment and were careful and stayed cool, calm, and collected, you could do it. In the old days, he had been told, these were easy runs, and a pilot could fly at 500 feet with no sweat.

Now, with the war on drugs, a pilot had to stay hard on the water.

The reflection of the yellow moon scooted across the water below him; the shadow of the D-18 Twin Beech rushed across the chops. The sea was clear of fishing boats and other vessels, as far as he could tell.

Dead ahead, a pinpoint of flashing light.

He piloted the Beech toward the light until he could see the silhouette of the waiting cigarette boat.

As he passed over the boat, Burlane tapped the button that launched the duffel bags seaward, and, gaining altitude, banked northeast for the short run to the Miami Airport.

He followed the air controller's instructions and circled the airport twice before he was given permission to land, sandwiched between an incoming United Airlines Boeing 747 and a Delta Airlines Lockheed 1011.

Burlane climbed into his Jeep Cherokee in the covered long-term lot. The Cherokee was filthy with accumulated dust and crud, and dented in several spots. The ugly ding in the windshield had been put there by Burlane himself to depreciate the vehicle in the eyes of thieves.

In the back of the Cherokee were four air conditioners, one on its side, together with two greasy starter motors and a radiator fan. Judging from the missing knobs and rusted, dented bodies, the air conditioners were on their way to be scrapped. In fact, they disguised Burlane's three Mixed Enterprise safes, which were secured to the rear floor.

In the first: weapons, munitions, and diving gear.

In the second: high-tech cameras, mikes, and intercept equipment.

In the third: transmitters and receivers for coding and encoding secure communications.

In the fourth: nature guides and manuals and Burlane's Macintosh laptop.

The starters and radiator fan were worthless crap.

Burlane drove to his apartment in South Miami Beach, located on a peninsula across Biscayne Bay from Miami proper.

On the way, he turned on the radio and tuned to the news. It seemed the Jah Ben Jah uproar had momentarily been replaced by the story of more human bones being found, apparently gnawed on by a dog. In this latest case, two teenagers had come upon a skull and other, less dramatic bones on the edge of the Tamiami Canal.

11

James Burlane worked on his report for Sheridan Harnar, then, with more than an hour to kill, decided to walk up Ocean Drive past his rendezvous point and double back by the beach. If he was clean, he would meet Ara Schott in the News Café as scheduled. If he was dirty, they'd shift to their alternate.

He set off for his rendezvous with the sun low in the west, behind the rooflines of the colorful art deco cafés and hotels facing Ocean Drive. The wind felt cool against his face, and the humidity was mercifully low.

Owing to the litter of beer cans, bottles, and paper bags, South Miami Beach had the appearance of a carnival on a Sunday morning. In a festive inspiration, the sidewalks had been painted a light purple, but it was now faded and splotched by squashed chewing gum, rendered black by the passing of feet. The blackened splotches were everywhere; except for the dog turds in Amsterdam, Burlane had never seen anything like it. Had the sidewalks ever been cleaned? How many years, or decades, did a wad remain?

Burlane turned down Fifth toward the ocean. He paused before the window of License to Spy, an establishment that sold clandestine listening devices, antibugging gear, equipment to detect phone taps, parabolic mikes, and—the ultimate assurance for the wary—a television set with a transparent chassis.

This was the kind of gear Burlane had once been issued by the Company—and still received via Ara Schott, who maintained connections in that redoubtable enterprise. Burlane wondered how many cities in the U.S. had a retail market for spook gear. How many customers used a credit card? And why had the enterprising owners chosen to spell it *licence*, which made them appear to be boneheads, rather than *license*? Was it clever or hip to be illiterate? Was there an in-joke there that Burlane did not appreciate? Perhaps *licence* was the way the Brits spelled it, and so suggestive of James Bond and his gadgets.

Beyond the shop, a mammoth demolition crane was reducing an entire block to rubble. Twenty or 30 people on the sidewalk stared transfixed at the virtuosity of the black man in the crane. Working levers coolly and methodically with a bored look on his broad face, he swung the ball *ker-unch, ker-unch* upon wood and cement.

Burlane crossed Washington Avenue. On the corner was Roosevelt Ivory's 5th Avenue Gym. The 5th Avenue was famous, the place where Muhammad Ali had trained for some of the biggest fights of his career. Here, under the watchful eye of Angelo Dundee, Ali had perfected his legendary ability to float like a butterfly.

It saddened Burlane that the gym was almost entirely boarded up and looked empty. Was it abandoned? Next up for the demolition ball? He stopped. He had heard something. Voices? For a moment he thought voices were coming from a single second-story window that was unboarded. Then he heard the slapping, a faint slapping as though from a jump rope hitting the floor. Or had he?

He continued on his way. Perhaps it was the spirit of the unstoppable Ali, still in the 5th Avenue, immortal, his jump rope *slap, slap, slapping*.

He turned the corner onto Ocean Drive and headed north. He skirted a camera crew, pausing to look up at an entire wall of magazine covers in a studio located just above the sidewalk. Rows of pretty girls stared out from the covers of *Cosmopolitan*, *Vogue*, and *Glamour*. When they didn't shoot indoors in Manhattan, New York's fashion photographers adjourned to Miami Beach. They never strayed far from Ocean Drive, which had everything they needed for background: good light, outdoor cafés, colorful art deco architecture, palm trees, a beach.

In order to get the most dramatic light, that is, the sun at an angle rather than straight above, the RVs, containing clothes, makeup rooms, photographic gear, and diminutive darkrooms, assembled on Ocean Drive and its side streets early in the morning or late in the afternoon. The Xtacas, Pathfinders, and Highwaymen parked end to end, sometimes taking up an entire block.

Burlane couldn't see the beach from the sidewalk, owing to a hundred-yard-wide park across Ocean Drive—a long narrow strip that flanked the street. The park was divided by a meandering sidewalk set out in long curves for the enjoyment of those who wished to stroll or skate or cycle on something other than the hard rectangles of city streets. There were benches where one could simply sit and enjoy the ocean breeze, and open spaces for the kite flyers who gathered in the late afternoon.

The News Café was, Burlane had repeatedly been told, *the* watering hole of choice for the hip in-crowd that frequented Ocean Drive.

The young men among the patrons, a few of them perhaps gay, affected an air of casual masculinity, as though they were auditioning for a spot in a Dockers' trousers ad. The young women knew what they had to show, and showed it. She who had tits showed tits. She whose butt turned heads wore trousers that were too tight.

Burlane had to watch he didn't trip on the step up to the bar level. He knew the place was supposed to be romantic, but he couldn't imagine why. Maybe because the bartenders and most of the self-assured patrons were too young to have been disillusioned. He hoped to find a good-looking yet soulful woman, perhaps an adventurous marital refugee from northern climes.

As Burlane had instructed, Ara Schott had gotten an inside table away from a window. In fact, he had snagged the best one, in a corner, the gunfighter's position, but Schott looked somehow very ungunfighterish with his long, thin nose, eyebrows in the form of an inverted *V*, and sharp cleft chin.

Despite Burlane's amused suggestion that Schott should adopt a hang-loose look for the rendezvous, he certainly didn't look like a tourist. He wore his usual costume, blue jacket, light-gray shirt, dark-gray trousers with a sharp crease, and polished, black, wing-tipped oxfords. His mix-and-match clothing was in fact bought by his sister in Philadelphia, who did all his shopping.

On this occasion, he had added a touch of daring and wildness with a tie of muted red-and-green diagonal stripes.

That Schott found hanging loose difficult was made even more obvious by his archaic crew cut. He wore short, mowed hair because it was pragmatic, not because it was associated with the military.

Burlane plopped down, his back to the wall, and surveyed the room.

Schott licked his lips and looked around. "Is it, uh, okay?"

"What do you mean, okay?" Burlane looked puzzled.

"I mean for us to talk and everything."

Burlane laughed. "Oh, hell, yes. Do you think I'd be here if there was someone following me? For Christ's sake, Ara! Give me a break. Have you found out if Guzmán turned in the run I sold him?"

"Yes, he did."

"How did it test out?"

"It was cut ten percent with speed."

"It was pure cocaine when I flew it out of Panama."

"Guzmán's work?"

"Who else? The government doesn't have any idea how pure it was when it was loaded. Guzmán's square with the weight, but takes a nick on the purity. Who's to know the difference?"

"He's just a little bit crooked."

Burlane smiled. "He's a nibbler, Ara. A kernel of corn here. Some oats there."

"Huh?"

"Never mind. I wonder what he does with his money? Do you suppose you can make some discreet inquiries for me, Ara?"

"Sure. You know, James, the people in the Bureau think Guzmán's one of their best agents. He's got a superb record of busts."

"Why not, if he wants to keep his job."

"Do we tell them now? When?"

Burlane shook his head. "There's plenty of time for that. I don't want anybody yanking him in until I've had a chance to learn more. The more he's interested in me, the more I find out about him. You know, Ara, what I need most is a direct link to Banda-Conchesa himself. Any cop worth his salt would be all over me if I was one of Conchesa's pilots, wouldn't he?"

"A person would think so."

Burlane grinned. "Well, let me tell you, old partner, fortune shineth upon Mixed Enterprises. Word gets around. Just two flights for the Bolivians, and I've been invited to Chetumal to talk business with a Colombian gentleman named Manuel Lopez, who is Banda-Conchesa's nephew. You may remember him from the Medellín list Harnar gave us."

Schott grinned broadly. "He's a Medellín regular!"

"Yes, isn't it sweet. The Colombians obviously've been watching me—sort of like baseball scouts assessing minor-league players. I think I'm about to be called up to The Bigs, Ara."

"You be careful, James. Harnar says you must be careful. You must take all precautions. And you know I agree. If you think you've been burned, you should withdraw immediately. Without hesitation." Schott gave Burlane a firm, no-nonsense look.

Burlane rolled his eyes. "You and Harnar've been watching too many movies."

"Bullshit too," Schott said. "Pay attention to what the man has to say."

"What about the coke I sold Fernandez?"

"The DEA says he turned it all in."

"Cut?"

"One hundred percent pure."

Hmmmmmm. "I don't think there's any doubt Luis is straight, but he's also disappeared."

"Oh?"

"Gone for several days now. Guzmán says he probably followed his snake north. Chased a blonde to Seattle or somewhere. He'll show up grinning, he says. What do you say we eat?"

"How can you eat at a time like this?"

"Why, I'm hungry! A person's gotta eat, Ara. Doesn't

matter how many chislers and disappearances are out there, people being fed to a dog, life somehow stumbles on."

Schott said, "You know, they call this place the News Café, but they don't have much in the way of magazines or newspapers. There are more magazines in a drugstore back in Maryland."

Burlane laughed. "People don't come here to buy magazines, Ara." He followed Schott's eyes to the sidewalk outside. "Those are all models. This is a mecca for fashion photographers. They're out there every day, everywhere up and down the street. Enjoy!"

"I hate this place. You have to drive forever to find a bookstore, and they almost all stock best-sellers and how-to titles. I like the musty smell of used books. Besides, I hate the traffic."

"You're trying to tell me there's no traffic in Washington? Ara! A little time in Fort Lauderdale won't hurt you. Harnar given you some good contacts, has he?"

"Oh, yes. Whatever I need, I can get."

Burlane thought about it. "You know, it doesn't make sense to overuse police contacts if part of my job is to give Harnar a sense of how many cops might be crooked. Harnar may be doing his best to help us, but he lives in Virginia. How can he be sure a particular cop in Miami is safe?"

"He can't."

"In Miami if you drive shit, you are shit. Marimbeiros can't bring themselves to drive old beaters. They just can't. You don't have to be a cop to find the registered owner of a car, do you? In most states, a license plate and a few bucks for a fee is all you need."

"Same here."

"I want you to do as much as you can without the use of cops, including checks of license plates. And when you do that, I want you to use one of your fake IDs."

"Got it."

"Crooked cops won't like assholes like us coming down here asking unwanted questions. I don't want any trails leading back to us."

A beauty walking by on the sidewalk caught Schott's eye, and he nearly did a double-take. "Dammit, I want to go home."

Burlane said, "You don't like girls? What's happening to you, Ara?"

"Come on, James."

"If you flashed a Rolls and had a yacht, you could have them two or three at a time."

"Aw, James."

"Sure you could, you know it. Sex is what the marimba is all about. You believe Jackie Kennedy married Aristotle Onassis because he was a good-looking stud? Ara! Marimba bucks make the players all mini-Onassises. They can earn in weeks what would otherwise take years, screw the consequences."

"I'll pass."

"You know, Ara, the problem now is to prove my Sid Khartoum *bona fides*. They say Lopez likes to put would-be Conchesa pilots through fun little tests."

"Fun little tests?"

"To prove we are who we say we are. But hey, you're talking Sid Khartoum here."

12

James Burlane met Manny Lopez at a sidewalk café on a broad avenue that led to a lovely park along the Gulf of Mexico. This part of Chetumal was clean and prosperous; Burlane understood why it was popular with tourists, especially Belizians and Mexicans seeking free-trade prices on television sets and electronics gear, which Chetumal offered.

The wary Bolivians had paid newcomer Sid Khartoum $2,000 a kilo for each of two 1,200-key flights. Lopez said he would pay Khartoum $2,500 a key for a full 1,500-key run from an airstrip carved out of the jungle in north central Nicaragua. Khartoum was to dump it to a boat waiting 20 miles off Islamorada in the Florida Keys.

"There is plenty of money for everybody, May-jor Khartoum. There is no reason not to treat your pilots right. No reason at all. *Coño!* If you can't get your crop to market, it rots in the field. Is that not correct?"

"I agree entirely. Not to mention that it's my ass in the slammer if I get caught."

"Not to worry, May-jor. Not to worry. If anything happens, we will see that you are taken care of. We have our connections in the United States, you may rest assured. They only paid you two thousand a key? Really? I find that hard to believe."

"That's it."

"Two thousand a key is *mierda*. I'm surprised that you accepted."

Burlane shrugged. "I had to start somewhere."

Lopez shook his head. "And they didn't even give you a full load! *Maricóns*."

"I suppose they didn't trust me entirely."

"Fair is fair, May-jor. But that's in the past. Now, you are working for the best. Professionals. You may be sure of it. You do professional work, you will be rewarded."

The South Americans had been charging marimbeiros in Miami $28,000 a kilo before the Gulf War diverted attention from the cocaine traffic, and the price plunged to $17,000. A few marimbeiros had hoarded at the higher prices and had gotten stuck.

But now, with the heat back on, the price had risen to $25,000 and was holding. More dealers were landing in jail, but the Colombians didn't care. Nothing had changed for them; they simply moved less coke at higher prices.

According to Sheridan Harnar's numbers, there was far more profit in crack than toot; a $25,000 key of pure cocaine, ballooned sufficiently with soda to form crack, brought a middleman $50,000 to $60,000 in the ghettos. Kids on the street doubled their money for every gram they moved.

While he approved of a $500-a-key raise, Burlane felt the Colombian was uncomfortably vague about the length of the runway.

"It is plenty long. *Grande. No es problema*, May-jor Khartoum." Lopez had a tough time handling the English *j*.

Khartoum said, "I need three thousand feet for a reasonably safe takeoff. Twenty-seven hundred at a minimum."

Lopez said, "We will have it measured, May-jor. We are Colombians, not Bolivians. If more jungle has to be cleared, we will of course have it done. Men with machetes are cheap in Nicaragua. *No es problema*."

"I'd appreciate it."

"Word of your reputation precedes you, May-jor. They say you have *cojónes grandes*. Big balls." Grinning, he grabbed himself by the crotch.

Burlane said, "I get paid to do a job, I do a job." He thought:

> *To market, to market, to buy a fat pig*
> *To market, to market, riggedy jig.*

TWO

THE FEEDING
OF MARIMBA

13

James Burlane could hardly believe it when he first saw the dim outline of the airstrip in the late morning haze. What the hell was that? He was supposed to land on that?

No es problema? Es bullshit too!

It was a screw-up. Had to be. He rechecked his bearings on the Loran.

No! This was it! This was the place.

The crude strip hacked out of the forest was maybe 1,700 feet long, 2,000 at the longest.

Burlane refused to return to Mexico with his tail tucked between his legs and plead for a longer runway. That was not Sid Khartoum's way. Burlane had to go in.

He circled twice to build up his nerve. Then, with sphincter tight and heart thumping, he went for it. He nearly clipped the tops of trees, but made it, bouncing wildly down the crude path before he lurched to a stop two yards in front of a wall of trees and tropical underbrush.

He took a deep, grateful breath and climbed out into withering heat and humidity.

Lopez, laughing, piled out of a Toyota Landcruiser to meet him. "May-jor Khartoum! May-jor Khartoum!"

Señor *Gringo Cojónes*, laughing, had won the first round. He triumphantly tapped his crotch with his forefinger. "*Besame la pinga!* I thought this strip was going to be twenty-seven hundred feet at a minimum? *Hijo de puta!*"

As Señor Lopez was fully aware, landing was one thing; gaining the airspeed necessary to take off was something else. Lopez said, "If you like, I can have my people chop some more brush for you, May-jor." He half grinned, his lizard eyes saying:

Okay, May-jor Khartoum, let's see if you're as crazy as everybody says. You speak softly and swing una pinga grande. Is that mierda or is it real? Landing is one thing. You got cojónes? Let's see 'em, gringo.

Burlane needed 2,700 feet minimum to clear the trees at the far end of the runway. But 1,700 to 1,800 feet? No, no, no.

He remembered watching a television documentary on the Gulf War in which the battleship *Wisconsin* launched remote-controlled spotter planes to find targets for its 16-inch guns. The spotter planes—halfway between large model airplanes and Piper Cubs—had video cameras in their bellies.

A large rope net was mounted on the *Wisconsin*'s stern. The controller slowed it down and drew its nose up into a stall and snuffed the props. *Ker-plop* into the ropes! Such clever American sailors.

He considered the trees at the end of the ridiculous runway. The bushy treetops offered a cushion of sorts, although perhaps not as good as the net on the *Wisconsin*.

Burlane thought: *All right, you little Colombian cocksucker. You want to see Sid Khartoum flying, I'll show you Sid Khartoum flying.*

He said, "Naw, I'll pilot that mother out of here the way it is."

Lopez looked in disbelief from the plane to the end of the runway. "Are you sure? I can have it cleared. You can leave tomorrow night. It is nothing. There is plenty of rum and *muchachas* back in town."

"The deal is for tonight, Señor Lopez. Tonight it'll be. But anything I fuck up because of those trees, you get to replace."

"Oh, *sí, sí.* It goes without saying. I am good for it."

Burlane, watching him, said, "You mean Conchesa is good for it."

"Ah, well, May-jor." Lopez wanted everybody to know he worked for The Man himself, but would never say so directly.

"The next time, I'll want a proper runway. This is *mierda*, and we both know it."

Lopez looked surprised and concerned. He said, "Oh, *sí*, May-jor. *Sí, sí. Por supuesto.* The next time it will be longer."

An hour later—Lopez had said he would need an hour—Burlane waited for Lopez in a sleazy bar that doubled as a brothel. He'd ordered a beer and a plate of red beans and rice; no sense facing those trees on an empty stomach. It went without saying that Lopez would be late.

Burlane tried not to think about the short runway. While he waited, he listened to Hispanic men shouting in unison on the jukebox, guitars hammering—rather like mariachi out of control. Burlane assumed he was guilty of cultural bias; the prostitutes seemed not to mind.

Should Burlane include a whorehouse scene for Harnar's edification? Yes, he thought he should. These women were willing to do Khartoum's bidding for the equivalent of three U.S. bucks. Burlane didn't believe a critic of the marimba could fully appreciate the meaning of the music without listening to the full song.

One scantily clad hostess, about four foot ten and 150 pounds, had dyed her black hair blonde, with disconcerting results.

Two of the ladies had gone for the more common red-headed look. One had a tattoo on her shoulder and a thin white scar across the top of one of her almost almond breasts; the other, with investments in mascara companies judging from the layered black paint around her eyes, had huge, glistening red lips.

The third prostitute, the youngest, in her early twenties, was also the best looking. Her rump had not turned to blob and she had extraordinarily long, eye-turning nipples, dark brown and spikelike, that she displayed by wearing a filmy wisp of a bra. The nipples poked right out there, saying: *Hey, gringo, have you ever seen anything like these? Can you imagine these numbers rock-hard and scraping against your chest?*

The ladies performed their duties as hostesses either behind the building, where stalls hardly larger than closets lined an alleylike courtyard cluttered with old tubs, or upstairs in a regular room, which cost more.

Lopez arrived. Burlane was fed, with his gear stowed in his backpack.

Lopez said, "Ready for it, May-jor Khartoum?"

"If you are." Burlane rose, tipping his hat to the women. "Do have a good evening, ladies." He wanted them all to remember the inimitable Sid Khartoum.

He bowed to the one with splendid nipples, a low, graceful bow. Had he world enough and time . . .

He laid one of Harnar's benjies on the bar as a parting tip. A hundred bucks was *nada* to Sid Khartoum. "Split this among the ladies," he said with a wave of his hand. *"Qué bellas muchachas!"* He thought it was far easier to lie in Spanish than in English.

Behind him he heard the nippled one say, *"Buena suerte,* Major Khartoum."

He turned and gave her a wink. He thought it was not without logic that luck was a feminine word in Spanish.

Burlane followed Lopez out to his four-wheel-drive Toyota Landcruiser. Burlane tossed the pack into the rear; the wok lashed to the outside banged on the metal floor. The Colombians would be looking for Khartoum to lug a wok around; ergo, Burlane had a wok strapped to the back of his pack.

Lopez, who knew what it was, said, "What's that on your pack?"

"A wok." Burlane closed the rear door and started walking around to the passenger's side.

Lopez opened the rear door again. He thumped the bottom of the wok. "To cook on?"

"Of course to cook on. We have windows to piss out of."

"It's black."

"That's because I use it all the time."

Mmmmmm. Lopez didn't understand men who liked to cook. Women cooked.

Burlane said, "You can fry, boil, or steam food in a wok. Take your pick."

Lopez shut the rear door. "A kitchen in one instrument, then."

"You can use a wok over any kind of burner or over charcoal. All you need is a wok and a Swiss army knife and you can cook anywhere. Food from all cultures. Perfect cooking for one or for a banquet. New recipe each time out, simple and straightforward, mix or match, depending on your mood."

"Beans and rice?"

"Sure, beans and rice. Blessed are the Chinese. Forgive them gunpowder, for they gave us the wonderful wok, the best cooking tool in the world."

Lopez started the Toyota.

14

They set off on a butt-numbing ride down a road with a
pothole every foot, or so it seemed.

Burlane said, "You know, Señor Lopez, woks never
caught on in Europe and the United States because there's too
much money being made hustling unnecessary pots and pans.
Next time I'm down, I'll stir-fry snook and chayote à la
Khartoum for you. A beautiful combination. Plenty of garlic in
the oil and a hit of salsa to finish it off."

"No soy sauce?"

"If you lug soy sauce and sesame oil around with you,
you're missing the point. The idea is to match the wok's
efficiency with whatever food you can lay your hands on. An
elegant simplicity. It's okay to buy food, but if you can score it
wild it's even more soulful."

Khartoum the wok-man was easy for Burlane to pull off; he
liked to cook, and he wasn't bad at it.

Burlane's heart slumped when he saw the top of the high
canopy at the end of the runway. True, the trees were silhou-
etted by stars. And yes, peasants at the far end started waving
flashlights as soon as they saw the Toyota's headlights.

Burlane glanced from the flashlights to his D-18 Beech sitting in the moonlight. Ho, ho, ho.

Crap. Maybe Harnar was right. Maybe he and Ara had over-extended themselves. That is, maybe *he* had over-overextended *him*self. Ordinarily Burlane survived on confidence. Without an unshakable belief in himself, he'd be out of business.

Failure was no disgrace. Lack of balls was. He had to call Lopez's bluff. Or at least he had to try.

If he destroyed the plane, word would get back to Colombia as well as Miami, and his Khartoum cover would make him what he wanted to be: one of Banda-Conchesa's regular pilots.

All he had to do was survive.

Flashlight in hand, he walked to the plane, confidently, with a long, casual stride. He checked the low-point fuel drain for water in the fuel, squinting his eyes as he did. He examined the oil level in each engine, and then all the control surfaces. He checked the landing gear to make sure it was sound.

Burlane said, "I'm ready, Señor Lopez. If you can load 'em up."

In Spanish, Lopez ordered the duffel bags loaded aboard the Beechcraft. Each duffel bag contained 50 kilos of cocaine; each kilo was eight-by-four-inches in size and wrapped twice, first in transparent plastic, then in brown paper, and sealed with light-brown tape. The Colombians had packed Styrofoam around the kilos so the duffel bags would float, and then waterproofed them with a blue elastic rubber coating.

They packed 48 such duffel bags in position behind the cargo door. The door, to be operated by the pilot, was located halfway between the cockpit and the tail.

"If you could tell your people to aim their beams at the tops of the trees there. The ground won't do me any harm."

Burlane stepped up into the cockpit with a wave of his Sid Khartoum mane. He turned on the ignition and went through the drill of inspecting the instruments: was the gyro working? Was the compass okay? Did the fuel pump and the mags check out?

He took a deep breath and popped the engine. He sat there with it idling, staring at the stupid flashlight beams waggling to and fro on the top of the bank of darkness at the end of the runway.

He revved the engines. Foot hard on the brakes. Revved them to 2,700 RPMs.

Revved them higher still.

Then, eyes on the tops of the trees, red-lining the engine, he released the brakes.

The Twin Beech jumped and bounced down the crude runway.

Ka-bump! Ka bump!

Too big a bump would pitch the D-18 forward on its nose. Shit!

Burlane held his breath.

Ka bump! Ka bump!

He clutched the stick tightly, his eyes, unblinking, still on the trees. Mouth dry.

Ka bump! Ka bump!

Stick back, engines blasting, the plane lifted.

For a moment, Burlane thought, *Wait a minute, I can make it. I can.*

Then he knew otherwise.

He stalled the plane, nose up.

He snuffed the props.

Losing speed.

Falling.

Trees coming.

Ohhhhh shhhhiiiiiiiiiit!

Burlane braced himself . . .

15

James Burlane's left forearm throbbed with pain, and his left cheek and jaw burned. Although it hurt like hell, his arm was just badly bruised, not fractured. He touched his face with his right fingertips. Ouch! He'd lost some skin on the side of his face, but nothing seemed broken there either.

Below him in the darkness, Lopez's people shouted in Spanish as they ran toward him.

He unsnapped his safety harness with his right hand. As he did the plane shifted slightly. He stood, holding the top of the seat with his right hand. The plane shifted again.

He sat back down and resnapped his safety harness. He bounced up and down in the seat. The plane shifted, then held.

He bounced again.

The plane was stable.

He unfastened the safety harness.

A light flashed through the windshield.

From below, Lopez shouted. "May-jor! May-jor! Are you okay, May-jor?"

With his right hand, Burlane popped the door open.

He was pinned by beams of light flashed from below.

"I'm fine. I have a bruised arm and a bloody cheek but other than that I'm okay."

On hearing that, Lopez and his companions began laughing and babbling in Spanish. The insane gringo pilot was alive.

Lopez yelled, *"Hombre loco!"*

"Mierda! Can you get me down from here?"

"Not tonight, May-jor. It is dark, and you are in the top of a mame tree. You will have to wait until daylight so we can see what we are doing."

"Aw fuck!"

"We are very sor-ree, May-jor," Lopez said.

"Maricóns!"

They laughed. They didn't mind him calling them faggots in Spanish. He'd earned the right. He was now one of them.

James Burlane, having thus proven his Sid Khartoum *bona fides*, spent the night on top of the tree in high spirits despite an aching face and sore arm.

Burlane sat in the open door the next morning with his swollen arm in his lap and legs dangling. The Colombians gathered at the base of the tree to assess the task before them. It took them two hours to climb the ree and lower Burlane with a rope looped under his armpits.

He climbed back into Lopez's Toyota, and after some obligatory pissing and moaning about *mala suerte*, Lopez admitted he had been impressed by the virtuoso, if perhaps crazed, display of Sid Khartoum's *cojónes*.

Burlane said that, by God, a deal was a deal. The D-18 Twin Beech was 40 years old, but it was the only plane he had, and he had kept it well maintained. Lopez owed him a new plane. A decent model, too. Banda-Conchesa could afford it. No way Burlane was going to swap a perfectly good, dependable airplane for a piece of shit.

Lopez kept his word about replacing Khartoum's plane. Banda-Conchesa sprung for a King-Air with twin-turbine jet-prop engines. Conchesa also saw to it that the King-Air was fitted with an automatic door and ejection device far superior to the one on the Beech.

* * *

On the drive back from the airport after his first run in his new King-Air, Burlane listened to the radio as usual, turning the dial until he settled on public radio station WAXY 106, where none other than the Colombian drug baron Guillermo Pena de la Banda-Conchesa was being interviewed on his ranch outside Medellín. The session with Señor Banda-Conchesa was being simultaneously telecast on Miami's public television channel.

The interviewer referred to Banda-Conchesa as "Don," the Spanish equivalent of "Sir." Don Banda-Conchesa? The interviewer was rowing his boat with one oar; Guillermo Conchesa was in charge of the latest incarnation of the Colombian cocaine cartel.

Burlane had to admit the Colombian sounded like an amiable, perhaps even jolly, Satan on the radio, speaking serviceable English sprinkled with American homilies. He was a tease, obviously having a good time with the interviewer.

Don Conchesa said he was a businessman who dealt in a commodity. Simple as that.

Thus inviting the answer: "Cocaine, Don Conchesa?"

Conchesa, laughed, *ha, ha, ha, ha!* "Cocaine? Oh, no, no, no. Coffee! Coffee, señor. I have coffee in the mountains. Haven't you heard the American commercials for 'Rich Colombian coffee'?" Rrrrrrrrolling the *r*, Conchesa imitated the mellow voice-overs of the commercials.

"The American secretary of state says you inherited the Medellín cartel from the Gachas."

"Yes, you Yankees got the poor Gachas and Manuel Noriega. You had to invade Panama to get Noriega. Look at what all that cost you. Billions of dollars. The Colombian government allowed American troops to kill Colombians on their own soil and try Colombians in American courts—may all Colombians hang their heads in shame.

"And what did it accomplish, all that flexing of Yankee muscle? *Nada*, señor. It accomplished *nada*. You Americans claim to believe in the marketplace. Let the market do it, you say. This is your political ideology. Here, you have created a black market for cocaine and complain bitterly about the results. Do the intelligent thing for once. Eliminate the black market, señor."

"And how would that be accomplished, Don Conchesa?"

Conchesa laughed, *ha, ha, ha, ha.* "Why, make it legal, of

course. It's cheap enough to produce. Find the people who are using it and ease them off the stuff."

"Surely you're joking."

Ha, ha, ha, ha. "Not at all. You asked the question, señor. I am nothing if not an honest man. I gave you an honest answer. Spend your money on education and treating addicts."

"Wouldn't that put the Colombians out of business?"

Ha, ha, ha, ha. "Of course it would. Eliminate us completely. And everybody in Miami, too."

"If you will pardon me, Don Conchesa, surely that is tongue in cheek. You are joking. You would never offer advice that would destroy the traffic."

"No? You think not? Please, señor. Give me some credit. I offer it precisely because I don't want it to be followed. I'm a public devil in the United States. If I declared the Earth was round, your leaders would claim it was outright flat. I give you this perfectly logical, sensible advice in order to taint the solution and protect myself. Since it was suggested by the evil Banda-Conchesa, your Congress would never follow it. Never. It is impossible." *Ha, ha, ha, ha.*

"Impossible?"

"American politicians prefer the pious, grand statement, señor. The righteous gesture. Internationally, they are famous for it. I suppose it is effective; it gets hem reelected. But the costs!" *Ha, ha, ha, ha.* "Exercising power is far more fun and dramatic than education and treatment, señor. There are too many American bureaucrats whose budgets depend on the war on drugs, you see. It is a bureaucrat's dream: a constant need to launch operations and spend the taxpayers' money. And for a cause that's above criticism!"

"An enemy in perpetuity."

"Correct. Señor, there is more than plenty of money for everybody involved, from the time the coca leaves are gathered until the cocaine arrives in the consumer's nose or lungs. Plenty for everybody—including the police, of course. You've seen the poverty here in Colombia. Do you truly expect these people to starve their families in order to appease American morality? Do you? *De eso nada, hermano! Ha, ha, ha,. ha.*

"Such a terrible price you Americans are wiling to pay for your piety and moral certainty. A nation of saints. You never cease to amaze me. Señor, señor! The enemy was never the

Gachas. You Americans created the Gachas. Someone else will replace them. It is inevitable."

"Is it true what they say about you, Don Conchesa? Did you, in fact, inherit the cocaine cartel from the Gachas?"

"Of course not. What kind of nonsense is that?" *Ha, ha, ha, ha.* "I told you I grow coffee, not coca. I am a coffee merchant." *Ha, ha, ha, ha.*

16

Roberto Guzmán was sitting near Burlane's bed on a chair of rusted metal tubes upholstered in cracked, flowered plastic. He was in a talkative, that is to say, stoned, mood as he watched Burlane wield a Chinese cleaver in the tiny kitchen.

"How's that arm of yours, feeling better?"

"Oh, sure." Burlane used the cleaver, *chop, chop, chop,* to quickly slice a stalk of bok choy.

"What is that stuff?"

"Chinese cabbage."

"Man, you really know how to use that cleaver."

"Practice," Burlane said.

"And your flight last night was from where?"

Burlane stopped chopping. "You want to buy coke, I've got it to sell." He gave Guzmán a look.

Guzmán, chastened, said, "I was just curious is all. No big deal."

"Last night's run was from Panama." Burlane laughed. "But I could be lying, you know, a question like that."

"Ahhhhh . . . Manny Lopez again?"

Burlane, pretending he hadn't heard the question, opened

a cellophane package of dried Chinese mushrooms and put them in a bowl of warm water to plump them up.

The apartment building where Burlane lived was two stories high, and long and narrow—two units wide—taking up half a block. Then came an alley filled with garbage cans, and more rows of two-story art deco apartments.

In the evening, the cooling breeze off the Atlantic picked up, whistled over the sand, scurried across Ocean Drive, and darted between the buildings on its way across the peninsula.

The apartments here were beaten up, neglected, and in some cases closed. Almost all of them, including Burlane's, had glass louvers in the windows—the kind found in the tropics everywhere—designed to divert cooling breezes through the house. Burlane had an air conditioner in his apartment, which he sometimes used after sweaty afternoon walks. At night, he preferred the wind, and slept naked on top of his sheets to enjoy it to the fullest.

Burlane deftly chopped his way through a spear of broccoli, laying it out in neat green strips, each cut at an angle. "You did say you liked broccoli, Roberto?"

"Oh, hell yes, broccoli." He took another hit from his little pipe. "Khartoum, you're not going to mess up that shrimp, are you?"

"If you don't like garlic, tough shit."

"Hey, I'm Cuban. We Cubans like our garlic."

Burlane began ripping cloves of garlic off a small white bulb. He said, "You know the grocery stores in Miami Beach suck, don't you, Roberto? It's damn near as bad as Manhattan. Why do you suppose that is? What have you got, wise guys down here scamming the grocery trade?"

Burlane splashed a dollop of oil in the bottom of the wok and watched it heat. When the oil was hot, he swirled it around the sides of the wok, then tossed in several slices of something.

"What's that?"

"Ginger."

"Ah, good." Guzmán looked about the apartment as though he was seeing it for the first time. He was amazed. "Where does that back door go?"

Burlane started stir-frying the shrimp and vegetables, using a spatula with a rounded tip to keep the food moving. "Down a narrow flight of stairs. It serves as a fire escape."

"Oh. Do you know what that is next door, Sid? A crack house that's been closed by the city. Talk about sleaze."

"Closed? People live over there."

Guzmán laughed. "That doesn't make any difference. They tack a sign on the door saying it's officially shut down, but the crackheads and sleaze balls move right back in. Free rent. They're like roaches. Nobody knows how to stop 'em." Shaking his head, he looked at Burlane in disbelief. "You've got the bucks, man. Get yourself a decent place. There are some good ones up a few blocks."

"Where's your taste, man? All in your mouth? Hey, I thought this place was hip."

"Hip?" Guzmán couldn't help laughing.

Burlane walked in from the tiny kitchen bearing two plates of shrimp and vegetables. He handed one to Guzmán. "I don't think it'd taste a damn bit better if we had a table to eat it on."

Guzmán, grinning, accepted a pair of chopsticks. He sampled a piece of shrimp and his face brightened. "Say, that's good!"

Burlane sat squat-legged on his bed and tried some too. This hole of an apartment was painted the color of French's hot-dog mustard. The linoleum counters were cracked; the old-fashioned sink was stained beyond redemption; there was no pilot light on the old gas stove.

Guzmán peered out the window in disbelief. "What goes on over there?"

Burlane speared a piece of shrimp and contemplated the former crack house. "Well, I got a woman who likes to scream at people in Spanish. She likes that music they all listen to."

Guzmán grinned.

"When she spanks her kids I turn on ESPN and hope for some kind of ball game so I won't have to listen to it. I hate it when people beat on their kids."

"They're South Americans," Guzmán said. He was busy with his chopsticks.

"I don't care where they're from. It gives me the willies. It's in and out, in and out over there. Coming and going. Every once in a while an ear-splitting alarm must go on for an hour before anybody shuts the damned thing off."

"Cops?"

"A couple of times. I can hear them sitting in their squad cars talking on their radios. A woman over there really teed off on her boyfriend the other day. Much yelling in English. Many charges made. Countercharges. Threats. High drama. Hysteria. William was the poor bastard's name."

"You ought to know about the South Americans, Khartoum, you and Manny Lopez being old pals and everything. I know people who'd give their left *cojón* to be tight with Manny Lopez. Conchesa's nephew!"

"Not exactly old pals, the fucker. And I didn't know him in South America. Met him in Chetumal."

"I'd have thought you'd go down to Medellín to visit Uncle Guillermo. Thank him for your new plane and everything. Shake on it."

Burlane laughed. "Sure, sure. Me and The Man himself. Best buddies. Sat around drinking rum and coke at his ranch."

"You should go see him sometime. I sure as hell wouldn't pass on a connection like that." Guzmán ate in silence for a moment, thinking, then said, "Crack houses all around here, Khartoum. That's one across the street over there."

"The building beside it that burned down was a crack house too, I take it."

"Probably. Shit, I hate to park my BMW on the street." Guzmán reloaded his chopsticks. "This stuff's good, Khartoum."

"You're stoned."

"No. I mean it. I don't mean good; I mean really good."

"It's the black bean sauce. I got it out of a bottle."

"Ahh!"

"Not Cuban. Chinese. Made in Taiwan."

"Oh." Guzmán sounded disappointed. "You're a strange guy, you know that, Khartoum? Slamming your airplane against the tops of trees. Living in a place like this."

Burlane pretended to be surprised. He looked around his pad. "Oh? Here I was starting to admire the mustard-colored paint."

"It's a dump."

"I figure what the hell. I've got a gas stove here, which is what you want if you like to cook."

"You don't even wash that stupid Cherokee of yours."

"Mmmmmm." Burlane seemed indifferent. "I spend most of my time flying back and forth from Central America. Better to spend my energy on engine maintenance, wouldn't you think?"

Guzmán said, "Shit! I tell you what I'm going to do, Khartoum. I'm going to show you how people live in Miami."

17

Roberto Guzmán slowed his BMW, turned off Eighth Street, and drove past Alhambra Entrance in Coral Gables. The 20-foot-high gate was a fortresslike arch and embattlement made of cream-colored blocks of coral—all Ponce de León and Spanish Florida.

Guzmán watched Burlane admire the Alhambra Entrance. "Pretty hip, eh, Khartoum? Built in the 1920s. A Cuban in Miami might grow up in Hialeah, but his eye is always on Coral Gables. If you're worth a shit, you have an address in Coral Gables or Cocopalm."

Beyond the entrance, the houses were suddenly larger, sitting back in the cooling shade of tropical hardwoods. They passed a white mansion with a red-tiled roof, barely visible through a thicket of manicured hedge. "Old money, I take it," Burlane said, wondering what Guzmán would define as old money.

"*Con cojónes!* Very old."

"How old?" he asked.

"From the nineteen-twenties, easy," Guzmán said. "You can't find a bungalow here for less than two hundred and fifty thousand dollars."

"Ah, well, I see."

"We'll be getting into it now. Art deco, Khartoum. Beautiful. You're gonna like my place. You really are."

Guzmán's house, Burlane was pleased to see, turned out to be rather less grand than the mansion inside the Alhambra.

In fact, Burlane thought Guzmán had made a remarkably good choice. His house was sizable, but not overdone, a white stucco art-deco bungalow with rounded arches over the windows and doors, and red-clay tiles on the roof. The lawn was a rich green, and the tropical shrubs had been trimmed and groomed.

The only people who had yards like that were gardening nuts, or people with enough money to hire someone to have it done. Burlane couldn't imagine Guzmán behind a lawn mower. What if his neighbors saw him?

It was on the inside of his house that Guzmán truly spent his marimba bucks. Burlane stepped under the rounded arch of the front door onto a polished hardwood floor, and into what could have been a *Playboy* or *Penthouse* magazine spread. Straight ahead, he could see the Jacuzzi and hot tub, which made him smile.

To his right, a fake fire burned on plastic logs in the elegant black-marble fireplace. A polar-bear skin in front of the fire supported a small, royal-blue, tiled table. There was a brace of matching black leather sofas, one on either side of the polar bear.

Current issues of *Fortune, Gentleman's Quarterly,* and the *New Yorker* were displayed on a magazine rack at the end of the far sofa. Burlane wondered where Guzmán kept his *Playboy*s and *Penthouse*s. Under the towels in the linen closet? No, the cleaning woman might find them there.

The dining room had a sparkling, cut-glass chandelier over an elegant glass table surrounded by slender chairs, lightly cushioned and covered in soft turquoise leather.

"Careful, Khartoum. Those're twelve hundred bucks each," Guzmán said.

Burlane, who had put his hand on the back of a chair, yanked it back. "What's that?"

"What the chairs cost. Twelve hundred bucks."

"Each?" Burlane was amazed.

"*Que guajiro!* Of course, each. They didn't come from a flea market. What did you think, Khartoum, twelve dollars and ninety-five cents? You been holed up in Asia too long. Those ain't bamboo, man. Wake up!"

"Oh, oh. I see. They're beautiful." Burlane had to admit, they were lovely chairs. Very elegant.

The kitchen had a high-tech Japanese stove with burners heated by vibrating magnets designated by patterns on top of the counter. Burlane half expected the arm of a robot at the ready to wipe the top clean after every use, but there apparently was none.

Guzmán said the stove sucked; he wished he had gas.

His dishwasher had digital controls that looked more complicated than the cockpit of Burlane's King-Air. Guzmán cheerfully admitted he didn't know how to operate it.

A leather love seat commandeered the center of the glistening hardwood hallway. Guzmán said it was Italian. Here, presumably, one could simultaneously whisper sweet nothings to one's beloved and contemplate the $5,000 Mijares original oils on the walls—anthropomorphic shapes and objects in primary colors, surreal gears as breasts, tangles of meticulously rendered cable as vaginas, braided wire for hips. If you were Cuban and were hip and had a few bucks, you collected Mijares.

Guzmán's Roman tub and Jacuzzi were at the end of the hall, the water lit by a pale-blue spotlight, standing before an exterior wall of glass brick. The tub faced a side wall with Guzmán's big-screen Sony and his bank of Sony and Fisher sound instruments that played audio- or videotapes, records or compact discs. A second wall featured shelves of antique and exotic chess sets.

Adjoining this was a room with an antique Coca-Cola machine, a full-sized Brunswick slate pool table, and a wet bar. Only the pool table and bar looked used.

Then Guzmán showed him his bedroom, the centerpiece being a king-sized waterbed surrounded by floor-to-ceiling mirrors—in addition to the mirror over the bed itself. The walk-in closet was a full 12 feet long.

Guzmán had four $1,200 Confar 100-percent virgin-wool suits. He had several classy $250 Burini shirts, and about 90 humbler shirts. For casual wear, he had 32 pairs of Burini slacks. For more formal occasions, he had a $1,700 Belvest suit, purchased at Franco B, Miami's classiest menswear store. As to shoes, well, among his two dozen pairs Guzmán had a $250 pair of Bruno Maglis and a $150 pair of Brutinis.

This, plus an apartment in the Manatee in Miami Beach for those nights when he didn't feel like driving back to Coral Gables. The Manatee, he told Burlane, was featured in several books on art deco. This wasn't vanity stuff, either; it was New York-published, respectable shit. If an apartment wasn't featured in an art book, Guzmán didn't want any part of it.

"Well, what do you think, Khartoum?" he said, as he watched Burlane looking about.

Burlane, slightly awed at the stuff Guzmán had bought with his marimba money, said, "This is the set, Roberto. Where do you live?"

Guzmán looked momentarily puzzled. "The set?"

"Like a stage. Nobody lives in these rooms. There's no soul here. For example, nobody can get near your dining room table without leaving fingerprints on the glass."

Guzmán laughed. "Ahh." He opened the door behind him, revealing a room that was a clutter of newspapers and magazines, and shelves crammed with books, and a television set. The carpet was shabby and the only furniture was a futon rolled back into a sofa frame and heaped with pillows.

"Now this is my kind of room," Burlane said.

"I thought so. Get out your pipe, I've got some good hydro."

Burlane gave Guzmán his Sid Khartoum pipe, and Guzmán pinched off part of a seedless green bud and loaded the bow. Then he retrieved three shoe boxes from a teak bureau. "I got something I want to show you, Khartoum. You're gonna like it. You're a pervert, I can tell."

Burlane opened one of the boxes. It was filled with color photographs of nude young women posed in various parts of Guzmán's house. On the love seat. In the Jacuzzi. In front of the fireplace. One slender brunette wearing nothing but a smile and black high-heels was even spread out on Guzmán's glass table.

"Go ahead, enjoy, Khartoum."

"My heavens!"

"Coke whores," Guzmán said.

"This is truly extraordinaly. How many are there?" Burlane flipped through the photographs.

"Close to four hundred. I like the blondes especially. You

want to know how we do it, Khartoum? How a Latin man scores pussy? Let me tell you."

"Sure," Burlane said. Four hundred? Burlane wasn't sure how he should react to that kind of statistic. Awe was no doubt proper.

The photos truly were remarkable. Burlane and Guzmán were both male Homo sapiens; but it occurred to him that his companion might have received a megadose of testosterone. And possibly HIV.

Guzmán said, "The house really does it. They know when they come in the front door there's plenty of coke here. They'll do anything for it."

Burlane said, "Judging from these, they like to have their picture taken."

"They love it. At first they'll try to act all shy and shocked. Blink, blink." Guzmán batted his eyes and lapsed into falsetto mimicry. *"A photograph? Me? Nude? Oh, I couldn't do that."* He dropped the falsetto. "Give them a line or two, and they go for it. Spread enough lines and they'll eventually do what they're told. There is one drawback, however."

"There always is."

"A lot of guys can't get it up if they've had too much coke."

"Oh, shit!"

"But I've never had any problem, though." Guzmán looked wistful.

"I hope not."

"Most of those pictures were taken in the good old days. Mind you, there are plenty of women who still love to toot, but it's not like it used to be. Crack is out of the question for me. Crack is not a recreational drug. It's a loaded pistol."

Burlane had stopped to appreciate a sleek young blonde.

Guzmán reached for the picture. *"Qué enferma!* You like this one, Khartoum? You do, don't you? I saw you, man. You stopped when you saw her. Look at you. Haven't been laid since Rangoon, I bet. Tired of playing with your snake?"

Guzmán gave Burlane the next picture. It was the same blonde. Here she was with another Latin man.

"Who's this?"

"Jaime. Buddy of mine from high school days."

"The lady entertained both you and Jaime? I see."

Guzmán said, "You really picked one, Khartoum. This one will do anything, I mean anything. For a line, she'll open her mouth and spread her legs. Mouth, pussy, asshole, take your pick. You got the coke, she's got the time. That's the night we took these pictures."

"Well . . ."

"You like her, don't you, Khartoum? You do! *Qué cabrón!*"

Guzmán got up and slid back the panel of a sleek teak cabinet and studied a rack of videotapes. He selected one and popped it into his VCR. He turned on the TV and VCR and punched the play button. He said, "That blonde you picked out, Khartoum. Me and Jaime had this little pussy run the camera for us."

"Should I know Jaime?"

"Naw. Guerrero is a straight dude, man, wife and four kids. He's in real estate. We've been buddies since high school when we ran cross-country together."

"He likes to knock off a little on the side, I take it."

Guzmán laughed. "He says after ten years and four kids, screwing his wife has all the thrill of spitting in a shoe box. Watch this action, Khartoum. It's a kick."

18

The tape, made in Roberto Guzmán's mirrored bedroom, opened with Guzmán talking.

"*. . . her suck our cocks and then maybe play some tie-down games. Give her a little spanking. Something like that. What do you think, baby?*"

The blonde's eyes were glazed, "Whatever you guys want." She looked from Guzmán to Jaime Guerrero.

"You must see a lot of skin in Asia, I bet. Huh, Khartoum?"

Burlane shrugged. "Not so much. Depends, I guess. You can get anything you want in Bangkok, of course. Incidentally, Japanese pornography is the most violent. Bondage and discipline and all that. You see businessmen enjoying S-and-M comic books on the commuter trains."

"Mighty samurai!"

"They show everything except pussy in Japan. Pussy they don't show."

Guzmán, naked, grinning, got up and disappeared in the direction of his bedroom.

(Everybody wanted to be on the Senate Select Committee on Drug Policy, but nobody especially wanted to be in charge of it. The senators finally prevailed upon Senator Graciela

Boulanger, the independent-minded Democrat from Montana, to take the job. Let a woman take the heat.)

Guzmán returned with leather anklets and bracelets and snap-on bonds, plus a pair of metal tit clamps, a vibrator, and an enormous black dildo, nearly as big around as a man's fist and more than a foot long. He said, "Helen knows all about this gear. Don't you, Helen?"

"So what were you doing in Japan, Khartoum, working for the Yakuza?"

"I've done chores for the Yakuza, yes." Guzmán's idea of getting Burlane's mind on his cock and off his business wasn't a bad one, but Burlane didn't mind Guzmán's questions. His Khartoum legend was well documented. In fact, the more questions the better.

"What did you do?"

"Smuggled shabu and guns."

"Shabu?"

"Amphetamines."

Helen swallowed, looking down at the mirror. "Do you suppose you could lay me a couple more?"

"Sure, sure, baby." Guzmán laid two more lines on the mirror with the edge of a jack of diamonds. "We got lots of coke as long as you're willing to earn it. Right, Jaime?"

"Right."

(The males on the committee immediately had second thoughts about Boulanger. They suggested that women did not understand the nuances and subtleties of power; and there were times women positively refused to listen to reason. Sure enough, Boulanger asked real questions of the heads of various state and federal agencies who paraded before the committee as expert witnesses.)

Guzmán gave her the anklets and bracelets as she snorted the white powder. "You remember these."

She closed her eyes. "I remember."

"What kind of guns, Khartoum?"

"Huh?"

"You said you ran shabu and guns for the Yakuza. What kind of guns?"

Helen offered Guzmán her wrists, which he clipped together at one end of a black nylon bond.

Guzmán popped to his feet. "Be right back."

"Imitation Smith and Weston revolvers and fake Uzis."

"From the Philippines?"

Burlane had never mentioned the Philippines before. Guzmán had obviously run an Interpol check on Khartoum. "The Filipinos have got this place at Danao City on Cebu. They'll duplicate and produce anything you want. Name the weapon."

While they waited for Guzmán to return, Guerrero said, "What happens next?"

Helen rolled her eyes and gave him a half grin. "A paddle, probably. I get mine."

"Are they any good?"

"I can't tell the difference from the real McCoy except the Filipinos engrave Uzi-Dan on the barrel instead of Uzi-IMI like the Israelis do. They call their revolvers Smith and Wasliks."

"What's Waslik mean?"

"It's something you use, then throw away with a scornful gesture. They're so cheap Yakuza killers pitch them in the ocean after one use. They say if the badass is closing in on you, and your pistol misfires, you Waslik—backhand him with the barrel and run like hell." Burlane liked the Filipinos and appreciated their sense of humor.

Guzmán was back, paddle in hand. "Forget this," he said. "Basic stuff. We want it to be fun."

"Bounce her buns a bit?" Guerrero said.

"Oh, hell yes." Guzmán laughed. "Give those numbers some color."

(Boulanger remained polite but open-minded as, one by one, administration officials testified that, yes, the current strategy was correct. They were doing the best they could under the circumstances. They would eventually triumph. In the meantime, Congress should appropriate more money.)

"Two more first," she said.

"Then we make 'em hop."

"Then you do whatever."

Guzmán gave her two more lines.

Burlane watched, his mouth dry. "How long ago was this tape taken, Roberto?"

She took the lines with tethered wrists, then turned to deliver her end of the bargain.

Guzmán, eyes on Guerrero spanking Helen, said, "Oh, I don't know. Eight or ten months ago. A year ago, something like that. Isn't she hot? She'll do anything for coke. Anything.

When they were finished, Helen stood, rubbing her reddened behind. "That really hurt. Ouch!"

(The law-enforcement expert witnesses implored Senator Boulanger's committee to be judicious before contemplating any cuts in their budgets. The senators should think of what their agents could do if only they were properly funded.)

"Time for the big black one." Guzmán brandished the huge dildo as he unsnapped her wrists.

"Oh, shit no, Roberto."

"Baby, baby. You got off on it last time, remember?"

(Since taxpayers were then springing for $9 billion a year to maintain the drug war, Boulanger suggested that the committee send its own investigator to the front for a report and evaluation. Was this money being spent effectively, or were they merely subsidizing high livers and good times? In short, were the taxpayers getting screwed? How?)

Guzmán gave Helen two more lines, then oiled the dildo.

She tooted the lines and sighed in resignation.

"You move heroin too, or just amphetamines?"

"Huh?" Burlane was stunned by what Helen was willing to endure for cocaine. It was incredible.

"When you were in Asia. This girl's something, isn't she?"

"Yes, she is. I ran a little heroin. From Chien-Mai. The speed was from South Korea, which is where the Yakuza have their factories."

"Ooooohh. Watch this, Khartoum."

"Hands behind your back."

Helen did as she was told.

Guzmán clipped her wrists together with a snap. "On your back, legs wide."

Again, she did as she was told.

Guzmán, watching himself use the dildo on the girl, said, "Chien-Mai is where, Khartoum?"

"Northwest Thailand. West of Vientiane, northeast of Rangoon. God, that must hurt like hell!"

"Look at her. Shit! Near the Golden Triangle?"

"It's the principle interior port of entry."

"Doesn't this one have a real port of entry? What's Chien-Mai like?"

"They say the best-looking Thai girls are from Chien-Mai. Then you've got biggie drug lords. The CIA put 'em in business to fight communists after the Second World War, and they're still there."

"I can think of some people in Miami who got the same kind of help. Look at that sweet bitch. Just look. Ooooooh!"

Guzmán removed the dildo and unfastened her wrists.

"You bastards."

"You loved it."

She blushed. "That's too much. Shit!"

(Sheridan Harnar, the committee's chief legal counsel, was asked to recruit a committee investigator with international experience. Boulanger suggested that Harnar talk to Ara Schott, a retired former director of counterintelligence for the CIA, who had once impressed her with his meticulous and thoughtful testimony before another committee.

After talking to Schott and Burlane, Harnar hired Mixed Enterprises. The taxpayers had a right to ask, Harnar said. What were the taxpayers getting for their money?)

"What do you think, Jaime? Time for the old sausage sandwich? Me on top, you on the bottom. She likes the old sandwich routine too, don't you Helen?"

(Harnar said the committee was concerned about the confident assertions made by those attempting to suppress the marimba through force. How many cops were straight? How many were crooked? And how crooked?)

Helen looked at the floor, licked her lips, and swallowed again. "Do you suppose I could have a couple more lines first?"

"Sure, baby. You earned a couple more."

(Harnar added that Senator Boulanger was tired of numbers. Numbers, numbers, numbers. She wanted to know how it felt to play the marimba.)

Helen leaned forward and scooped up two more white lines with her little straw. Then she sat upon Jaime Guerrero and leaned forward, rump up, to accept Roberto Guzmán.

19

James Burlane tried not to show concern as Roberto Guzmán, going too fast, wheeled his BMW convertible in and out of traffic, tailgating every car he came to. He said, "You really think you can find out what happened to Luis in this place?" Luis Fernandez had now been missing 10 days.

"Luis plays the marimba. There'll almost certainly be somebody in Oysterman's who has an idea what happened to him. Let me circulate a little, ask a question here and there. I'll find out something. Meanwhile, if you put some effort into it, maybe you can get laid. Be good for you."

"I don't want to stay up all night. I've got a flight tomorrow. Manny's opening up a new airstrip."

"Oh, where's that?"

Burlane laughed. "Would you like me to draw you a map, is that it?"

Guzmán looked disgusted. "What an eagle scout."

"I don't talk. I do my job. I stay in business. What's more, I stay alive."

Guzmán drove in silence for a moment, then said, "Oysterman's got a pink pearl on top of their swizzle sticks, Khartoum. Orgasman's." He, laughed, darting the tip of his tongue in an out. "Unfortunately there's lots of Cuban girls there, and they're all looking for husbands. It's a lot better in Fort Lauderdale because of the Anglo girls. I'll take you there some night."

"Fort Lauderdale?" Burlane thought about Ara Schott, grinding his teeth in Fort Lauderdale, hating every minute of his stay there.

Guzmán laughed. "Up the coast. Tell you the truth, Khartoum, the farther you get away from Miami, the easier it gets. By the time you get to Georgia, it's paradise. The males up there have all been trained to be big stupes."

"I see. Good old boys."

"In Atlanta they stand around twiddling their *cojónes* while we Cubans move in with our lines. You should see them, slapping one another on the back, *har, har, har,* while we're screwing their women. But you know, I think I've lost my touch in the clubs, Khartoum, that's the truth. I'm rusty. Can't throw a line worth shit."

Burlane raised his eyebrow. "Lost your touch? Do you have to practice?"

"Naw, shit. It's all natural, man, but of course you've got to work on it."

"I see. Are you sure it's not just the coke they're after?"

Guzmán gave him a look. "No, man, it's more than that. They don't want to hear that you're a dealer, so you have to tell them something else. You've got the bucks and can afford the coke, but you don't sell it, see. Also, you don't want to get too friendly at first. You let them know you think they're good-looking, but you've got so many bucks you've got your choice of women. There are coke whores in these places, of course, and they'll do anything for a few lines."

Burlane himself was unable to strike up a bullshit conversation with a strange woman while disco music hammered in his ears. "Oh? You don't want to get too friendly? I'd have thought . . ."

"Naw. It's the worst thing you can do. The first thing you've got to do is establish eye contact. Look 'em right in the eye. Tell 'em they've got good hair or a fabulous face or a hot dress or whatever. They want to hear that crap, so you have to give it to 'em."

"I see."

"They want a man with a bulge in his pants, not a pal.

They've got brothers and stuff for that shit." Guzmán lit a joint and took a hit. "So many women. So little time. It's impossible, Khartoum." In wistful silence, Guzmán braked his BMW for a stop light. "Not long ago, six or eight months, something like that, Stringfellow's was the in spot, but it sort of lost its poop."

"Oh, why is that?"

"No real reason. It'd been here for years and finally got boring. We like action down here in Miami, Khartoum. We don't like to be bored."

Guzmán wheeled his BMW convertible into a parking lot that was a sea of hot-damn automobiles: BMWs, Mercedes-Benzes, a sprinkling of Saabs and Volvos, and top-of-the-line Peugeots, Toyotas, and Hondas.

Burlane said, "My heavens, look at all this expensive metal! We're making progress, Roberto. A chicken in every pot. A foreign car in every garage. This is what makes America great."

"Some of these guys got their *pingas* mortgaged trying to keep up with the payments."

Guzmán got out of the BMW. Burlane imagined that the gold chain around his neck weighed half a pound. Guzmán's gauzy white shirt was open three buttons down to reveal the hair on his chest. His pleated turquoise trousers were cinched in at the ankles and buckled into place with silver buckles studded with tiny rubies. His alligator-skin shoes had silver tips on their pointed toes.

Guzmán said, "I've got the locks." When Burlane was clear, he locked the doors electronically with a plastic clicker on his keychain.

"Hey, that's real downtown," Burlane said.

"It also controls the burglar alarm. Bump it. Go on."

Burlane gave the BMW a gentle rock, setting off a high-pitched squeal.

Guzmán snuffed the squeal with his clicker. "You gotta have this stuff down here, Khartoum. You gotta." He checked his reflection in the car window. Mr. Gold Man. Mr. Silver. Mr. Bucks.

Guzmán flashed everything but a beeper. No dealing in grams for him. No midnight beeps from cokeheads. A beeper was bush and stupid. Guzmán wanted to come off as big-time.

Burlane thought if Guzmán's FBI superiors should see him in action, they'd give him a raise. Here was a real undercover agent in action. He wondered what kind of reports Guzmán was filing on him.

Burlane followed Guzmán through Oysterman's parking lot and stopped when he saw the line of people waiting to get inside the nightclub. There had to be over a hundred.

Guzmán saw the astonished look on his face and waved his hand no. "No problem. No problem. Follow me."

Burlane followed as Guzmán strode past the young women and pairs of lone wolves waiting to get in. Burlane was amazed; virtually all of the young men wore gold chains and jeweled stickpin earrings. Did they all play the marimba?

Guzmán and the bouncer were obviously old pals. After a little good-humored bantering in Spanish, Guzmán slipped him a benjie, along with a couple of twenties for the cover.

Burlane, following Guzmán inside, said, "A hundred bucks. I can see why he's glad to see you."

Guzmán gestured to the line. "You see those guys back there? They've got gold chains. They've got cool threads. But look at them. Waiting in line." He shook his head in pity. "Unfortunately, there's one thing they don't have."

"Benjies to lay on bouncers."

"You got it, *amigo*. They could be grocery-store clerks or pizza deliverymen. They might sell a few grams to support a little habit, but that's it. They all have at least one cool outfit. They might not have shit, but they look good when they go out."

"Embarrassing to be waiting."

"I certainly wouldn't do it," Guzmán said. "Wouldn't get caught dead waiting. No way."

20

Oysterman's pink-pearl swizzle sticks were a slightly risqué ha-ha for the gentlemen fancying themselves macho cocksmen. James Burlane assumed that the twenty-buck cover charge, ten-buck beers, and fifteen-buck cocktails kept the riff raff out. As was the custom, the gentlemen took care of the cost for the young ladies.

No macho cocksman, whether marimbeiro or up-and-coming young executive, dared flinch at the prices. If a gentleman's hand hesitated at his wallet, he was finished. If milady's every step did not merit open admiration by the gentlemen with the long green, she did not belong in Oysterman's.

On his own, Burlane would never have gone anywhere remotely approaching Oysterman's. But he was working. When he worked, he did what he had to do. If he could crash his Beech into the tops of trees, he could endure a crush of people who collectively smelled like a French whorehouse. Well, in a manner of speaking. Burlane had been in whorehouses before, but never in France.

Guzmán said it was customary to begin an evening at Oysterman's by knocking back a few five-buck raw oysters to stimulate the manly juices, and so Burlane followed him to the oyster bar. While Guzmán threw back a he-man dozen, Burlane took care of half that many, seasoned with generous hits of Tabasco.

"Isn't this wonderful?" Guzmán said. "Look at the women! Look at them! Have you ever seen anything like it?"

"No, I don't believe I have," Burlane said. The young women—largely Cuban, judging from their black hair and brown eyes, but with a sprinkling of invading blondes—were dressed and naked at the same time. While they had not painted the clothes on their figures, they came as close as possible. The material of choice stretched. Short, one-piece knit dresses were popular among those advertising impressive *culos*. These outfits hugged every curve from breast to flank. Young ladies with admirable breasts showed naked shoulders, demonstrating to the gentlemen that no bra was required to keep those firm numbers in place.

Burlane took a sip of ten-dollar draft beer. Once, in New Orleans, he'd gotten hooked for six bucks, but the place had had a jazz band. He didn't mind supporting musicians; Oysterman's was something else.

"There are four or five rooms here. You should cruise for a while, Khartoum. Take a look around. Look, look, look at that one. There's one for you. She sort of looks like that one me and Luis did the number on." He nodded with his head at a slender Anglo woman in her thirties.

Burlane glanced at the woman, a natural blonde. Roberto was right; she did look like an older version of Helen. She was good-looking and somehow had a way about her. But she couldn't be for him if she hung out in a place like Oysterman's.

And yet, there was something about her that said she didn't belong here. She wore black slacks and a blouse that was merely white, not translucent. The neckline was sexy without plunging to her waist. Her slacks fit her well enough, taking advantage of her long legs and showing off her rump, but she had passed on the fashion of splitting herself in half at the crotch.

"Ahh, I was right," Guzmán said. "You like 'em tall, don't you?"

"I take it you're going to practice your lines while you scout leads on Luis, Roberto?"

"Oh, hell yes. Can't waste all this *concha*." Guzmán was

amused that Burlane was watching the blonde out of the corner of his eye. "She's got great legs. She knows they're hot, too, believe me."

A young Hispanic woman with huge brown eyes walked in front of them, causing Guzmán to lick his lips and moan audibly. She wore a pale-yellow knit dress cut across the top of breast that, while pushing against the fabric, still managed to jiggle provocatively when she walked. The dress, molded to her rump and the backs of her thighs, ended six inches above the knees. She wore dangling gold earrings and gold bracelets on both wrists. She had long, shiny black hair, large brown eyes, and a perfect nose that was more beautiful than cute. It was sweet. She had a sweet face, provocative in its sweetness.

"Oh, shit, do you see that, Khartoum? Do you see that face? Look at that *culo!* That's a real Cuban ass, man, the genuine article."

"She's trolling," Burlane said.

"She's got a lot to troll with. I've got to have her, Khartoum. Got to."

"Don't let me stop you, Roberto. Go for it."

Guzmán did, leaving Burlane alone in this place that might have been imagined by Hieronymus Bosch. There was literally nowhere Burlane could go without bumping up against somebody or standing between two people trying to talk—or, more accurately, trying to shout. It was impossible to hear anything because of the music, and so people took turns shouting at one another.

Would Roberto be forced to shout his lines like a circus barker? Burlane assumed so.

Guzmán, grinning broadly, hands gesturing, engaged the lady with the jiggly breasts and outsized *culo* and sweet/beautiful face. Behind them, dancers bumped body-to-body on a diminutive dance floor; colored lights, synchronized to the beat of the music, blinked against their gyrating forms: blue, green, red, and yellow; blue, green, red, and yellow.

The sweet/beautiful one giggled at Guzmán's opening line. He quickly added another. Obviously charmed, she asked him something in return. Guzmán's reply made her little body shake with laughter.

Guzmán put a hand on her shoulder, and she seemed not to mind. He moved closer until their bodies nearly touched. That was okay too. She was obviously taken by him. Then they were into it, as though they were the only two people in the room. Their bodies even closer, they took turns leaning toward the other so he or she could hear. It appeared as though nothing either of them could say failed to draw a smile, a giggle, or laughter.

Guzmán suddenly turned and pushed his way through the crowd, headed for the bar.

Burlane joined him just as he'd given the bartender his order. "I saw you jabbering with the little sweetie with the *culo*, Roberto. Working your lines, I take it."

"You don't throw lines to one like this, Khartoum. No. No. No." Guzmán looked serious.

"Whatever happened to looking for Luis?"

"We'll find him. First things first. Isn't she beautiful, Khartoum? Isn't she something? Look at her." Guzmán beamed, his eyes glazed.

"Are you sure you're not getting too friendly? Remember what you said about not getting too friendly at first. Surely you don't abandon your game plan that quickly."

"It doesn't make any difference with this one, Khartoum. Sometimes you have to know when to take your time. I know what I'm talking about, take my word for it. This one's different."

"Ahh! Different? More than just a *concha*."

"A sweetheart, Sid, I mean it. A little sweetheart. She's twenty. A junior at the University of Miami. A trophy. This one's a trophy."

"And her name is?"

"Lourdes Martinez. Her brother Eduardo is cruising around here somewhere." Guzmán accepted the drinks from the bartender.

"Her brother? Oh, shit. No *concha* tonight, I take it."

Guzmán gave him a reproving frown. "When I tell you this one's different, Khartoum, I mean she's truly different. Isn't she beautiful? She could be a model. That face! And that *culo*. Oooooo! I gotta go."

He started pushing his way back through the crush.

Burlane watched. He imagined himself, momentarily, as a zoologist. Guzmán's behavior upon meeting Lourdes could very well be taped and shown as an episode of "Wild Kingdom." Here was evolution in action, hormones expressing themselves.

As the immortal Elizabeth Browning wrote:

How do I love thee? Let me count the ways.

Roberto Guzmán looked like he was prepared to count all night if he had to.

Oysterman's was not Burlane's natural habitat. He needed a corner. In a corner, he could nurse his drink in relative peace. From a distance, he would watch Guzmán charm Lourdes Martinez.

Repressing outright panic and leading with his left shoulder, Burlane plunged through the crowd like a human icebreaker. The nearest corner was occupied, as they all were, but he was determined. If necessary, he would loom crassly and without embarrassment over the occupying couple, drink in hand, until they yielded the space. He needed relief. Had to have it.

But . . . he was in luck. The couple joined the gyrating crowd on the dance floor before he got there. For a wonder, owing to a quirk of acoustics, the corner was relatively quiet.

He located the animated Roberto Guzmán, by now well into his campaign to impress the little sweet/beautiful Lourdes.

Burlane's feet were tired. He leaned his rump against the wall, but that didn't help his feet. He was staring at his feet, wondering how long he would be forced to suffer, when hair brushed against his ear.

A woman said, "Not a partying type of guy, I take it."

It was the older woman whom Guzmán had seen earlier. He repressed a giggle.

"A few minutes ago I saw you hanging out with a drug dealer."

Burlane shook his head. "Businessman."

She shook her head. "Marimba player. Are you a dealer too?"

"I'm a pilot. I fly airplanes."

"Ahh, a smuggler then. Or a cop pretending to be one."

"No, just a pilot."

"What do you fly, if you don't mind my curiosity?"

Burlane shrugged. "You're the one who sounds like a cop."

She laughed. "My name's Katherine Donovan. I run a boutique in Baltimore."

Burlane shook her hand. "Sid Khartoum. Pleased to meet

you. I am just a pilot, by the way, not a smuggler. I sometimes fly tropical flowers from Honduras. Sometimes trained horses from Mexico, and once in a while rich people to scuba-dive off Belize or shoot white water in Costa Rica. You'd be astonished at how much money there is in exotic flowers. They have to get them to market fast. But mostly, I fly businessmen."

"What kind of businessmen?"

"All kinds. If you've arrived, you don't associate with swine on commercial flights, even in first class. No self-respecting CEO would be caught dead on a commercial flight—all that waiting with sweaty proles in the airport. Why do you suppose congressmen hook rides on corporate planes when they know damn well it's ethically wrong? It's ego. Status."

"Where do you take these businessmen?"

"In the fall, I fly them south to north to hunt ducks. In the winter, from north to south to fish for bonefish and tarpon. Once in a while I fly a party all the way to Alaska to fish for salmon or hunt for moose. Tomorrow I fly two guys and their girlfriends to Bimini to fish for marlin."

She pulled a photograph out of her handbag, and showed it to him.

Burlane blinked. It was Helen from Roberto Guzmán's videotape. She was younger and very fresh looking in the photograph.

She said, "You know her. I can tell by your face you know her."

Burlane turned the picture over. On the back was printed "Helen Donovan" followed by a telephone number.

"My sister." She waited for him to say something. When he didn't, she said, "You notice all the models in Miami Beach?"

"How could I not? They're everywhere."

"Helen was a sophomore at Johns Hopkins when she quit school and came down here to model. It didn't work out."

"Probably doesn't work out for most of them."

"She was good looking, but not quite good enough. She was a waitress for a while before she got hooked on coke. I'll bet your 'businessman' friend over there has stories about what a cokehead will do for a line."

Burlane frowned. "Hey! Give me a break. That guy's one of my best customers. Businessmen like girls too. He's a rich Latino. He likes nightclubs and flash and dazzle. So what?"

"So what is right. When I saw you over here staring at your shoes, I knew you'd help me out if you could."

"My heavens! You're a regular Sherlock Holmes."

"That's my number on the back of the photograph."

"You came down here like Nancy Drew looking for your sister?"

"Do you know where she lives?"

Burlane considered her question. Guzmán probably had a good idea.

"My family can't afford private detectives, Mr. Khartoum. I can't either. My parents and I want her back. I don't care how you came to know her. That doesn't matter. What matters is Helen."

"I see."

"Now then, will you please help me find her? You don't have to answer now. Think it over and give me a call."

21

James Burlane woke the next morning with Katherine Donovan on his mind. He had lived by himself long enough to have become largely used to it. Being around too many people for too long a period of time—especially those with predictable imaginations—gave him the jitters.

But there was no denying—even Burlane had to admit—that he nursed the hope that one day The Right One would, however miraculously or unexpectedly, appear off his bow. She with the right stuff would first of all be *soulful*—an open-minded, adventurous woman, secure and intelligent enough to be a nonmaterialist.

Burlane believed feverently that remembered experience, passion, rather than things owned, was the stuff he would value most at the end of his measure. Burlane's father had made moonshine whiskey for 12 years; in the weeks before her end, the greatest treasure of Burlane's dying mother had been her memories of life on the run with a wild-haired whiskey-making man.

The leggy woman who had cornered him at Oysterman's had all the earmarks of being soulful. It was impossible to tell just yet, but there was something about her.

Burlane got up and started the morning ritual of buzzing coffee beans and making his coffee.

When it was ready he sat down, took a sip, and studied the picture of Helen Donovan. Katherine and precocaine Helen had remarkably similar faces, only Katherine was probably 10 years older. Did they inherit their facial bone structure from their father or their mother, he wondered? And what of the contours of their interior world, the emotional inheritance that had allowed one to plunge herself into cocaine whoring while the other remained in control of her life?

Also, was it possible that Katherine's zeroing in on him at Oysterman's was accidental? Burlane's survival depended on a hard-assed, never-ending, professional paranoia.

Helen was Katherine's sister. Their facial structure did not lie. And Helen was a coke whore. There was certainly no getting around that.

He turned the photograph.ever, holding it carefully by the edges.

If Katherine were indeed truly soulful . . .

If . . . if . . . if . . .

Burlane bit his lower lip. Harnar wouldn't like it a damn bit. Burlane had work to do, and chasing after Helen wouldn't get it done. But he couldn't just blow Katherine off. He couldn't. It wasn't in his nature.

He knew he could postpone his scheduled flight to Honduras with a simple telephone call. All he had to do was tell Lopez something was wrong with the King-Air's fuel system, and that he had to get it fixed before he flew anywhere. No way was he going to chance splashing his plane in the middle of the Caribbean. The world wasn't going to stop turning because the load arrived in Miami a day or two late.

He punched Katherine's number.

The phone rang. Once. Twice. Maybe she wasn't home. Should he hang up? This was his chance.

For a heartbeat, he thought of slamming the receiver down. To hell with it.

But no.

She picked up the phone, answering hello.

There was no turning back. "Ah, Katherine, this is Sid Khartoum. From last night in Oysterman's. The man with the hair. You gave me the picture of your sister, remember?"

"I thought you'd call. No, I take that back. I knew you'd call."

"You were right. Maybe I can help you find her."

"I thought so."

"But there must be no discussion of how I know her. I prefer not to go into that."

"You have your privacy, Mr. Khartoum."

"Thank you. Sid."

"Sid. Sid, let me tell you again, in complete candor: all I want to do is to get my little sister out of this place and back home where she can be helped. It's help she needs. Help. Not lectures. Not slogans or television ads. Not courts and legal bullshit. Not jail. Not any of that. Help. She needs help. Support and understanding. That may sound mush-brained, but it happens to be true."

"I don't disagree with a word of what you say, but to tell the truth, I only know where she hangs out." After meeting Katherine in Oysterman's, Burlane had asked Guzmán where the blonde Helen lived. South Beach, Guzmán thought. "We can't just cruise the neighborhood looking for your sister. The people down there will be wary of getting involved. What I have in mind to find her may or may not work, Katherine. It will require imagination, and it may be dangerous."

"I'll do it. No problem."

Burlane cleared his throat, remembering Manny Lopez's *no es problema.*

"That is, I'll see if I can keep up," she added quickly. "El Sid."

"I've been called that."

She laughed. "I thought so. Had a bet with myself."

"You look like your sister, but not so much that a stranger would immediately pick up on it. You'll have to dress in such a way as to take attention away from your face, and we'll need multiple copies of that photograph of Helen. Do you speak Spanish?"

"*Un poquito.* Tell me what you have in mind."

Burlane put some effort into inventing his pimp drag. He had nothing if not professional pride in his ability to outpimp Katherine Donovan's hooker. He wanted to roast her brains.

The wok-man slipped his daypack over his shoulders, took

a hike up Collins to the mall along Lincoln Road, and went shopping.

In Medco Drug Store, he chose a metallic-black elastic band to fashion a ponytail out of his mane of hair, and a silken scarlet headband. The headband called attention to the one-half-carat ruby on his stickpin earring. There was no question but that the ruby was genuine.

At Palma, he bought an avocado-green Bugle Boy shirt; he left the top two buttons undone, demonstrating that yes, here was a man with hair, however silver in color. He also bought a pair of pale-blue, lightweight denim trousers that had pleated front pockets and wide, stylishly baggy legs; and for his feet; the most expensive, show-off Nikes currently on the market.

It was Harnar's money; Burlane threw caution to the winds. In place of ordinary gold chains, he strolled into Gray & Sons Jewelry and Coins and forked over 450 bucks for a single strand of tiny gold nuggets that had been drilled and strung like beads.

Then he carried all this stuff home to his digs.

Burlane was dressed and ready to go when he heard the buzzer downstairs. He was feeling good as he bounded down the short flight of steps to let her in.

And when he did, he let out a whoop and said, "Oh, shit, lady, you win the turkey!"

Katherine grinned broadly. "You think so? You didn't do badly yourself."

"No, no, I look like a Wall Street banker by comparison. Turn around. Let me appreciate the subtleties."

"Subtleties?" Katherine, wearing dark glasses and now raven-haired, pivoted on the three-inch heels of her black sandals, saying, "I went whole hog. Can't have them think we're cops. You like the skirt?"

Her form-fitting lycra skirt, with a silver-studded leather belt, ended inches below her buns.

Katherine's transparent, fuschia-colored Christian Dior blouse was open at the throat. In fact, open to the belt. This exposed a vast V of skin, including the insides of her breasts, around which were coiled tatooed boa constrictors of lethal yellows and coppers and greens. The tail of one boa disappeared behind her belt. The head of the other, flickering a blood-red forked tongue, rested on her breastbone.

"I feel compelled to say the snakes are truly wonderful."

She smiled. "You said to take attention away from my face."

He laughed. "Guaranteed nobody's going to pay any attention to your face. They wash off, I take it."

She studied the insides of her breasts. "It takes a special solvent. Soap and water won't do it. They're boa constrictors. Do they look real?"

Burlane shook his head, grinning. "Oh, yes. They look real."

"You really think so?"

"Believe me."

"I found an artist who has a thriving business painting these things. Painless, removable tattoos. She does beautiful work. Aren't they something?"

"Do they, uh, go all the way around?"

She raised an eyebrow. "And the earrings? How do you like the earrings? Move attention from my face to my ears, do you think?" She wore dangly gold loops; a tiny parrot perched on the bottom of each.

"The earrings are good. Nice touch, but I bet nobody gets above chest level. I bet those are whole snakes. Who'd want to paint half a snake? Would you like a cup of coffee before we start?"

Katherine followed Burlane up the stairs to his apartment. He unlocked the door, and she stepped inside, shaking her head at the mustard-colored walls. He had made the bed in her honor, and hung up most of his clothes.

"Pretty hip, eh?" he said. "Tranquil mustard. Don't you think it's grand?"

"I'll admit other adjectives come to mind."

Burlane bunched up his lower lip in a mock pout, and went to his kitchen to make the coffee. He threw a handful of oily black coffee beans into his grinder, talking louder as he started the buzzing. "It takes some years to become a proper Bohemian, Katherine. It doesn't come automatically or over-night."

"Oh?"

Burlane finished with the grinding. He dumped some coffee into a paper filter and poured hot water over it. "It requires an examined life, the intellectual and emotional ability to step outside of fashion and the herd. It may begin with youth, but doesn't flower until a person is old enough to be aware of his or her mortality. Nor does it necessarily connote a left-wing attitude, as some people believe."

He returned from the kitchen with two cups of coffee in hand. "For example, for all their colorful costumes, hippies were never true Bohemians. They were followers, not individualists or contrarians."

Katherine took a cup. "Thank you. I take it the ability to appreciate a mustard-yellow apartment comes close to being a test."

"Exactly. Two hundred and seventy-five bucks a month, four blocks from the beach."

"All right!"

"They'd probably have to pay most people to live here. Did you get the copies of the photograph?"

"Got 'em. I think this is a hip pad, too. It must be like living on a stage set."

"That's how I look at it."

"Coffee's good, Sid."

22

The warm wind coming off the Atlantic caressed their skins as James Burlane and Katherine Donovan set off in search of Helen. They decided to reconnoiter the neighborhood first to give Burlane a chance to perfect his pimp walk and Katherine to blow the minds of passersby with her amazing snakes.

They walked south on Washington to the tip of the peninsula, surveying the narrow apartments as they went, then turned north again and started with the Sea King, an apartment building on Meridian Avenue. A solitary, bluesy trombone wailed from one of the ground-floor windows, playing along with a jazz tape.

Through the open glass louvers, they could see the trombonist, a white man with a great pale belly, and his lady, a black woman with pillowy breasts pushing against a flowered dress. The man with the trombone had thin black hair slicked back over his head in glistening furrows frozen into place with hair spray. He sat in a tattered easy chair. His eyes were closed. He soared in his private space, his wrist fluttering a silken vibrato. He was a professional. Had to be.

The woman in the flowered dress ate popcorn and read *Ebony* magazine through horn-rimmed glasses.

"We start here?" Katherine asked.

"Surely a soulful couple. They look like they speak English. You get the Spanish speakers, I get the English, what do you say?"

"Fine by me."

Burlane rang the doorbell. The trombone stopped. The door opened.

The woman looked up at Burlane through the tops of her horn-rimmed bifocals. "Yes?" Her eyes went quickly from the nuggets around Burlane's neck to the tattooed snakes around Katherine's breasts. She grinned a half-grin.

Burlane said, "My associate and I are in the entertainment business."

"I see." She said to Katherine, "You don't mind if my husband enjoys your snakes? He appreciates the exotic."

"Not at all," Katherine said.

Over her shoulder, she said, "Harold, I think you should come here. Lady here got something I know you're gonna want to see." She turned back. "Now what is it I can help you folks with?"

"We're in the business of providing custom entertainment for executive spenders. We're in the market for model-type young ladies to serve as hostesses."

Harold, with trombone, appeared at his wife's side, and, seeing the snakes, broke into a grin. "I bet you are."

Katherine stepped forward so he could see the snakes better in the dim light.

Burlane said, "Our clients are all professionals and the compensation is truly remarkable. Wouldn't you say so?" He looked at Katherine.

Katherine said, "Perhaps they've seen Helen. Didn't she say she lived in this area?"

"You're right. Perhaps they did." Burlane fished a photograph of Helen from his pocket. "This young woman was quite anxious to work for us. She's very good-looking, as you can see. We called her back to tell her yes, but her telephone was disconnected."

"Are you cops?" Harold said.

Burlane burst out laughing. "Do we look like cops?"

Harold laughed. "You don't look like Don Johnson."

"If you see Helen or know of any other talented young ladies who would like to be entertainers, you might give us a call." He turned the photo over and wrote "Sid" and "Katherine" on it, together with their telephone numbers. He fished a one-gram, 50-buck Ziplok packet of coke from the pocket of his baggy trousers and laid it on the edge of a bookshelf by the side of the door. "I found this on the sidewalk back there. Somebody dropped it. You can sell it or do what you want with it, I don't care. It must be worth a few bucks."

"Don't use that shit," Harold said. "Learned that lesson long ago."

"Like I said, I don't care what you do with it."

"Much obliged," the trombonist said.

Burlane and Katherine strolled along the sidewalk under the spreading branches of an areca tree. Ahead, rock and roll music boomed from a ghetto blaster. They rounded the corner; lights glowed from the dark doorway of an apartment that faced the street. Cigarettes being lit. After the glowing, laughter. Then more glowing. In the dim light of the cigarettes: three teenaged boys.

Dodging a broken bicycle, a battered skateboard, and a deflated inner tube, Burlane and Katherine headed for the open door. As they went into the apartment, one of the boys said, "Shee-it," and they all laughed.

Inside, someone turned on a dim lamp. It was a slight, bald man in his late 30s, with two days of graying stubble on his face, and his eyes reddened by drugs.

The only furniture in the room behind him was a sagging, threadbare sofa on the far wall and an old card table with folding metal chairs. The sofa was missing the middle cushion; stuffing poked out of a hole in the left arm. The card table was piled high with dirty plastic plates and two empty Gator Delight pizza cartons. That and empty Busch beer cans.

The floor was littered with filthy cushions, dirty clothes, old newspapers, and three empty beer cases.

The bald man's reddened eyes widened as he checked out Katherine's snakes.

Burlane gave their pitch. He ended by giving him Helen's photo and four one-gram bags of crack.

The man slipped the baggies into his pocket without a word and studied the photograph. "I've seen her around, but to be honest with you, if you want much in the way of entertainment out of her, you'll have to keep her supplied with something to get her up and going."

Burlane sighed. "No problem."

"Good luck with that, man."

"You don't know where she lives?"

"No, man. Don't have any idea. Lady, I gotta tell you, those snakes are something else."

The cooking beans smelled good.

The aged, tattered sofa and easy chair were of a type that Burlane called proletarian modern: the legs and frames were black metal tubes, the seats and backs cushioned in a now illegal variety of inflammable plastic that hardened and turned brittle with age. The three unmatched kitchen chairs were simply that.

The black woman's hair was done in natty dreads. Her eyes were red. She was hugely pregnant and skinny at the same time, as though someone had jammed a golf ball into a soda staw. The elastic waist of her cotton shorts was pulled so tight that the top button had popped. It had been replaced with a safety pin.

Her woman friend, larger-boned and dressed in a muumuu splashed with faded azaleas, was equally pregnant.

There were five children in the room. The two youngest, a boy and a girl two or three years old, were naked. The three oldest, two girls and a boy about five or six, watched "The Cosby Show" on the television.

On the set, the beautiful, impeccably dressed black lawyer Claire Huxtable was baking a cake in her spotless, high-tech kitchen. In came Dad, cheery Dr. Huxtable, and boy, did that chocolate cake ever smell good! He gave his wife a big hug and kiss. She made a wry comment. The laugh button was punched. Everybody laughed. Cosby mugged, looking chagrined, then ho-ho-ho, joined in with his beautiful wife and the happy laugh track.

The pregnant woman, studying the photograph of Helen, said, "Kids love to watch Bill Cosby."

There was a test tube in a small pan of boiling water on the stove, but Burlane tipped the woman with one of Harnar's benjies instead of dope.

After they left, Burlane said, "I figure twenty for groceries and eighty for crack. No chocolate cake for the kids, but they might score a Twinkie out of the deal. I'm glad they're watching something they can relate to."

"You don't understand, Sid. Dr. Huxtable and his wife are role models."

"Role models?" Burlane looked amused. "I'd always been told religion was the opiate of the people."

The 10-foot-by-10-foot yard in front of the Ocean Breeze apartment building contained a pile of broken cement garden blocks, an automobile transmission, and a plastic tricycle with no wheels.

In the middle, a sign posted by the city of Miami Beach said the building had been condemned and closed for violations of drug laws.

A light, too bright for candles, flickered in the windows at the rear corner.

As they got closer they heard the heavy bass beat. Reggae being played on a ghetto blaster.

Burlane rapped on the door. The music stopped.

A teenager with hard, reddened eyes opened the door a crack, latch chain still in place. His body hid whatever was behind him.

Burlane could smell fried chicken.

"What you want?" His reddened eyes went from Burlane to Katherine and held fast on the snakes.

Behind him, somebody said something Burlane couldn't make out.

Red Eyes said, "Ain't no cops. Ain't no cops got tits like these."

"You wouldn't know what to do with no tits if they was pokin' you in the eye."

Burlane glanced at Katherine and back at Red Eyes.

Over his shoulder Red Eyes said, "Just hold on to your dicks for a second, will you? Let me hear what the people have to say."

Burlane fished a benjie out of his wallet. "We're after some help."

Red Eyes snatched it from his hand and slipped it quickly into his pocket so his comrades couldn't see. "Everybody's after help of some kind or other. My friends'd like to lay eyes on those." Red Eyes nodded toward the snakes. He started to unfasten the latch chain.

"We talk," Burlane said.

"Sure, sure."

Behind him, someone yelled, "Hey! Fuck you doing, pisshead? Leave that alone."

"Shut up for a change, will you? Turn up the lantern."

"What?"

"Just do it." He opened the door so everybody could see Katherine in the dim light. He held a bottle of champagne by the neck. Foam spilled out and over his hand. He took a swig.

Twelve teenage males, Hispanics, blacks, and a couple of Anglos, all wearing expensive running shoes, squatted on the bare floor in a circle around bottles of champagne, plastic baskets of Pollo Supreme chicken, and crack paraphernalla.

In the corner behind them: a stack of 30 or 40 unopened cardboard boxes containing Toshiba computers and half a dozen cases of Dom Perignon champagne, one of them opened.

Seeing Katherine, the merrymakers rose to their feet, holding their bottles of champagne by the necks.

"My ladyfriend and I are talent agents," Burlane said.

Red Eyes laughed. "Talent agents! Sheee-it too."

Burlane said, "Dom Perignon. You've got good taste."

Red Eyes said, "We've got good taste in everything. Champagne, women, whatever . . ."

One of his friends said, "Spoken by a man whose mouth tastes like his asshole," and everybody laughed.

Red Eyes said, "Say, lady, you wouldn't be interested in . . ."

Burlane interrupted. "Uh-uh. Sorry. There'll be no screwing with the snakes."

Red Eyes put his hands up in mock fear. "Hey, hey. No offense there, Rambo."

"Oh?" Adrenaline squirted through Burlane's body.

Looking up at Burlane, Red Eyes blinked. He took a quick step backward.

One of Red Eyes' buddies said, "Way to go, dickbrains," and they all laughed. They were high on crack, drinking $65 bottles of champagne. No one felt like fucking with Burlane.

Red Eyes, covertly staring at Katherine's chest to show he wasn't completely defeated, said, "What kind of help is it you're looking for? Are you buying or selling?"

* * *

Up ahead, under a corner streetlight, a huge, thick-necked black man wore a tank top to show off the great slabs of muscles on his shoulders. He was joined by a second black giant, and a third, then a white behemoth. All wore tank tops to show off their incredible muscles.

An apartment door slammed.

Between the slammed door and the young hulks, voices in a courtyard. The courtyard was separated from the sidewalk by a hedge.

The muscular young men on the sidewalk laughed nervously, and leaned up against the fenders of three cars parked under the light. The cars had Miami Hurricane decals on the bumpers.

Katherine lowered her voice. "What do we have here?"

Burlane stepped under the branches of a spreading cypress, which partly shielded them from the streetlight. "Shhhhh. Listen." The wind was blowing from the direction of the young men, and they could hear their voices.

One of them said, "I can't fuckin' believe there's supposed to be a mystery about how the 'Canes score the best football players in the country, or how come it is Nevada, Las Vegas, is so hot at hoops. Can you believe living in Lawrence, Kansas, or Bloomington, Indiana? Spend your time fuckin' jackrabbits."

"Shee-it! Or Athens, Georgia. My cousin Carl's a safety there. He coulda been a 'Cane. That's where religion'll get you. Spent too damn much of his time studying the Bible. Think she'll do it?"

"I'm betting on it. It's not like it's the entire traveling squad, for God's sake. There're only eleven of us. No biggie. She's hot for it, I know she is. I told her we'll all throw in and make it right by her."

"Make it worth her while."

"She'll do it, believe me."

Voices from the hedged courtyard. Men's. And a young woman's.

Katherine said, "That's her. Helen."

"What?"

"Listen."

More men.

Helen again.

Burlane opened the gate and, followed by Katherine,

stepped into the courtyard of the apartment building nearest the cypress. No canines. They could hear better in the courtyard. The wind carried the conversation through the chain-link fences that separated the buildings.

Burlane squatted in the shadows and waited for his eyes to adjust to the dim light.

Helen said, "Oh, you guys."

A young man—a linebacker? fullback?—said, "Come on, now. What'll it take? Tell us what it'll take? We're game. We like to have fun, too. We like to party. We know the score."

"Oh, you."

"Come on, tell us. What'll it take?"

"Oh, I don't know."

"Like to toot a little?"

"You guys really are Hurricanes?"

"We ain't from Jupiter, honey."

"Ah, steroids, I bet."

The young man laughed. "Can't get away with that *shit* anymore. We got big mamas and daddies and a helluva weight room. We're big all over, ain't we, guys?"

"God!"

"I bet you love to toot, don't you?"

"Oh, you."

"You're shy, aren't you? She's shy, guys. See how shy she is. Shit, doesn't that give you a hard-on."

Helen said, "All of you? Eleven? Oh, you guys."

"You want to go party, let's go party. We'll show you a good time. We're all friends. We're teammates. Know all about teamwork. We know how to treat a lady." He raised his voice to address his companions on the sidewalk. "Right, guys? What do you say out there? Little teamwork, called for. You all ready to pitch in?"

The hulks on the sidewalk applauded. Hey, hey, they were ready for it. They knew about teamwork. They knew how to treat a lady. Just give them the chance.

The negotiator in the yard said, "Isn't she a sweetheart? Look at her! You want to do a little toot, sweetheart? She does, guys. I can tell she does."

Helen said, "Oh, you guys. Take me for a ride, and I'll think about it."

The chief negotiator said, "Sure. We'll take you for a ride all right."

Burlane whispered, "Well, what's next, Katherine? It's your sister."

"I want to talk to her, but if we both show up at once, we'll spook her for sure."

"What do you want me to do?"

"Stay here unless I need help, then come running, and we'll see if we can't somehow get her out of there."

Burlane nodded. "I agree."

"I have to try."

"Of course you do."

Katherine stepped through the open gate and strode rapidly in the direction of her sister.

Burlane waited, listening to her footsteps and the murmur of conversation in the wind.

One of the men, seeing her coming, said, "What the hell?"

"Helen!"

"Aw, shit!"

"Please, Helen."

"Hey, would you get a load of this woman's snakes!"

Helen said, "Let's get out of here."

"Helen, I want to talk to you. Please."

The hulk said, "Back off, snake woman. The fuck you think you're trying to do?"

"This is my sister, if you don't mind. Give me a minute, Helen. One minute."

"By God, I do mind," the hulk said.

"I said, let's go," Helen said.

"Please, Helen."

"Maybe your snake-lady sister would like to go with us," the hulk said. "We could entertain her for a minute or two. What do you think, guys?"

"We go now or the deal's off," Helen said.

"Helen, listen to reason, for God's sake. One minute. You owe me that much."

"It's my life, Katherine, not yours. I'll live it how I damn well please. Now go away and mind your own fucking business!"

"You are my business. You're my sister. Hey, hands off my chest, asshole."

Burlane stepped through the gate and sprinted toward the sisters on the sidewalk. He plunged into the group, grabbing Helen around the waist, and kept going.

A hulk swung on him.

Burlane turned to avoid the blow, but couldn't because of the wriggling Helen. He took a hard shot on the ear, and Helen twisted from his grip.

Burlane fell to his knees, dizzy, nearly passing out.

Another hulk give Katherine a hard football block with his elbows outstretched, knocking the wind out of her and sending her sprawling on the sidewalk.

The hulk who had hit Burlane said, "I think I broke my fucking hand."

"Let's go! Let's go! Let's go!" Helen yelled. She piled into the front car with the hulks, and all three cars sped off.

Katherine, gasping to regain her breath, got up from the sidewalk and watched them disappear. Her shoulders slumped. "We'll never catch them."

She was right, Burlane knew. "At least you know she's still in Miami."

Katherine sighed. "So close. So goddamn close."

"You'll find her again."

"You're goddamned right, I'll find her again. Dammit, if she'd just listen a minute!"

"She didn't seem in the mood to do very much listening, that's a fact."

"God, did you see her face? She used to have a lovely complexion, Sid. You should have seen her."

Burlane said nothing.

"Why would they be interested in somebody in that shape?"

Burlane bit his lower lip and turned up the palms of his hands. He felt helpless.

"The diseases she must be carrying around. Are they crazy?"

"Their brains are turned off."

"She was beautiful. Beautiful! Now look at her. Why, for God's sake? What's wrong with them?"

Burlane sighed. "They're not thinking about diseases, and I don't suppose they're very much interested in her complexion or the way she used to look."

23

N eed to know. That was the first rule.

If loose lips did not literally sink ships, they were certainly capable of splashing a marimba pilot; in view of Roberto Guzmán's videotape of Helen Donovan, Burlane saw no reason to tell Guzmán about his South Beach adventure with sister Katherine.

The next night Guzmán asked Khartoum to go with him on a search of his own—for Lourdes Martinez.

Sweet Lourdes had told him at Oysterman's that listening to the music along Ocean Drive, especially reggae, was one of her favorite early-evening pastimes. That was where they would find her, Guzmán said. He and Lourdes were made for each other. They were perfect together.

"What else are you going to do, Khartoum? Sit around and read? Play with your snake?"

Burlane had been scheduled to make another run for Manny Lopez, but it turned out Lopez couldn't make it.

"*Mañana*, May-jor, or maybe Sunday or Wednesday. What-ever. There is no hurry," Lopez had said. It was not that Lopez didn't like Khartoum's work; it was just that he was delayed. To get laid. To go fishing. What difference did it make?

Burlane told Guzmán sure, he'd go along for company.

The Cuban and his pilot companion had been listening to Soon Come, a reggae band at Tropics; when the band took a break at sunset, they went for a walk on Miami Beach.

"I'll find her, Khartoum. Give me enough time, and I'll find her. She's out there somewhere."

"She probably is, I agree."

"She's out there looking for me."

"She could very well be."

"She is. I know it. I won't quit. And when I catch that brother of hers, I'll strangle the motherfucker."

"Patience, patience, Roberto. You'll find her. Also, you should remember there may come a day when you'll want to get along with her brother."

"*Coño*. He just grabbed her and yanked her out of there. Right in the middle of our conversation! What was I supposed to do? Run after her like a puppy dog shouting for her number?"

"Nothing you could do, I suppose. And there's not much you can do now except keep looking."

"Have you ever seen how many Martinezes there are in the Miami telephone directory? Ooof! It's like Jones or Smith. Impossible."

The beach was a perfect white rectangle, three hundred yards wide and three miles long. Burlane said it looked like it had been cut by a giant cookie cutter and said so.

Guzmán looked around as though seeing the beach for the first time. "You're right about that, you know. Nature doesn't tidy up the corners."

They walked toward the water. Burlane discovered that the only real sand, which he had always thought a requisite for a beach, was located in a narrow strip along the water. The rest of the "beach" was a packed white substance—clay? chalk? crushed limestone?—over which was sprinkled an indifferent layer of sand. In some areas the wind had eliminated the sand, leaving scars of packed base.

To find the kind of sand they could wriggle their feet into, or make castles out of, beachgoers had to go to the water's edge. Although they were now packing their gear to go home, this in fact was where most of them had gathered with their blankets and suntan lotion and beach gear. Here were drying strands of purplish seaweed and a few cracked shells and bits and pieces of wood.

Here, almost, was nature.

Burlane kicked at the white base. "Where'd they get this stuff from, anyway, Roberto? I bet it doesn't even come from Florida."

"Beautiful women come down here and lay around nine-tenths naked, and you complain because there's not enough sand. You'd bitch if they hung you with a new rope, do you know that, Khartoum?"

Burlane looked foolish. "I was just wondering, was all."

"Coño, tu eres de pinga!"

Burlane stood with his back to the water, in the middle of the beach, on the packed white substance, and enjoyed a bath of color. He didn't know anything about the history of art deco architecture, but one thing seemed obvious: the roses, subdued oranges, lavenders, fuschias, plums, pastel yellows, soft greens, and off-blues used to accent the hotels and cafés on Ocean Drive mirrored the panorama of color that the sunset was reflecting off the bottoms of the clouds. The result was rich and sensual, languorous. Mysterious. Perhaps a little dangerous.

"All this color isn't bad, I have to admit," Burlane said. "You people have got something here with your sunsets."

"See. See what I told you. No matter what everybody says about you, Khartoum, you're not all bad. I tell people all that stuff they say about you is *mierda sólo. Mierda todo,* I tell them."

Laughing, they pushed on to the water's edge. The light surf was that pale blue-green Burlane associated with ads for Caribbean vacations. The color was truly wonderful. Burlane thought the version the Miami Dolphins used for their uniforms, which they called aqua, was somehow lacking.

As the sun set, a dazzling white liner, enthusiastic holiday-goers crowding her layers of decks, nurturing fantasies of romance and getting laid, made her slow, grand way past the southern tip of the peninsula.

"That's the *Carnival,*" Guzmán said. The *Carnival* was followed by another liner, and yet a third.

"Ahh, do you know them all?"

Guzmán said, "Most of them. The second two are the *Fantasy* and the *Norway.*"

As darkness settled, the three huge ships, moving farther offshore, became a dazzling, splendid show of twinkling, blinking lights, and disappeared slowly, slowly into the advancing night. Burlane watched the wonderful sight, thankful for the wind that kept the mosquitoes at bay. The two men headed back toward Tropics. In the distance, they heard Soon Come begin another set.

When they got to the bar, Guzmán ordered them each a rumrunner. He had no sooner taken his first sip than he said, "Shit, Khartoum, would you look there."

Burlane saw what he meant. Lourdes, the sweetheart from Oysterman's, was at the edge of the crowd, watching Soon Come.

"All right! Yes!"

"By God, you found her. Okay, Roberto!"

"I knew it. I knew it. I knew if I just didn't give up. No fucking way I'm not going to get her telephone number this time. Just no way."

Burlane, watching Guzmán from the corner of his eye, said, "Got your strategy and tactics?"

"You don't need strategy and tactics for a sweetheart like this, Khartoum. This is something entirely different."

"Then go for it. Show her your stuff."

Burlane watched, amused, as the amiable, animated, rejuvenated Roberto Guzmán engaged Lourdes Martinez in conversation. He had found her, and they were both obviously delighted, floating in their private, special zone.

A few minutes later, Guzmán motioned with his hand for Burlane to join them.

Guzmán said, "Lourdes, I want you to meet my friend Major M. Sidarious Khartoum."

Burlane shook her tiny hand. "Sid," he said.

"Retired major?"

"Sacked major," Burlane said.

"He's a wok master," Guzmán said. "You should taste his gingered chicken."

Burlane bowed. "My gingered chicken is said to be of the heavens, but I would never be the one to say it."

Lourdes giggled.

Guzmán said, "She spent the last three nights looking for me, Khartoum. While I was looking for her, she was trying to find me, just like I said. Can you believe it? Isn't that what I said?"

"That's exactly what you said."

"I knew it. I just knew it. She said she liked reggae. That was the key."

Lourdes said, "I could have throttled Eduardo, grabbing me like that."

"It turns out we just missed each other at Shooters. Ay!"

"See what I told you, Roberto. Patience," Burlane said.

"We almost missed each other again tonight. She was about to give up and go home when we came back from the beach. *Que suerte!* What do you think, Khartoum? Time for a little celebration?"

"I think so. You're both young. The night's warm. The breeze feels good. You've found each other. Soon Come isn't a bad reggae band."

"She drives a Yugo, Khartoum. A Yugo! Isn't that a kick? Got it parked down the street."

Lourdes giggled.

"A sensible car. How do you like it?" Burlane asked.

"It's cheap, but fun. Gets me where I want to go. It's yellow and black. The bumblebee, I call it."

"Well, good for you. You know, Roberto, I've had enough reggae for one night. Now that you've found your lady at last, I think I'll walk on home and maybe watch a movie on the tube. Give you two some time to celebrate alone."

Guzmán, holding Lourdes's hand, eyes glazed with happiness, swayed with the reggae rhythm of Soon Come as he watched the wild-haired Khartoum, with that loose-jointed walk of his, stroll down the sidewalk toward his South Beach apartment.

After listening to Soon Come until well past midnight, Roberto Guzmán and Lourdes Martinez walked hand in hand down Ocean Drive, taking a detour down a side street to check out Lourdes's bumblebee Yugo, then back again, past the Waldorf Hotel and the Clevelander, heading for Guzmán's pad in the stylishly art deco Manatee Apartments.

A gentle breeze was at their backs, caressing their bodies, and the night was warm. They'd both been looking for each other, and they'd found each other. Life was good.

Communicating by a squeeze of the hand and occasionally bumping together, they walked past a long line of gay men in Bohemian attire waiting to get inside the Warsaw Ballroom. On Washington Street they strolled past the Industry Club, another night spot, and the Cameo Theater, which showed skin flicks.

Guzmán slipped his hand around her body, feeling her move against him.

Suddenly they were there, at the Manatee.

Lourdes was wide-eyed."You have an apartment here?"

"This is it. What do you think?"

"It's beautiful, Roberto."

Guzmán opened the front door with a key. He ushered Lourdes inside, then, holding her hand, took her up a flight of stairs to his apartment.

Her eyes lit up when she saw the restored interior of the corner apartment, done in light blues and grays.

Guzmán beamed."You like it, then."

"Do I ever! It's lovely, Roberto."

"I keep it so I won't have to drive back to Coral Gables if I have too much to drink."

"What's this?" She flipped open the handsome art deco book on Guzmán's coffee table and quickly discovered that it featured a colored spread of the Manatee.

Guzmán slipped his arm around the sweet, sweet Lourdes. She was the one. So innocent. So unaffected. Capable of such joy. He could hardly believe it. Had he ever lucked out! She was the one. Delightful, was the word. He had lost her, then found her. *Sí, sí, sí!*

The sweet, sweet Lourdes, her hair smelling so wonderful, nuzzled up against him. Her body was so warm and soft, he could hardly believe it.

Roberto Guzmán, inhaling the fragrance of Lourdes's hair, felt so grand he wanted to shout it to the heavens, wanted to jump right out here and belt it out, sing it, like a hero in one of those dorky old Hollywood movies. Had he ever lucked out. *Que felicidad!*

He kissed her. Those lips! Her breath so sweet. Ooof!

Her breasts were warm against his chest. Ahhhh! He could hardly stand it.

Later, Roberto Guzmán lay back, listening to the splendid Lourdes singing in the shower.

I got a dog, and his fur is black
Pet him on the head, and you won't go back

The sheets smelled of Lourdes.

Black, black, black

Guzmán couldn't get enough of her. He breathed deeply, enjoying her smell.

Pet him on the head, and you won't go back

Guzmán had been told more than once that he should find a girlfriend like his mother. Guzmán's mima was a plump little sweetheart. She loved Roberto passionately and would do anything for him. Roberto knew that.

Now, he had found one just like her. A Cuban sweetheart. Lourdes would do anything for her man. And she'd be sexy when she got older, too; she was more petite than his mima had been when she was younger; her delicate frame could carry a few more pounds, no problem; as she got older she would round out just right.

And her *culo!* Ooooh!

Guzmán wanted to tell Lourdes everything about himself. That he had once caught 183 croakers in one afternoon off the Miami Herald bridge on Biscayne Boulevard. That he had hit a triple his first time at bat in Little League. That he was a special agent for the FBI's Organized Crime Unit and had been scouting marimbeiros when he met her.

Well, no. He couldn't tell her *that*. But everything else about himself.

And he wanted to know everything there was to know about her. What kind of movies she liked. What she liked to cook. It sounded corny, he knew, but it was the truth: his heart just soared. Everything suddenly smelled better and tasted better. Life was good. Life was grand. He was renewed. *Un hombre nuevo!*

He would take Lourdes for a ride on his 34-foot sailboat. She would pack a lunch. No, he would buy a fancy wicker picnic basket with French cheeses and foo-foo goodies and patés in it, and a cooler with champagne on ice. Good champagne. Proper champagne. The best. Not any of that cheap bulk-processed California swill. Now when the Bureau paid the bills.

They would go skinny-dipping with scuba gear. He would

follow her down in the clear Caribbean water, and, side by side, they'd cruise naked with groupers and skates.

Later, when she had played the kazoo for him naked, and they had made love, they would fall asleep in one another's arms, comforted by the gentle rising and falling of the calm sea.

After an afternoon on the water, he would take Lourdes shopping. He would buy her clothes beyond her dreams.

Then he'd take her to dinner, Dominique's maybe. They'd have rattlesnake salad and buffalo sausage and lobster and a bottle of Cristal. He'd get himself a new jacket for the occasion. Maybe buy it at Franco B. Spend a few bucks. Go for it.

Roberto Guzmán's insides twisted with desire. Fantasies of Lourdes Martinez tumbled one after another in a collage of beautiful dreams.

24

J ames Burlane lay naked in the dim light that spilled through the open glass louvers into the mustard-colored room. He wondered what Dante would make of trying to go to sleep in a room this color. Was there a level of purgatory painted French's-mustard-yellow?

In the apartment next to Burlane's, a soccer match, broadcast in Spanish by a gentleman with one hell of a set of lungs, came at last to an end, a one-nil victory for the home team, Real Tampico. The wonders of nighttime radio!

Burlane's third flight for Manny Lopez—from the Yucatán—had left him exhausted. His agreement with Harnar didn't include cooperation by the Coast Guard because the Coast Guard too had its share of marimba players. So each time out, Burlane had to fly pancaked all the way, never for a moment letting his attention wonder. When he got to Miami he was always pooped.

Lying there, his muscles aching, he supposed that he ought to follow Roberto Guzmán's suggestion and worm an invitation to visit Conchesa in Medellín. Manny Lopez could arrange it, he knew. The risk was that Conchesa's curiosity might be aroused, and a double-check of Burlane's credentials could cost him his life.

Besides, the idea of stopping the cocaine traffic at Colombia's borders was like trying to fix a leaky tire by putting a patch on the outside. What Harnar was most interested in was what happened to the coke after it got to American borders. There, theoretically, the patch of Coast Guard and Customs Service was at least correctly applied.

The cool wind racing across his skin felt good.

Burlane remembered the warming easterlies when he was a boy. Chinooks, they were called. After hard-assed north winds blew snow and ice down out of Canada for two or three months, the warming Chinooks followed. Oh, they were sweet. But after a sweltering tropical day or a tiring flight from Central America, the night winds of Miami Beach were right up there, Burlane had to admit.

Next door, the sportscaster delivered an excited recap of the soccer match. Burlane gathered that Tampico had played exceptional defense. The Guadalajara players had done everything within their power to penetrate the area in front of Tampico's goal, but they could not score. In the end, the Tampico manager had gone so far as to move every man forward. *Nada. Hijo de puta*!

Perhaps when winter baseball began in Mexico, Burlane would feel more at home. He could keep up with a Spanish account of a baseball game, but not *fútbol*.

Was the gentleman next door from Mexico? Burlane doubted it. More likely El Salvador or Nicaragua, although Burlane's Spanish wasn't good enough for him to spot the country. And was he using a shortwave or regular-band radio? He had either hit a lucky patch in the ionosphere or had a good radio. Burlane suspected the latter.

Burlane guessed that his neighbor longed for home. For *fútbol* matches. For a place where everybody spoke Spanish. Burlane imagined that for this steadfast radio listener, American football, with that ridiculous plastic armor, was incomprehensible.

Burlane knew that Cubans were especially passionate baseball fans; when Miami's Jose Canseco started slamming them out of Oakland Coliseum, they went bananas. Burlane had passed through Miami in that September and had seen the craziness for himself. Forty home runs and 40 stolen bases in one season? It had never been done before. Not even by Mickey Mantle! *Viva Jose!*

The neighbor turned the radio off. Burlane drifted off to sleep.

Then he awoke. He listened to the wind rustling the curtains by the louvered windows. He scratched himself, and thought he heard a voice.

He sensed movement outside the windows. Somebody said something. He caught one fragment clearly: " . . .omrade Molotov," followed by suppressed laughter. Somebody else shushed him up.

Burlane grabbed his .22-caliber machine pistol, his wallet, to which were fastened the keys to his Cherokee, and a pair of boxer shorts.

He grabbed an armload of shirts and jeans from a bureau drawer and threw them and the pillows under the single sheet. Quickly, he did his best to make a decoy body under the sheet.

Voices. Downstairs.

He slipped the shorts on.

Movement on the stairs.

He tiptoed quickly to the back door.

He paused. Should he stay and attempt to ambush the fuckers with his machine pistol? He wanted to in the worst way.

But then again maybe not. No telling how many there were.

He heard a faint metallic click at his front door.

Whoever it was had a key.

And his companion very likely had a Molotov cocktail.

Burlane darted into his kitchenette and grabbed his wok, unlocked the back door, and stepped onto the steep flight of interior stairs that served as a fire escape. He had checked it out when he moved in; the stairs led to a narrow courtyard littered with dog shit and broken toys.

Should he venture out into the courtyard? No. Do that and he'd likely be a had dad. The disgrace was to be killed out of stupidity.

He eased the safety off his pistol and waited on the stairs.

Behind him, an explosion. His apartment burst into flames.

He stayed put.

Somebody had casually decided to torch him in bed. Now just who in the hell had pulled that stunt?

When he could hear sirens, he slipped out the back door into the moonlight, wok in one hand, pistol in the other. He dodged a broken beer bottle with his left foot, but stepped into fresh dog manure with his right.

He hustled quickly down the alley in the direction of his Cherokee. A few minutes later, the attention of the area diverted to the fire at the corner of Third and Meridian, he slipped into the vehicle and headed west on Alton Road toward Miami.

25

James Burlane rolled his eyes toward the heavens, pretending to be shocked. "Isn't this something, Ara? I told you—why meet in a park or a shopping mall when we can meet someplace civilized?" Burlane sipped his six-dollar rumrunner.

Burlane and Ara Schott were in Shooters in the Bay Side at Biscayne Boulevard downtown. Shooters featured oysters and chicken wings and waitresses with wonderful butts.

Schott tried not to be obvious as he scoped the waitress behind Burlane, a petite brunette with an outrageous Cuban *culo*. "Civilized? Say again, how did you find this place?"

"Roberto brought me here when he was looking for Lourdes. They have bands here on the weekends. They had a reggae group the day we were here. His lady likes reggae."

"Tell me again about last night. You say you grabbed your wok and hid on the stairs when your apartment went up?"

"Actually, cowered on the stairs would be more accurate. Knees clicking like castanets. Those apartment buildings sit cheek by jowl with only narrow passages between them."

"Perfect for ambush."

"You better believe it. I risked getting pranged if I went

outside. But I did wake up, and I did protect myself so everything's hip."

"Hip for the moment. If we had any brains we'd make like a couple of Arabs and steal silently away into the night."

"Oh, come on, Ara. You're talking to Sid Khartoum here. El Sid does not run, especially when some asshole tries to blow him up in bed."

"If I told Harnar, he'd give you the hook, James. No doubt about that."

"Yes, but you're not going to tell him, are you, Ara? By the way, before we forget Guzmán, did you learn anything about who pays for what to keep him in his role?"

"For starters, the government leases his house in Coral Gables and his apartment in Miami Beach."

"Who buys the furnishings?"

"Guzmán, I think, but I'm not sure about that. The government has leased a sailboat for his use, but he owns his own car, a BMW."

"Who arranged the leases?"

"The government takes Guzmán's recommendations. The house, the apartment, and the sailboat are all leased from the same man, a real-estate developer named Jaime Guerrero."

"Ahh, Guerrero the cocksman. The circle closes."

"What's that?"

"Jaime Guerrero is Guzmán's buddy from high school days. Did they tell you that, Ara?"

"No, they didn't."

"They probably don't know. If Guerrero is the legal owner of Guzmán's property, the government can't confiscate it if he gets busted for his little scam." Burlane sipped his rumrunner. "I've been straight arrow with Manny Lopez. He doesn't have a bitch that I know of. He thinks I'm nuts, but I've been delivering for him."

"I wouldn't be too casual if I were you, James. Here's some more disconcerting news. What the cops aren't telling reporters is that the gnawed hand belonged to a Miami cop who once broke his little finger. The fracture matched the X-rays in his medical records. The skull in the last find belonged to your DEA friend, Luis Fernandez."

"What?" Burlane was stunned.

"That's right."

"Luis? Fed to a fucking dog? How do they know that?"

"The skull the kids found by the Tamiami was his. They identified him by his teeth."

Burlane sighed. "Aw, shit, Ara."

"I'm sorry, James."

"You know something, I knew intuitively Luis was straight. He was an okay guy, he truly was. Loved his fishing. Blue jeans were good enough for him. He honestly didn't give a shit about the squid."

"Squid? What are you talking about?"

"Nothing. It's a long story, Ara."

"You have to keep in mind, James, Fernandez was Roberto Guzmán's friend, too."

"So? He was probably checking Guzmán out, just like me."

Schott shrugged. "Maybe that's why he got fed to a dog."

"MacRae was doing what? Did you find that out?"

"Monitoring the drug traffic from ship to shore via harbor boats. He was trying to trace Conchesa's water connections."

"Tell me, what does Harnar say about dead cops and dog-food killers?"

He wants you out of here yesterday if not sooner. He says he doesn't want to be responsible. Et cetera. You know Harnar, James."

Burlane shook his head; yes, he knew Harnar. "What does the senator say?"

"She says it's up to you."

"A stout-hearted Montanan," Burlane said. "Good sense obtains. We stay in business."

Schott watched two waitresses giving their orders at the counter. He slurped the dregs of his rumrunner through a straw. "These are good, but I thought they were from Hawaii."

"You're probably thinking of mai tais. Mai tais are generic tropical, Ara. They're sold wherever tourists gather. I'll take you down to Penrods on the beach, and we'll have more rumrunners there. Rum, grenadine, and ice."

Burlane slipped an envelope out of his jacket pocket, and took out the photograph of Helen. "This young woman's name is Helen." He watched his friend examine the photograph.

Schott said, "What's the story here?"

"Last Friday, I went with Guzmán to a bullshit nightclub called Oysterman's looking for Luis."

"Fernandez?"

Burlane nodded. "At least that was Guzmán's story. I

retreated to a corner for some peace from the insane disco music when this long-legged blonde, Katherine Donovan, suddenly had me pinned, asking me some damned specific questions."

"How specific?"

"She suggested I was a cop or played the marimba."

"Uh-oh."

"She was after her sister, she said. Her sister had come down here to be a model and wound up hooked on coke."

"The truth, do you think?"

"The family resemblance is clear enough, besides which Guzmán showed me a videotape taken nearly a year ago of a night he and his friend Jaime Guerrero spent with her. In return for coke, Helen gave them a performance straight out of Krafft-Ebing. Hard core."

"Oops!"

"A casualty of the marimba. The next day I helped Katherine run Helen down in South Beach, but we lost her to a gang of football players."

"Football players?"

"Hulks. A whole gang of them. Katherine's still looking for Helen, but Helen is doomed."

26

Helen Donovan woke up late.
     She had to pee.
     Little pee pains. Stab. Stab. Crap!

An old-fashioned electric clock hummed on the wall.

She was exhausted. Her brains felt mushy. Her mouth tasted awful.

It was one o'clock. What now?

Stab. Stab. She had to pee.

She turned on the couch. A Pollo Supremo wrapper tumbled to the floor.

She should get up and get moving, but she couldn't. She had to pee, but she was too tired to get up.

Her stomach growled.

Katherine wanted her to go back to Baltimore. Wanted her to sign up with some fucked treatment program. For what? To do what? Ration her pussy to some boring dork? Spread her legs for fried clams at Howard Johnson's on Friday night?

Was that what they wanted her to do? Was that it? To turn herself over? To be owned?

She wanted a man who would walk naked with her on the beach with the moon above and the surf crashing and throw her on the sand and pull her legs wide, crazed by the animal inside him, and by God give her a proper fucking.

Helen's left tit was sore. She poked at a hickey by the side of her nipple and winced.

She wished she had a gram to perk her up. It wouldn't take much, a couple of hits, and she'd be up and going.

Whose couch was this? What's-his-face's. She couldn't remember his name. Robert or Richard or Ronald. Someone.

Couches, couches, couches. This one, at least, was long enough for her to stretch out on. Everybody's couch but hers.

She wanted her own couch. With soft pillows and a nice comforter. She wanted a television set with a remote, too, so she could lie on her own couch, tucked in with her comforter and beholden to no one. She'd eat Fritos and sip Diet Coke and flip through the channels until she found a good movie.

She'd watched a war movie after what-his-face had finished, having gotten his pathetic cock up for the last time and tumbled off to bed.

The soldiers in the movie—serving their hitch one day at a time—marked Xs off what they called a short-timer's calendar. They were from Brooklyn, San Antonio, Walla Walla, and so on, and they wanted to go back.

She wanted . . .

She wanted someone. No, she didn't. Not that shit.

She wanted . . .

She wanted freedom.

She wanted fulfillment, but the quality of fulfillment eluded her. What was it? What was there, locked in her imagination, but ever vague and elusive?

She didn't know what she wanted anymore.

No, that wasn't true. She did too want her own couch. What was wrong with that? Why shouldn't she have her own couch? And a comforter, and Diet Coke and Fritos, and remote television set? No having to fuck some shit to make it through the day. She wanted all that, and she wanted a bed, too. Her own bed. A bed with proper sheets. When she finished with her movie, she wanted to slip into a bed with sheets that didn't smell of sweat and pecker tracks.

It seemed like the only time she saw a bed anymore was when someone wanted more space to fuck her. When this one had finished with her, he'd thrown her onto the couch like a dirty pair of shorts. He liked the privacy of sleeping alone.

If he'd let her sleep with him, maybe put an arm around her shoulder, she might have felt differently. That wouldn't have taken much. But no: face it, she'd swapped pussy for coke, a deal was a deal, and what's-his-face had delivered.

She'd gotten what she was after. She didn't have any complaint.

She wanted some coke.

She had to pee.

She listened to the clock hum.

She started to cry. She lay there, sobbing.

She summoned the energy to retrieve what's-his-face's remote from the floor. She punched up a channel and tapped the mute button.

A preacher with a florid face and nose of Rushmorian proportions lectured passionately to his far-flung flock. There were enough alcoholics among their flocks that it didn't pay for preachers to get too high and mighty about booze as they did about other drugs. Despite attempts to promote the neutral euphemism "substance abuse," there was, in the popular imagination, a moral hierarchy among the "substances" that politicians worked to the hilt.

She watched the minister. The face surrounding his nose was so earnest. He looked so sincere. She wondered what he was talking about. She tapped the mute button.

". . . you have to understand that we're not talking about money. We're talking about seed. Some of the seed you eat. Some of the seed you save. Some of the seed you sow. If you sow your seed in God's furrows, then He will give you more seed to eat and save. There is more talk in the Bible about money than about sin and salvation. Did you know that? So remember, when we're talking about the church's projects, we're really talking about furrows, and when we're talking about money, we're really talking about seed . . ."

She punched him off, marveling at the simplicity of his logic: The present is screwed, so his flock lived for the future. Seed for salvation.

Helen's future was screwed, so she lived for the present. Pussy for coke.

Her life was pussy for coke.

She was getting tired of it.

Gang bangs weren't exciting anymore. But when they were finished, and Helen had reduced their mighty cocks to limp little weanies, the profitable guilt really set in. None of the participants wanted to look cheap in the eyes of their friends.

The shrinks would say she was punishing herself.

Well, fuck the shrinks.

Helen sighed.

The clock hummed.

She watched the red second hand sweep slowly around the face of the clock.

She had lost the ability to dream, and that was the spooky part.

She was so tired. Exhausted. She could hardly turn over on the couch. She needed a pick-me-up. Something to get her going. If what's-his-face had had any class, he'd have left her a little hit on the coffee table, but she knew he hadn't. The two of them had gone through his entire three-and-a-half-gram baggie.

She thought about Baltimore. She'd like to have a boyfriend. She'd like to have a boyfriend and hold hands with him at a foreign movie on Charles Street. The Orioles had replaced their old stadium. She'd like to watch the Orioles play in their new park.

Was that still possible? Could she have that? An appreciative arm around her? A hot dog loaded with chopped onions and mustard? Applauding Cal Ripken, Jr., at bat with that determined look in his eye?

She knew when what's-his-face woke up, he'd be groggy too. Buzz all night. Sleep all day. That was the cycle.

She had to pee.

The clock hummed.

She watched the second hand. It swept, inexorably, past the three. Past the four, on its way to the five. Past the six.

She wanted some coke. She had a need. A void. She wanted to live. She needed to get up and get moving. Had to have it. Had no choice.

She remembered being 16 years old and going to something called Young People's at the Presbyterian Church down the street from where she grew up in northwestern Baltimore. The Presbyterians were predestinarians; they argued that since God was omniscient and everything, He obviously knew the screwed future. What a wonderful God!

One night the minister confidently asserted that dogs didn't go to heaven.

Well, why was that?

Because dogs didn't have souls, he said, citing chapter and verse.

Helen had been stunned by his arrogance. She later understood that the conceit that dogs didn't have souls was the underwear of the larger, repressive drag that people wore without being aware of it. Over this transparent garment was worn layer upon layer of fantasy, delusion, and outright lie.

Perhaps it would have been better to have been born a dog. A dog could at least look forward to some peace at the end. A dog was allowed to be a dog. A dog lived. A dog died. His cycle completed, he returned to earth, as did all animals.

What's-his-face was still sleeping. The odds were he kept his stash in his bedroom. They almost always held something back, the bastards. If she slipped into his bedroom there was no telling what she might find. She needed something to get her up and moving again.

27

Mima Martinez fingered the large green and black beads at her throat, then punched open the garage door with her remote. As the door slid skyward in expensive, high-tech silence—devoid of the slightest annoying hum—she adjusted her Ray-Ban sunglasses against the tropical sun.

Mima had always had more sense than to unnecessarily fry her face, and so was given to stylish broad-brimmed hats—today's hat, on the seat beside her, being a $250 Bill Blass.

It never entered Mima's mind that the assertion that she looked like Natalie Wood might be abject bullshit. She believed it and clung to it passionately, in near religious fervor.

Mima believed the wearing of a hat enhanced the physical similarities between herself and Natalie Wood. Separately—and spontaneously, Mima thought—Lourdes and Marta had both mentioned the Natalie Effect when she wore a hat.

She asked Eduardo about it and modeled an outfit both with and without a hat. Eduardo agreed that the hat did the trick, although he couldn't lay his finger on the specific reason why. Hat on, Mima was Natalie Wood; hat off, she was almost, but not quite, Natalie. He said maybe hats concealed a basic difference in the shape of their heads.

Looking her youthful Natalie Wood best, Mima cruised down Palmetta Drive in her $125,000 Rolls-Royce.

Of the many twisting, winding streets and cul-de-sacs in Cocoplum, not all were equal in status. Everybody could cite reasons as to why his or her street was a touch classier. A rock star lived on their street, or a certain millionaire financier, or an impossibly rich drug dealer the cops couldn't touch.

In fact, there were so many rich and momentarily famous residents of Cocoplum that none of them carried too much weight, except for one: the Oakland Athletics slugger Jose Canseco. Although Jose's street was perhaps not the best in Cocoplum, the value of his neighbor's property had shot up when he moved in.

There was hardly a woman in Cocoplum, including Mima, who had not at one time or another indulged in the fantasy of accidentally bumping into Jose and his muscles while out for a stroll in the neighborhood. Although Mima was some years older than the slugger, she was undeterred. Age was on the outside, and Mima had taken care of that nonsense.

The canal looped around Mima's property, turning it into a peninsula of sorts, the water becoming, essentially, a moat. This privacy and suggestion of exclusivity added a quarter of a million bucks to the value of her house. The two-story imitation English country manor was made of stones imported from Devonshire; it was flanked on the left by an imitation Alamo owned by Colombians of no visible means of support, and on the right by an outsized Swiss chalet owned by a commodities broker.

But Mima truly did think Palmetta was one of the classier streets in Cocoplum. Thank God, the rich on Palmetta had so far stopped short of reconstructed Castilian castles—as had happened to one embarrassed area of Cocoplum. The fact that Palmetta was featured in a heavily promoted WTVJ story on Cocoplum cinched its reputation. Much pride, as well as property values, was at stake, and the residents along Palmetta had been jubilant. The WTVJ cameras had dwelled on the houses with yachts anchored out back—including the Martinez residence. Since that story was telecast, Mima had been able to walk with extra pride at Cocoplum gatherings.

As everybody knew—or an astute passerby could quickly discern—the insiders' competition in Cocoplum had to do with porticos. If you didn't have a house on a canal, you definitely couldn't go cheap on the portico. Even Mima had to admit the competition had sometimes gotten out of hand; there were cases in which the entrance was very nearly as large as the house itself. There was hardly any arguing that Mima's portico was the best on Palmetta. The interior of her portico featured a green and black jade mural, carved in relief, of peasants throwing hand lines into the surf.

The residential area next to Cocoplum, luxurious by most standards, made Mima smile. Proles lived there. Wage slaves.

She drove to a run-down black neighborhood at the fringes of the Cuban community in Hialeah, to a *botánica* run from the home of a tiny black man, the *babalawo* Jorge Rodriguez. The leathery-skinned, jet-black Rodriguez—who was well past 80— had received his religious instruction as a boy in Cuba.

Rodriguez grew sacrificial animals in the fenced yard behind his dilapidated one-bedroom house. The house was white on the outside, but the interior walls and ceilings were jet black, and he had painstakingly painted constellations of the stars on them.

A year before his birth, Rodriguez's mother had gone to a santero complaining of pains in her stomach. She subsequently delivered a toad, a sign her next child was destined to become a *babalawo*, a master of Ifa, the way of divination.

Everybody knew that Rodriguez, through proper cere- mony, could see the future.

On seeing Mima Martinez park her white Rolls outside his modest shack, Jorge Rodriguez got up to turn on the tea kettle. Mima liked tea when they talked.

Mima was the most powerful santera in Miami and his best customer, but, as befitted his status as a *babalawo*, Rodriguez took his time.

The longer he took, he believed, the more apt his visitors were to buy one of the colorfully painted, plaster-of-paris saints he displayed on a table behind the barred window beside the front door. He was old and had arthritis; his visitors needed time to reflect as he slowly went about the business of turning the gas under the kettle. This was not a *botánica* for tourists; it was his sole source of income.

Everybody in the Santería community knew that on the nights of *ebo*, Mima's *orisha*, Ogun, rode the night wind in the form of a jet-black Doberman.

Once, she had confessed to Rodriguez that she had violated a fundamental law of Santería by feeding the dog flesh as well as blood for *ebo* to Ogun. On hearing this startling admission, Rodriguez repeated the old rule: *the blood is for the saint, Mima, the flesh is for the priest.*

Rodriguez knew nothing good would come of this awful trashing of Ogun's *ashe*. It confirmed Rodriguez's long-held conviction that Carmela's mother had made a grave mistake in assigning her main *orisha*. A santera could not handle Ogun. That required a man.

But Rodriguez would say nothing. It did not pay to make enemies among the santeros, besides which Mima was his best customer—buying sacrificial animals for several different *orishas* worshiped by her family. What she wanted for her ceremonies, she bought. She never hesitated at the price, and never tried to worm credit.

Mima's dog suffered from an extreme restlessness that had his mistress worried. Mima once confessed to him that the dog slept most of the day in a form of funk or malaise, and could only be revived by appeasing his ravenous appetite with a special diet she would not reveal, even to him.

She hinted that a white rooster, Ogun's traditional favorite, was no longer sufficient *ebo* when the *orisha* inhabited the dog's body. Even more spooky was her suggestion that the dog required more than blood.

Rodriguez thought to himself: *You foolish, silly woman! The* ashe *is clear. Blood for your* orisha, *flesh for yourself. You should never have given Ogun flesh! Never. It was wrong and dangerous.*

Rodriguez suspected that Mima both worshiped and feared the dog's magical transformations. The power of Santería was awesome, but it could, and sometimes did, go bad. When a santero lost control of a spirit, or a spirit unaccountably turned evil, the results could be truly scary. The rule was to follow your *orisha's ashe*. Never, ever deviate from the proper *ashe*.

Rodriguez's own principal *orisha*, Eleggua, the messenger and way opener, had told him some real stories. Rodriguez had consulted Eleggua about Mima's transgression. Eleggua, shocked that the *orisha* involved was Ogun, suggested that Rodriguez stay on her good side.

Of all the *orishas* she could have fed flesh to, she had to choose Ogun!

Ay, Santa Barbara!

Mima liked to talk, and Rodriguez was pleased to listen, wondering what manner of bad end would come to this confident but profoundly ignorant santera who had so casually fed flesh to Ogun. Flesh!

She had hinted, but not said outright, that she had gone a step further, offering Ogun something other than his usual rooster or dog. Rodriguez hesitated to speculate on the outcome.

Mima Martinez didn't mind her waits on the porch while the old man heated the water for their tea. It gave her time to contemplate the plaster saints behind the barred window.

These saints had been assigned to the *orishas* hundreds of years earlier. St. Christopher, the priests said, was Agayu, *orisha* of fatherhood; St. Francis was Orula, source of wisdom and knower of destiny; St. Joseph was Osanyin, *orisha* of herbs; St. Barbara was Shango, who knew the ways of force.

St. Norbert was Eduardo's *orisha*, Oshosi, hunter and protector. *Ebo* for Oshoshi required clear rum, guinea hens, or white doves. Rodriguez stocked the correct rum, distilled in Cuba; he raised the guinea fowls and doves himself.

St. Mercedes was Marta's *orisha*, Obatala, the one who saw with clarity. Obatala demanded sacrifices of white goats or pigeons, which Rodriguez also raised and sold.

St. Caridad was Lourdes's Oshun, *orisha* of Eros. Oshun was satisfied with the blood of white hens, sheep, or goats. Rodriguez supplied all these, plus the special fans and peacock feathers Lourdes needed for *ebo*.

Mmmmmm. Rodriguez's window displayed a new statue of St. Norbert. She decided to buy it for Eduardo. Help him take his mind off the Cubs. Mima could not understand how her son could become fixated on a baseball team that never won a pennant.

The *babalawo* Jorge Rodriguez, having been slightly quicker than usual, opened the door, holding a tray with two cups of tea. "Ahh, Mima," Rodriguez said. "Eleggua told me you were coming so I put water on for tea. He gives me plenty of warning, but I'm so very slow these days. The arthritis. I hope I didn't keep you waiting too long. *Qué placer.*"

Mima frowned. She was not happy. *"Es sobre Marimba."*

Rodriguez looked concerned and sympathetic. *"Todavía está inquieto?"*

28

A balmy wind pushed the clouds like nocturnal four-masters, and the ghostly ships, sails furled in a billowing reach, stormed across the muted white of the ancient and honorable moon.

Nighttime. Feeding time.

The anxious Doberman paced.

Marimba's studded, black-and-green leather collar had a box on the underside that zapped the dog if he approached an electrical wire buried around the shore of the Martinez peninsula and under the driveway at the gate.

When Marimba was still a puppy, Mima had given Eduardo the unsavory Skinnerian task of teaching him the boundaries. Eduardo placed small white flags over the wire. Actually, the flags came atop small wire rods that he speared into the ground one by one. When the dog had been zapped enough to learn the danger zone, Eduardo removed the flags. By such discipline the dog was restrained without the property being marred by an unsightly and annoying fence.

Besides, it was not such a harsh restriction. The lawn was large, and when Ogun entered and became one with him at *ebo*, Marimba roamed the night wind.

Mima didn't understand people who walled their estates in with impossible barriers. What was the point of owning one of the grandest houses in Cocoplum if nobody could see it? *Eso es una estupidez!* It had cost her real bucks to import the proper stone from southern England. Why not let the proletarians drive by and stare in awe? A small pleasure.

Mima once mentioned her attitude toward fences at a ta-ta cocktail party and was stunned when a snotty bitch said, "My dear Mima, when you really have it made, you won't give a damn if people see your place or not. You'll drive an old beater and have pizza sent in. Confidence is the measure."

The comment made Mima furious, and on the next full moon she turned Babaluaye loose on the evil bitch, offering him an *ebo* of rum and tobacco to put him in the proper mood; sure enough, eight months later, the woman was diagnosed with cancer of the pancreas. To Mima's, sublime pleasure, she died in weeks, a testament to Marimba's power. Mima wondered if the bitch thought the privacy of the grave was so hotsie-totsie.

Marimba was four feet tall and weighted 115 pounds— with fist-sized paws and long, powerful legs. The sheen of his ebony fur was so rich the dog seemed almost iridescent; finely sculptured ropes of muscle rippled on his flanks; his back shimmered and glistened in relief.

The dog knew the drill of his nightly feeding.

First Eduardo came out, dressed in white, and gave Marimba a scratching behind the ears. "Sit," Eduardo said.

Marimba sat.

"Stay." Eduardo said. He stepped to one side.

Marimba stayed.

Then Mima, Lourdes, and Marta came out, in their white dresses and red beads.

Mima held a plastic Budweiser beer cooler in the crook of her left arm.

Marimba knew what was in the cooler. He tensed.

"Stay," Eduardo said.

Mima opened the cooler and pulled out Luis Fernandez's thawed left foot and threw it to the dog.

Marimba leaped on the foot, fangs bared. He ripped the toes off first and chewed them with obvious contentment. The bones and cartilage of Fernandez's toe bones *crunch-crunch-crunched* as he gulped them down.

Eduardo said, "He just loves the toes. Notice that? Sounds like he's eating celery."

Mima gave him a look.

Eduardo shut his mouth.

Finished with Fernandez's toes, Marimba held the foot between his paws and chewed off the heel. When that was finished, he examined his prize briefly, eyes glistening, then set about chewing the goodie layer of muscle under the arch of the foot. When that was done, he ripped the skin off the top and chewed it contently. Then it was gone, no more meat on the foot bones.

The dog looked up. He was still hungry. He wanted more.

Mima said, "Oh, poor Marimba." She reached in the cooler and grabbed a fresh rib roast of beef. She threw it on the ground in front of him.

Marimba sniffed the beef and looked hopefully up at Mima.

Mima said, "See, he doesn't like beef, Eduardo. And he's bored with roosters and goats and dogs. Bored."

Marimba returned to what was left of Fernandez's foot, and began gnawing on the bones.

"Ohhhhhh, he wanted more, poor baby."

Eduardo said, "Mima, he always wants more. When there's absolutely nothing left on the foot bones, he'll eat the beef."

"It's hard for him to eat it thawed after Ogun has been inside him, and he's had it fresh."

Eduardo looked hard at his sisters. "Lourdes, Marta, speak up, for heaven's sake. This can't continue."

His sisters said nothing.

He said, "*Coño.* Don't just stand there like bumps. Help me out. It's bad enough the dog has to have the stuff, but we've got to slow up a bit. Somehow ration it out to him. Got to."

Mima said, "Don't talk about Marimba like that in his presence."

Eduardo said, "You know, Mima, I've been checking out some possibilities. Do you know that those places around the country that sell horse meat add beef fat to it so it tastes like beef? The fat is what gives it the taste. The fast-food chains mix lean Central and South American beef with fat from grain-fed animals in the Midwest. The consumer never knows the difference."

Mima saw where that argument was heading. She said, "No, Eduardo, we will not adulterate his treat or otherwise try to trick him. The people who eat that stuff have all their taste in their mouth anyway."

Eduardo frowned.

"You could feed those people beef fat mixed with sawdust, and they'd never know the difference. But we can't have human bones found in our garbage, and we can't have you driving around slinging them out of the window anymore. That has to stop, I agree."

"Thank God!" Eduardo knelt and gave the gnawing Marimba an affectionate scratch behind his spiked ears.

Mima said, "Gardeners use bone meal, don't they? Where have I seen that? I've been thinking that if we got ourselves a power grinder with proper blades, we could grind the bones up into a nice meal. Get ourselves an industrial model. Do it right."

Eduardo blinked.

"We can enlarge our garden. Tell the gardener we'll furnish all the bone meal he can use. If that won't do it, we'll mix the meal with seeds and feed it to the birds. I've always wanted a bird feeder outside my bedroom window, down by the water."

"Anything that cuts the risk is fine by me."

"Marimba loves those bones, doesn't he? Look at him, Eduardo."

Marimba, chewing on Luis Fernandez's foot, looked balefully out into the darkness. Still gnawing, he glanced up at the mention of his name.

29

Eduardo Martinez used his remote to snuff the sound of the commercial while the Mets took the field. *"Carajo!* You two are something else. Do you realize you've been running in and out of those bathrooms for more than three hours now? What are you doing in there? It's incredible."

Lourdes, wrapped in a towel, stopped in the hallway. "You have a question, oh smooth one?"

Eduardo said, "You shower. You wash your hair. You brush your teeth. You swipe on some pit juice. You slap on some smell. You smear on some lipstick. What else is there to do?"

Lourdes raised an eyebrow. "Plllennnty! And besides, this is part of the fun. Better than laying around watching the Cubs and scratching your stupid testicles."

"The Mets this afternoon. Cubs are off. Why don't you put your beds in your bathrooms? You could take little naps in there between sessions of admiring yourselves."

"We don't tell you how to do your job. You don't tell us how to do ours." Lourdes stuck her tongue out at Eduardo and disappeared into her bedroom.

Lourdes and her sister Marta just loved to shop. They

savored each moment of their buying expeditions, especially the Friday afternoons when they capped their trip with a visit to Club Passions.

The trip to Club Passions was part of Lourdes and Marta's duties in the family business, but it was not an onerous chore by any means. Marimbeiros hung out in Club Passions on Friday afternoons to show off their bucks, and there Lourdes and Marta helped Eduardo spot marks.

The Mets were at bat again. Eduardo tapped the mute button.

Lourdes stepped out of her bedroom, looking fabulous. She checked herself out in the mirror.

Eduardo glanced at her and returned to the game. "It's a wonder you and Marta don't paste those 'Born to Shop' bumper stickers on your cars. The more conspicuous the consumption, the better you two like it. Have they talked about that in your economics class? Or do they read books at the University of Miami?"

Lourdes, turning to look at herself in profile, said, "What you don't understand, Eduardo, is that human cultures have evolved around a biological principle that is economic in nature: production and consumption. Men produce. Women consume. As long as you men think through your *pingas*, we're the ones who'll do the buying."

"Ay! *Cojónes*. Isn't that the fucking truth!"

Lourdes turned again and used her fingernail to flip a piece of lint off her hip. "There is no free sex, just as there is no free lunch. That's why we're in control, not you. If you think otherwise, dream on." She tossed her mane of black hair.

Marta stepped out of the bathroom. She'd been listening to the conversation and wanted to support her sister. "So who are we after at Club Passions, Eduardo, some geek peddling a few grams to support his habit, or someone moving keys? What do you think it'll take to score with Alejandro Pena or Ricardo Hernandez?"

"You think they go for bucktoothed fat girls in K-Mart outfits?" Lourdes said.

"No lo creo!"

Lourdes said, "Of course we have a good time spending money. Why shouldn't we? The bumper stickers are right: we *are* born to shop. So there, Eduardo. Make fun."

"Coño!"

Marta said, "So lay around watching baseball. But remember, we've got Club Passions this afternoon. Mima won't like it if you're back here glued to the bottom of the ninth when you've got work to do."

Eduardo made a farting sound by blowing between his thumb and forefinger. He turned up the sound on the Mets. Their rookie third baseman had made a sensational stop, and they were showing the taped replay.

Their handbags stuffed with comforting wads of hundred-dollar bills, Lourdes and Marta set off for Coconut Grove.

Lourdes drove her Mercedes convertible; it was a wonderful day for some sun, not sweltering hot, and if they really got into a buying mood, the Mercedes had more trunk space than Marta's Jaguar. Lourdes parked the Mercedes in a secure indoor lot opposite Mayfair, and the two sisters, looking fine and feeling good, set out in high spirits, their high-heels going *click, click, click* on the cement.

Lourdes and Marta were not J. C. Penney kinds of women. They didn't go to stores. They went to shops. A proper shop did not sell anything made out of oil. A truly respectable shop was someplace where the other customers were similarly slender, well manicured, and good-looking—and did not worry about price. A place where the help was attractive and solicitous. When Lourdes and Marta wanted to browse, they wanted to be left alone; when they wanted help, they wanted help now, not later.

Lourdes bought herself a pair of $55 French underpants, the better to carry out her part of the family business. Marta went for a $75 Christian Dior bra. They each bought themselves a $2,500 Bob Mackie dress.

Then, their stomachs growling after a day of not eating, they set off for Club Passions.

The owner of Club Passions understood, at an intuitive level, the nexus between sex and money. At Club Passions the waitresses, with extraordinary if not downright outrageous bodies, were formally dressed in tuxedo bikinis. They wore neat little black bow ties around their necks. Their formal jackets consisted of tiny white shirt pockets on black nipple cups. Their black leather thong bikinis barely covered the companionable neighborhood of orifices.

The cuisine at Club Passions, mainly seafood, salads, and

tropical fruits, was notable both for its exotic price—there was hardly a bar snack on the menu for less than twenty bucks—and its presentation. Everything served at Passions was a little work of art: a baked fish leaped out of the water; a fruit salad was sunrise at the beach; a round, open-faced sandwich was a flower with a stem of two green onions.

The price of this mock formality and pretentious food, with its attendant ho-ho-ho-isn't-this-clean-fun quality, made it possible for young ladies to dine and chat and be admired and compared without embarrassment. That is, a classy place to troll their *tetas* and *culos* among the assembled marimba players.

Club Passions was one of the best places in town to be scoped by marimbeiros, but Lourdes and Marta had to be careful not to overwork the territory. They didn't want to become known as regulars, but rather as two hot-looking numbers who popped in once in a while after a little shopping.

Mima required Eduardo's approval before either Lourdes or Marta accepted the attentions of a prospective mark. Mima trusted Eduardo's instinct for men. Eduardo didn't want one of his sisters cozying up to some Charles Bronson type who was too much to handle. He liked eager 24-year-olds with beepers on their hips, cocks at the ready, and so much money they didn't know what to do with it.

Eduardo had managed to tear himself away from the Mets and was sitting at the bar when Lourdes and Marta settled into one of Club Passions' classy, padded booths.

Hah, they were in luck. Both Alejandro Pena and Ricardo Hernandez were there.

Lourdes and Marta received a barely perceptible nod from Eduardo and ordered Cuba libres. Lourdes's attention was suddenly drawn to the entrance, where two men had stepped inside, a muscular Cuban and a taller Anglo, both with wild hair—the Cuban's brown and curly, and Anglo's a silver tangle.

Marta had watched them come in too.

Lourdes's face was suddenly flushed. She slid quickly out of the booth. "I'm not feeling good, Marta. I think I'll go home."

Marta looked dumbfounded. "What? You're sick?"

"My stomach. You can get a ride home with Eduardo."

"We'll both go. We can put this off. Mima certainly won't

care, and Eduardo can go somewhere and watch the rest of his game."

"No."

Before Marta could say anything more, Lourdes was out of the booth, weaving quickly through waitresses in tuxedo bikinis. She darted through the side exit and was gone.

Marta was dumbfounded. For one thing, the front door was by far the shortest way out of the building and to the Mercedes. She looked Eduardo's way.

Eduardo nodded in the direction of two men who were being escorted to a booth.

Marta didn't understand. She mouthed "What?"

30

Marta and Eduardo Martinez stared at the $10,000 oak floor, which had taken seven master carpenters a week to lay at a cool 35 bucks an hour. It was a handsome floor, competing with the best floors of art deco houses built 70 years earlier, and when it was properly waxed, it dazzled.

Only now the images it reflected were not happy; in fact, they were downright glum.

When Mima was in a mood, Marta and Eduardo had sense enough to keep quiet.

And Mima, on this occasion, was most certainly in a mood.

She looked at Marta again, her Natalie Wood lips compressed into thin white lines. "Tell me again what happened."

Marta cleared her throat, glancing at Eduardo.

"One or the other of you speak up. I don't care which."

Eduardo said, "She met him last week at Oysterman's."

"And?" Mima's lips grew even tighter, if that was possible.

"Well, you know . . ." Eduardo was hesitant. Neither he nor Marta liked finking on Lourdes, but they had no choice.

"Well you know what, Eduardo?" Mima mimicked her son, her voice heavy with sarcasm.

"He came on to her, and they talked and flirted. The usual

stuff. You know . . ." Eduardo shifted uncomfortably on the $1,500 handcrafted Italian leather chair.

Mima shook her head in disbelief. "He was not a mark?"

"Ah, no."

"Not on our list? Out there drenched with Brut and with a smile on his face. We didn't know who he was?"

"No. At least, I didn't know who he was."

"*Qué carajo!* Lourdes had a job to do. She knows that. And you did what, Eduardo?"

"Nothing at first. I thought she might have tumbled onto a hot one."

"We spot them first. We check them out. If we know it's worth it, *then* Marta and Lourdes do their thing. We can't have them waste their time with every used-car salesman or shoe clerk who gets a stiff dick. Who was she supposed to be after?"

"Alejandro Pena."

"Was Alejandro there?"

Eduardo nodded yes.

"But this guy, what's his name?"

"Roberto Guzmán."

"Guzmán got to her first."

"Yes."

"And then what?"

"Well, I was watching Pena, and it was obvious he had his eye on a piece. It was too late for that action, so I glided in and squired Lourdes out of there. Said it was her bedtime."

"Left Guzmán standing there."

"*Sí.*"

"Ay, Santa Barbara *vendita!* Thank God somebody in this family has some brains. Now then, what happened yesterday, Marta?"

Marta glanced at her brother. "Uh, Mima, I . . ."

Mima cut her off. "When I ask you what happened, Marta, I want to know what happened."

"Oh, Mima." Marta's shoulders slumped.

"Now go ahead and tell me what happened."

"Mima, Lourdes and I went shopping in Coconut Grove, and after that we went to Club Passions, where we knew Pena and Ricardo Hernandez had been hanging out on Friday afternoons."

"You were after Hernandez?"

Eduardo said, "Hernandez has some big bucks. Has to. If we can set it up. *Quién sabe?*"

Mima said, "You were in Club Passions, and then?"

"This guy Roberto Guzmán shows up with a tall Anglo with crazy hair."

Eduardo said, "This same guy was with Guzmán at Oysterman's, too. I saw them talking."

"Shut up, Eduardo. Let your sister tell us what happened. She's a big girl. She knows what she saw and didn't see."

Marta sighed. She didn't like blabbing on her sister. "Okay, so we were having Cuba libres when Lourdes sees them coming in the front door. They're standing there, looking for an open booth. She's suddenly rattled. She says she's sick and has to go. I can get a ride with Eduardo, she says. I say I'll go, but she says no and is gone, out the side door."

"So what do you think?"

Marta said nothing.

"Marta?" Mimi's voice rose.

"I think Lourdes might be in love."

"*Dios mío!* Now just what does she have in mind? What? Do you want to tell me, Marta?"

"I don't know, Mima."

"Marrying some fast-talking nobody and move in with him in a cute little bungalow in Hialeah? Kids? Is that It? Is that what she wants? She's going to trade her Mercedes and a quarter of a million dollars' worth of jewelry and designer dresses and shopping trips to Hong Kong for a houseful of squawling *chiquillos?*"

"Please, Mima."

"Is that it? Is that what your sister has in mind? She wants to eat black beans and rice every day and spread her legs every night for some go-nowhere do-nothing. *Un arancao sin futuro.* I want you to remember what I'm telling you, Marta. We don't need you pulling the same stunt. What would you rather have, lobster and champagne, or beans and beer? Are you listening?"

"I'm listening, Mima."

"There's plenty of time for that kind of nonsense. Have enough kids and you'll wind up looking like a fireplug with a big fat ass. You're young, enjoy it while you can."

"Mima."

"Listen to me, I know what I'm talking about."

"Yes, Mima."

"So tell me what you've found out about this guy, Eduardo. I take it you have had sense enough to find out something about this Romeo."

"It's possible we may have lucked out, Mima. He plays the marimba."

"Oh?"

"But it's hard to tell how much stuff he moves. The Anglo with him is named Sid Khartoum, a pilot, I'm told, and probably a player too."

"*Un muerto de hambre*, Eduardo. We have to be selective."

"What do we do now?"

"Nothing until I find out more about him." Mima put her left hand on her lip and glanced covertly at the mirror.

Marta said quickly, "Would you like to go shopping at International Intrigue, Mima? I saw a pair of Guess jeans that'd really look hot on you."

"Ms. Spacek butt," Eduardo said. "Twitch, twitch, twitch."

Mima turned her face to the left and the right, studying her reflection.

Marta said, "You know, Mima, I think you look more like Natalie Wood than most people give you credit for. Catch you at the right angle, and it's downright amazing."

"Really? You think so?" Mima ran her hand over her dark brown hair.

"Enough to give Robert Wagner a hard-on," Eduardo said.

"Eduardo!"

Eduardo laughed. He had his mother's number, and he enjoyed teasing her. "Maybe we could send him your picture anonymously. Here you go, Robert. Eat your heart out."

"Or maybe the movie people could do a Natalie Wood story," Martes said. "They'd have to have a Natalie who looks like Natalie."

"Oh, be quiet," Mima said.

Mima liked being complimented. She was happy again. Her children were forgiven. The Martinez family had its ups and downs like all families, but it was a Cuban family, and Cuban families stuck together. The problem with Lourdes was real and serious, to be sure, but it would be taken care of in due time and in the proper manner. For now, no use to dwell on it unnecessarily. There was a Cuban saying, '*No te ahoga en un vaso de agua*'—don't drown in a cup of water. For now, all was well. Life was to be lived.

Mima had responsibilities as head of the Martinez clan, but she loved her children. She said, "Sure, I'll go shopping with you, Marta. After that we'll go to Coral Gables and have dinner at Yuca."

"Maybe Lourdes could come too, Mima."

"Of course, Loudes can come too. That goes without saying."

Eduardo said, "We could invite Robert Wagner down for a visit, and you could take him out to the Everglades for a little splendor in the swamp. 'Mima! Mima!' 'Oh, Robert! Robert! *Te amo! Te amo!*'"

Mima, laughing, chased after her son. "You're not so big I can't give you a proper spanking, you *culo cacao*."

W   hen Roberto Guzmán, saying he had to meet a marim-
     beiro to move some keys, first mentioned the idea of
     "pumping up" at Scandinavia, James Burlane was amused.
He could imagine himself pumping up a tire or a basketball.
But muscles?

Burlane had been told, before he went underground as Sid
Khartoum, that the Miami fitness center—with a $1,200 annual
fee to keep out the riffraff—was a favorite gathering spot for
both cops and marimba players.

For men, it enshrined the cult of muscles and power. Also
the ritual exhibiting of one's masculine stuff, like peacocks'
strutting or gorillas' breast-beating, that zoologists called "display."

For the women, it was a battlefield, the site of eternal
combat against surface fat and the ravages of childbearing and
aging.

Burlane didn't regard exercise as a spectator sport or group
activity. He walked and did sit-ups with his calves on the seat
of a chair to spare his lower back. But the reason for communal
sweating and grunting was nothing to be looked down upon,

he knew. It was straight from the brain stem: the quest for sex. Sexy necks. Sexy pecs. Sexy tits. Tight asses. Sex. Sex. Sex.

And if the ladies had any reservations about exposing ripples of unsightly cellulite on the surface of their thighs and rumps, they were rescued by wearing colorful second skins, exercise costumes made of spandex Lycra. Thus they could walk around legally naked, the tights serving a cosmetic function. With a proper Lycra outfit, the most outrageous behind, no matter how jiggly or unsightly, was transformed into a glistening, stretched, hard-body sheen in which the promise of shape triumphed over in firmness of tissue or imperfection of color.

Also, Burlane knew, extreme physical exercise produced pain-killing chemicals called endorphins that were also produced during sex.

Scandinavia, the name presumably invoking images of blonde goddesses, was located in the Miracle Center Mall on Coral Way at 24th Street in Coral Gables. Malls were necessary in Miami, a city of neighborhoods rather than a metropolis with a functioning downtown. In fact, most Miamians seldom had any reason to go downtown; downtown was given over to jewelry and electronics stores catering to visiting South Americans. There were no skyscrapers downtown. No financial district.

The Miracle Center was an eight-story, light-blue-and-white building with an indoor parking lot where Guzmán, with Burlane's Cherokee right behind him, parked his BMW. Judging from the collection of overpriced automobiles in the garage, this was a favorite spot for those who, like Roberto Guzmán, confused expensive machines with self-worth. They knew the cost of everything, but the value of nothing.

Burlane followed Guzmán inside and found that Miracle Center was—as he had deduced from the automobiles in the garage—sterile and soulless, filled with predictable shops and overpriced boutiques.

On the ground floor there was a TGIF, Thank God It's Friday, a franchised bar and eatery featuring a clutter of antiques on the walls. TGIF was new and shiny, with a clientele of the young and ambitious, Miami having given itself over to the new—as opposed to the old, in other cities, where antique interiors might qualify as natural habitat.

Burlane assumed that TGIF and Scandinavia existed in

symbiotic relationship to one another. After milady cast the lure of her Lycra-encased form in the exercise rooms, and perhaps let a prospect observe her charms close-up in a hot tub or jacuzzi, she could, in good conscience and observing propriety—that is, without seeming desperate or easy—allow the gentleman to buy her a drink in the classy, that is, cheery and antiseptic, TGIF. After that, if the gentleman had promise—a sufficiently thick wallet—one never knew. Negotiations would begin with ritual, in which casual gestures and offhand comments were in fact elaborate code.

Her goal: security and a family.

His: a satisfying fuck.

Compromises were therefore inevitable.

Scandinavia's interior glass wall faced a yogurt shop on the balcony surrounding the mall's open interior. Burlane had never seen so many preposterous high-tech exercising machines in his life. On the wall immediately facing the yogurt shop, he counted a row of eight bodies walking on treadmills, glancing at high-tech digital gauges that recorded their performance and body reaction.

Casual visitors, that is, voyeurs, were not allowed in Scandinavia, but Guzmán took care of that obstacle with a little Spanish palaver with the girl at the counter. Burlane, threading his way through a maze of rooms filled with exercise machines, followed Guzmán behind the treadmills to the mirror-lined weight room.

Burlane sat on the floor, his back against the wall, as Guzmán screwed 275-pound weights into place on a barbell. Guzmán began doing bench-press repetitions while covertly scoping his bulging muscles in the mirror. He had a powerful upper torso, Burlane had to give him that.

Burlane noted that Guzmán was also using the mirrors to scope the interior of Scandinavia. He was trying to be casual, but it was clear he was eyeing someone in particular.

The mirrors were a great way to enjoy the female bodies twisting and bending on various machines behind the treadmills that faced the mall balcony. Was Guzmán just girl-watching, or did he have somebody else in mind?

Was this FBI work? Burlane was curious.

It took him a while, but Burlane finally spotted what he was certain was the object of Guzmán's interest, a man in red shorts working a machine designed for one's thighs. The machine required him to squat and straighten, squat and straighten.

The man on the thigh machine was obviously enjoying the ladies as he worked.

Any one female in particular?

Burlane checked out the women himself, and discovered a new arrival on a machine apparently intended to strengthen one's arms or pectorals: Katherine Donovan, wearing mint-green Lycra warm-ups.

Katherine looked svelte and sexy in her outfit, sleek as a greyhound.

Well, well . . .

Burlane shifted slightly, putting a pale-blue concrete column between himself and Katherine so she couldn't see him without using the mirrors herself. Burlane had to admit it was fun, even a bit sexy, to secretly watch her exercise. He counted to himself as he watched: one, two; one, two; one, two. He wondered what it would be like to peel that green outfit off her.

The man in the red shorts certainly admired her. There seemed little doubt about that.

Guzmán could see the man in the red shorts, but not Katherine.

Burlane said, "Who's the guy over there in the red shorts, Roberto?"

"What guy in red shorts? What are you, a *maricón*, Khartoum? Checking out men."

"The one you've been keeping an eye on, *cabrón*."

Guzmán rested, sweat pouring from his brow. He grinned. "You don't miss anything, do you?"

"I was just wondering is all."

"Khartoum, remember I told you that both cops and players hang out here? That's Captain Donald Fowler, the scourge of the marimba himself. I see him in here every once in a while. I was curious to see if he had any cop buddies with him today. They work in teams, but pretend not to know one another."

Burlane grinned. "I can see how that would be useful."

"They're like snakes with protective coloring. They blend right in. When you spot one, you don't fuck with him. You keep your distance, and see if you can locate any more."

"If you don't want to get bit."

"Right. You have to be careful. You remember their faces for future reference."

At this point, Katherine took a short walk, swinging her arms to loosen them up.

Seeing her, Guzmán muttered, "Ay! Oh, shit!"

Burlane thought: Screwed up, eh, Señor Crooked FBI man? He said, "What's wrong?"

Guzmán set the weights quickly down and grabbed his left shoulder, massaging it. "Pulled something. That's it for today, man. No more of this shit."

"I thought you were going to meet a player."

"He hasn't showed. He knows where to find me. If I don't get home fast and put some ice on this thing I won't be able to tie my shoes in the morning."

Without waiting for a reply from Burlane, and looking neither left nor right, Guzmán grabbed his gear and strode quickly out of Scandinavia.

Katherine, her back to him, was adjusting the tension on her machine as Burlane hurried past. Good. She hadn't seen him.

Captain Donald Fowler's wife, Norma, was a bigger-than-life woman—professionally, as a housewife, socially too, and, alas, physically.

Norma, a holder of a Ph.D. in psychology, was the reform-minded principal of a progressive elementary school in Miami that had developed a much-ballyhooed reading-skills program with evening classes for immigrant Haitians needing to improve their English.

All in all, a good woman, one would think.

The problem was that while Norma had had Amy's cheerleader figure at age 22, she was now six ax handles and a plug of tobacco wide. And then some.

Norma had become a neurotic eater, and was now positively bulbous. Her hippolike buttocks looked like buckets of chicken fat held in place by Glad Wrap. And her tits! Shit! Great bags of hanging fat. Screwing her had all the thrill of sticking it in cold library paste.

Some years earlier, Fowler's imagination had begun to wander, a fact of which he suspected Norma was well aware. But then, she got to read about her school in the "Living" section of the *Miami Herald* and in professional educational journals, and even, once, in the *Wall Street Journal*.

Now Fowler was aware that he was being watched by a svelte beauty in her mid-30s.

Most people in Miami knew Fowler by reputation, and many speculated that he was on the city's shortlist of candidates to head the Dade Metro Police Department, but few of them knew what he actually looked like. There were many reasons for his remaining out of the public eye. He was, after all, still an officer involved in police investigations.

He had scored before at Scandinavia, but he had been circumspect and careful.

Did the woman in mint-green know who he was, he wondered? Or was she attracted to him in a more desirable, that is, primal way, impressed by his form? Animal to animal. Man and woman.

Fowler, squatting and standing, checked out his reflection in the wall mirror behind his machine. His hair was graying at the temples. A man of experience, no pink-cheeked boy. Boys had yet to prove themselves, and so their mouths were always flapping: I'm gonna do this; I'm gonna do that; I'm gonna be this; I'm gonna be that. Gonna. Gonna. As any smart woman knew well, some would, some wouldn't. The trick was in learning to handicap their chances.

But Fowler had proven himself and was still riding the up escalator. And no potbelly, either. He didn't look bad. Not at all.

He watched her pull a weight with outstretched arms, closing her arms until she touched the heels of her fists in front of her. Then back again. Then forward, her pectorals rising in response under the mint-green workouts.

She looked him straight on with her green eyes.

Fowler swabbed the sweat off his forehead with the back of his wrist. He had to be careful. In what Fowler regarded as a reverse screw, Gary Hart had gotten knocked out of a presidential run because of a blonde on his lap—stopped cold six inches short of the White House.

Fowler wanted to be chief in the worst way, and was determined to be careful, and yet . . .

He walked over to the woman in green. "Say, you wouldn't be interested in soaking it off in a hot tub, would you?"

She gave him a smile that turned his mouth dry, and let go of the handles of her machine. "I don't know why not. That sounds like a great idea. My name's Katherine."

"Don," he said.

32

James Burlane hated trying to tail anybody the-way-they-do-it-in-the-movies-solo through traffic, much less in Miami, which, in his opinion, had exceptionally lousy drivers. Miami's streets were given over to the enthusiastic tailgating and weaving in and out that Burlane associated with traffic in Latin American cities. It took the nerves of a grand prix driver to tackle it.

Also, Burlane didn't want Fowler and Katherine to know he was behind them. Fowler was a cop, after all; he had to be a savvy driver when he needed to be.

Katherine was all charm when she left Scandinavia with her hand on Fowler's arm. It had taken her only a few minutes, and she clearly had Mr. Top Cop's brain fogged by testoterone and his heart thumping like a crook at plea-bargain time.

Fowler drove north a couple of miles on 37th, then turned onto an I-836 on-ramp and headed west.

Burlane assumed Fowler would have to get out of town if he was going to take Katherine anyplace public. Where would he go? To the Keys? To Fort Meyers? Or to some podunk village?

Or was he going to the airport? The airport was coming up.

A bit spendy, Burlane supposed, but then one never knew about cops. This was precisely what Harnar was paying him to look into.

Burlane suppressed a twinge of jealousy over the attention Fowler was receiving from Katherine. He told himself that the reason for Katherine and Fowler's coming together was due to professional rather than hormonal reasons on Katherine's part. He had to give her space. Still, Burlane was bothered. Allowing himself to be bothered was unprofessional, he supposed, but it was also being truthful.

Katherine hadn't struck Burlane as the type who would go to Scandinavia. She seemed even less likely to come on to someone in the exercise room. And she hadn't come on to any old hunk. She had chosen Captain Drug Buster.

Did she wear a white hat or black? Was she a cop checking Fowler out, or did she work for the Colombians?

Fowler turned off at the airport exit, and Burlane followed him to the second level of the long-term parking garage. Infrared binoculars in hand, he followed them to where private airplanes were hangared.

Burlane watched the small plane hangars through a chain-link fence. In a few minutes, a small yellow tractor pulled a black-and-yellow Cessna onto the tarmac.

Donald Fowler was the pilot. Katherine Donovan was in the passenger's seat.

Getting out of town in style. Well, well, well . . .

He watched with interest as Fowler taxied out to the tarmac and took his place in line for takeoff. A few minutes later, the plane was aloft. Burlane watched the red taillight. Fowler headed due east—to Africa if he had enough gas. More likely the Bahamas.

Burlane sighed. He was bummed out as he drove to his apartment in Miami Beach.

At home Burlane made himself a cup of coffee and retrieved his paperback copy of Henry David Thoreau's *Walden*. Impressed by Thoreau's meditations on solitude and self-reliance, he had read *Walden* numerous times over the years, and had himself reached an existential, nearly monklike ability to enjoy peace and privacy. But sometimes—and this was one of them—he very nearly desperately wanted a woman. There were times when there was just no substitute for their company, exasperating as they could be.

Burlane yearned for the talk. The sharing. The comfort of female softness. All of it. There was something about Katherine that had triggered his hormones.

He wanted her.

She was on her way to the Bahamas with Donald Fowler.

Ta, ta, Burlane!

Burlane wanted her, and he didn't like the idea of Fowler laying a hand on her. As his cousin Eddie used to say back in Umatilla, Oregon, tough tittie, Jimmy.

Crap!

33

Mima Martinez wore a hat when she met Donald Fowler in an overpriced, nearly empty restaurant in Fort Lauderdale, hoping he would tell her for God's sake to take it off, that he didn't want people remembering him talking to someone who looked like Natalie Wood.

But no. If Fowler noticed the resemblance, he didn't comment on it. This disappointed Mima, who had learned that people were somehow reluctant to point out the similarities between herself and the actress. She attributed this to envy, especially on the part of women.

Of course, Mima knew that in Fowler's case there was a reason for the lapse. Fowler was a worried man. He had troubles on his mind. She could have shown up with bright-red Elizabeth Taylor rouge and grossly painted lips, and he wouldn't have behaved any differently.

They ordered: a crab salad for Mima, lamb chops for Fowler. And drinks: Tanqueray gin with a twist for Mima, Pinch Scotch for Fowler.

When the drinks came, Fowler got straight to business. He said, "Mima, there's something we have to talk about."

"Oh?" This sound serious. Mima sat back in her chair.

"Mima, listen. I told you something had to be done about Luis Fernandez, yes. But for Christ's sake I didn't mean for you to feed him to your dog. My God! Mima, there were canine teeth marks on his skull."

Mima blinked. She looked pretend-contrite. "Well, you said to use some imagination."

"Jesus!"

"You said to distance ourselves. Eduardo said, hey, you want distance, how about a copycat murder. Copy the dog-food killer. That'd throw 'em."

Fowler shook his head angrily, his face tight. "All you had to do to protect the family was have Marta play it straight. Fernandez would have eventually concluded nothing was wrong and given up."

Remaining calm, Mima took a sip of Tanqueray. "You said distance, we gave you distance."

"There's such a thing as overdoing something. Shit!"

"Well, what's done is done. It was a one time thing. It won't happen again."

Fowler sighed, restraining his temper. "I've been through Fernandez's stuff, and I think I got everything that might connect him with Marta, but you never know. Has Eduardo gotten rid of the Jaguar? The Jaguar is a link."

"Eduardo's working on it. A guy in Seattle."

"Mima, I take it the family didn't have anything to do with the previous dog-food killings."

Mima's face tightened.

Fowler wet his lips. "I have to know."

Mima pushed back from the table, as though she was preparing to leave. "*Hablame claro!* I'm not going to put up with this kind of talk. Just what is this, anyway?"

"Please, Mima."

"Give us a break! Just because we have a dog, you conclude we're feeding him human bodies. Yuch! One time! A onetime copycat to get rid of a DEA agent that was nosing around. One time and you conclude that we're feeding people to our dog?"

"If you're clean, hey! No harm done." Fowler took a quick hit of Scotch.

"No harm done?" Mima narrowed her eyes. "Let's get something perfectly straight here. You think Eduardo liked doing what he did? He was disgusted, I can tell you. Disgusted. He did it for all of us. *Carajo!* I'm his mother. You expect me to sit here and hear you accuse us of something that outrageous and just sip my drink like a good trooper. That's not my style and you know it."

"Mima . . ."

"What on earth has come over you? Have you taken leave of your senses?"

"We've been through a lot together, and if it were anything ordinary I could figure out a way to let it ride. But not this. I had to at least ask."

"Eduardo is *not* the dog-food killer, I assure you."

"I'll say no more, other than this: there'll be no murders connected with your family. None. That's not part of the deal. There're other ways of handling people like Luis Fernandez. If something like this happens in the future, I'll want to know exactly what you have in mind to take care of it. No more killing, copycat or otherwise."

Mima sniffed. "Well, now that you've got that off your chest, do you suppose you could flag me another drink?"

Fowler caught the waitress's eye and pointed toward Mima's empty glass, then tapped his own on the rim. They waited in heavy silence, saying nothing, until their drinks were poured.

"Really!" Mima said, getting quickly to her new drink. "After everything we've done for you. We've delivered for you and kept quiet while you basked in the glory of being supercop. We made you. All those show-off arrests. You've got to be the most publicized cop since Dick Tracy. And to accuse Eduardo of something like that."

Fowler cleared his throat. "I'm sorry."

Mima's face mellowed. An apology meant she was in control again. "Who *is* doing it? Do you have suspects? I mean, who on earth? Yuch!"

"Beats hell out of me."

Mima cleared her throat. "I have to tell you, Captain, Marta and Eduardo and I think we, and I do mean *we*, all of us, may have a . . . well, a little problem with Lourdes."

Fowler looked concerned. "With Lourdes?"

"We think she may have fallen in love with a marimbeiro she met at Oysterman's."

"Uh-oh!"

"The problem is we don't know anything about this guy. We have to be careful, you said so yourself."

"We certainly do."

"Eduardo thinks the guy deals. Maybe you people could take him off the streets for a while. Give all this passion a chance to cool off."

"What does she want, kids and all that? Marriage? A mortgage?"

Mima frowned. "The whole disaster. It's entirely possible, unfortunately."

Fowler clenched his jaw.

Mima said, "We've talked about this before. You said to let you know immediately if anything like this happened."

"Yes, I did. Tell me the rest."

"It could be a harmless infatuation or even a false alarm. Or maybe he could work with Eduardo, I don't know. A family that plays together, stays together sort of thing. I'm telling you, we have some danger signs here."

"I'll see what I can find out about him. If we can find a reason to bust him, I'll let you know. If not, well have to come up with something short of knocking him off."

Mima didn't say anything.

Fowler grimaced.

She said, "Kids! What a parent does for their kids!"

Fowler sighed. "Kids. I know. I know."

The waitress arrived with their food.

Mima used her foot to slide a leather attaché case under Fowler's chair. "Of course, this is for you, as usual. Oh, doesn't this salad look wonderful? All that crab."

It had been impossible for James Burlane to get a parabolic microphone focused on Donald Fowler's tête-à-tête with the dark-haired woman, but Burlane knew from the start they were not lovers.

They were there to talk business.

All he could do with binoculars was watch their faces and read their body language. From that, he deduced that something serious was up.

First, Fowler had angered the woman.

Fowler pressed on, leaning slightly forward.

Now furious, the woman started to get up. Was she going to leave?

Fowler calmed her down.

They relaxed. They talked. Finally, the woman smiled. They had resolved their differences.

About what?

Then another discussion. Something very serious. Ominous. They were both in agreement.

Then the woman passed Fowler a leather attaché case. While chatting with Fowler above the table, she pushed the case under his chair with her foot.

When the waitress came with the bill, Burlane popped a 300-millimeter lens on his Nikon and got a close-up of the woman as she came out of the restaurant.

Also he got the tags of her Rolls-Royce convertible.

Unless it was on a holiday liner or someplace where there was an opportunity to flash a roll and screw blondes, Roberto Guzmán hated mingling with tourists. He was appalled by their stupid polyester costumes and disgusting bellies. Once, he had checked onto a liner loaded with high-school girls, wet pussy waiting in every closet. Blonde, every one. They couldn't wait to jump on his *pinga grande*. It was paradise.

But this?

Dolphin World?

No, no, no.

In Guzmán's opinion trained dolphin shows were the worst, or close to it; there was nothing to do but sit on board-hard bleachers under the hot sun and listen to some asshole with a microphone pretend he was calling the action on Monday-night football. *No comas mierda!*

But Adrian Kyle, the latest Grand Pooh-bah from Washington, visiting Miami to review the front and issue edicts, had said he wanted to watch trained dolphins while they talked. Kyle, who had begun his career with the FBI, had later taken a job with the Detroit Police Department, and was now back, a honcho in the Organized Crime Unit. This was his first trip to Miami; if Guzmán and Katherine wanted to get on his good side, they had to humor him.

Kyle wanted dolphins, he got dolphins. Guzmán hoped one time would be enough, and Kyle would get them out of his system.

The pooh-bahs in Washington were tired of reading sneering articles about the terrible cost of the war on drugs and about how the government was being made fools of by Guillermo Banda-Conchesa. Hence, Guzmán assumed, the appearance of Kyle, a slender, self-assured man with a neatly clipped, jet-black mustache, thick black eyebrows, and salt-and-pepper hair, silver at the temples. He wore an uptight power suit, dark blue with pinstripes, with a white shirt and muted red-and-green striped tie.

Guzmán was lucky he hadn't been assigned to Orlando. The agents there probably had to watch Mickey Mouse till they puked. But Guzmán was Cuban. Guzmán got Miami.

In the pool, two dolphins, one with a red garter around its tail, the other with a blue one, circled around a tall blonde referee in his early 20s. Each team had five dolphins: a goalie, two defenders, two attackers.

The referee readied the yellow ball.

He tossed it up, and the two dolphins rose from the water.

The crowd applauded.

The red-gartered dolphin caught the ball on its snout and flipped it down the pool.

The game was on.

A man's voice on the loudspeakers above the bleachers said, "The red team has it. That's Emil, a six-year-old male, who won the toss. Emil's a two-year water polo veteran. Give him a hand, ladies and gentlemen."

The crowd applauded, including Kyle.

A Blue defender swiped the ball with a nice move and passed to a teammate, and the Blues moved to offense. A determined dolphin flipped the ball down the left side of the pool.

The announcer said, "That steal was by Elsie, our top defender and a member of the original Dolphin World water polo team. We're not sexist here in Dolphin World. The best players play, male or female."

Guzmán wondered why on earth Kyle wanted to meet at

a jackass dolphin show. They could have spent the taxpayers' money in some nice quiet bar. Had some seafood on the taxpayers' tab. Flirted a little with Katherine Donovan. Do their business. Anywhere but this. This sucked. A dolphin show! Guzmán forced himself to pay attention to Kyle.

Kyle said, "After MacRae and Fernandez, the director is understandably worried about his own agents. You, Roberto. And you, Ms. Donovan. If all this explodes in the media, we have to be able to say, accurately, that we were aware of the dangers and took reasonable precautions against them recurring. Et cetera."

"Butt cover time."

"If we're too casual and the business of the bones breaks in the media, we risk getting roasted. The instinct obtains in Washington as well as in Detroit, I might add."

The red team intercepted the ball and began a fast break of its own.

The crowd was getting into it.

"Go, Reds!" a man shouted.

"Blues!" someone else replied, and everybody laughed. Both sides had their fans. Rooting for dolphins. Wasn't that funny? *Ha, ha, ha, ha.*

Guzmán could hardly believe it. Go, Reds? Blues? Were these people off their nuts? These weren't the Lakers or the Pistons. Cheering for fucking dolphins jumping around so they'd be fed. *Coño!*

Kyle said, "I once went to an ice circus in Novosibirsk, just across the Urals in Siberia. The Soviets called it the 'Chicago of the Soviet Union.' I'd never heard of an ice circus before. My friend and I got seats close to the ring, and guys wearing bear outfits and numbered jerseys skated out and began playing hockey. Well, you know, it took us a couple of minutes to realize the players had the skinniest ankles we'd ever seen. Hardly any ankles at all. Then, by God, the rest of it dawned on us: these actually *were* bears playing hockey! Bears! Skating, hockey-playing bears! It was amazing. When I heard about dolphins playing water polo, I had to come. Just had to."

Guzmán laughed. "Ahhhh, we were wondering."

Katherine said, "If you heard about monkeys playing baseball in Brazil, you'd buy a ticket. Is that it?"

Kyle grinned. "That's exactly it. With these two games I consider myself a world expert on trained animals playing team sports. But I get the feeling I've watched dolphins on the Discovery Channel or someplace. For some reason, the bears were more fun."

"Because it was unexpected," Guzmán said. "What have you learned about Sid?"

"Khartoum? Interpol says everything checks, down to his love of cooking. He's somehow managed to stay out of jail, but his dossier is rich with suggestion that justice, in his case, has been routinely, even cheerfully, thwarted. Say, that was a good play." Kyle applauded the dolphin defending the blue team's net.

The announcer said, "That fabulous stop was by Grant, ladies and gentlemen, the only rookie on this year's Blue squad, and already an all-star goalie. He was named by some visitors from Canada, after the famed Edmonton Oiler goal-keeper Grant Fuhr."

Kyle said, "They weren't able to give us a last home of record. The fact is they don't know where Khartoum was until he popped up here."

Katherine said, "Isn't that worrisome?"

"We don't see why. Guys like that go to ground all the time, then pop up again somewhere else."

She said, "Is it all bogus? A legend? Have you thought of that?" A deliberately planted legend that got by Interpol smacked of CIA involvement, and so was ticklish territory for the Bureau; if the Company went to that much trouble, there had to be a reason.

Kyle shook his head. "There's not much to question about the *bona fides*. Khartoum has all the ticks on Interpol's profile. And if the story of his crash in Nicaragua is true . . ."

Guzmán said, "I've heard several accounts by people I've got every reason to believe were there. He did it, all right."

Kyle said, "We think he's too outsized for Langley. The Company prefers chameleons. If it's true as you report, that Manny Lopez bought him a new King-Air to replace his Beech, well then, you never know. He may be our link to The Man himself."

The crowd rose. Yes!

"Gooalllllllllllllll!!!!!!!" The announcer mimicked the Latin American soccer announcers.

"A goal! All right! Nice shot!" Kyle joined in the applause.

"That goal was by all-star Bobby B-Boy, a record-setting

sixteenth goal this year. Bobby's known as the Pelé of dolphin water polo. You just saw a classic Bobby B-Boy move."

Kyle said, "Shit, that one's good! He really is. Did you see that move?"

Guzmán wanted to shove a wiggling Bobby B-Boy up Kyle's ass. "Hot fish," he said.

"And what do you think, Roberto? What's your opinion of our friend Khartoum? Isn't that great how they train those damned things? Water polo! Would you believe?"

"I don't know what to make of him, to be honest."

There was a time-out in the pool as the referee flipped herrings to all the grateful players, a reward for their nonstop, all-star action.

Kyle said, "No contract problems here. Just flip 'em a few fish. It's a wonder the animal lovers don't show up with lawyers and contracts for the players. You know, so many pounds of herring for each performance. Mondays off. That sort of thing."

Guzmán mopped his brow with the back of his hand. "Katherine, what did you and Khartoum do, anyhow?" He felt a twinge of envy as he asked the question. Katherine was a touch old for his taste, but not bad.

"He helped me look for my sister Helen. Helluva date, Roberto." To cover herself, Katherine had forwarded a note on her private search, and was obviously intent on staying squeaky clean with the Bureau. She wanted the new man on her side.

Kyle looked interested, although he probably hadn't read her file and had no idea what she was talking about. "Luck there?"

Katherine said, "Found her and lost her in South Beach. I'll keep looking." Katherine was supposed to look for her sister alone, on her time, although that was virtually impossible, and the people in Washington had to know it.

Kyle raised an eyebrow. "And what is your opinion of the redoubtable Major Khartoum, Ms. Donovan?"

Katherine said, "He's tight-lipped about how he earns his living other than to say he flies planes. If he's been flying coke for Manny Lopez as Roberto says, I think we should stay with him."

Guzmán suspected Kyle was sizing Katherine up as a first step toward easing her into the sack. Guzmán didn't blame him for this. Guzmán could stand a little of that action. "Katherine, wasn't that sweet how I led him straight to you at Oysterman's? Beautiful setup."

"It wasn't so sweet how you led him straight to me at Scandinavia."

Guzmán rolled his eyes. "I know, I know. *Mierda!*"

Kyle, riveted to the dolphins, half listening, said, "And Scandinavia is?"

"One of those fashionable workout spots. High-tech all the way. Body beautiful and all that."

"Ahhh."

"Do you think he saw me?" Katherine asked Guzmán.

"He picked right up on my checking Fowler out. But if he saw you, he didn't say anything, and I think he would have."

It was obvious Katherine wasn't so sure.

"Really, Katherine, I don't think he did. He was too interested in Fowler. When I spotted you, I hustled him out of there pronto. Did it look to you like he saw you?"

"Well, no."

"Then I think we're okay. We lucked out. He would have said something."

Kyle said, "Now then, on the matter of Captain Drug Buster."

Katherine said, "I came on to him in Scandinavia, the fitness place Roberto and I were talking about. I went out with him twice. Both times he had yards of benjies in his wallet. He has his own airplane, thank you. The first time out, he flew me to Eleuthera in the Bahamas. He gave me a wad to blow on roulette. I'd say he spent close to two thousand dollars for an evening of fun. The second time, he took me to his retreat on one of those mangrove islands in south Biscayne Bay. His little hideaway. A place where he can have privacy. His Japanese car cost eighty grand. Now just where does he get that kind of money? On his salary as a cop? No way."

Kyle groaned along with the audience as the yellow ball sailed high on an open goal. "Maybe there's an explanation for everything, Ms. Donovan."

Ahh, Guzmán thought, here it comes: the reason for Kyle's trip to Miami and Guzmán having to sit in the sun in the Dolphin World bleachers. *Manda cojónes!*

Kyle said, "The word from the Exalted Huns on High is that Donald Fowler is involved in a confidential, extremely successful operation the government doesn't want compromised in any manner, shape, or form. They want him to be given plenty of distance."

Guzmán looked surprised. "Even by us?"

"Especially by us. Us, they can control. Us, they want to butt out."

Katherine blinked. "Huh?"

Kyle said, "Fowler's been a sensationally successful cop. Famous. *Time* magazine. '60 Minutes.' One of the questions I don't think anybody has answered in any detail is just how in the hell did he come by all those busts? How did he do it when everybody else failed? That's never been made clear."

Guzmán said, "You think he's running a sting of some kind?"

"That's my bet," Kyle said. "Has to be. It's obviously a big success, a showpiece. Folks in Washington don't want a good thing fucked up by their own people. You can understand that, can't you? So they send me down to make damned sure it doesn't happen. But they don't tell me the details. I don't have a need to know details. They just say go, do it."

"Personally, I think he's as crooked as a dog's hind leg," Katherine said.

Kyle raised an eyebrow. "Donald Fowler? Crooked?"

"You can pull me off him, but you can't stop me from having my opinions. I don't think he was flashing government goodies at all. I think it was all his."

"All right! Another goal! Pretty good." Kyle joined the applause. "If it is a sting, they haven't dealt me in on it. All I know is what I've been told to do. I see that wishes get carried out. The current desire is that until the two of you hear otherwise, you are to back off Donald Fowler. Stick with Sid Khartoum and your other leads."

Guzmán looked annoyed.

Katherine rolled her eyes. "Wonderful!"

Kyle said, "Maybe Khartoum will help you put together the pieces of Conchesa's system. That wouldn't be bad, would it? If he seems to trust you as you say, stay with him. What do you say we get out of this sun and go someplace and have a beer?"

Guzmán said, "What's the point of having an Organized Crime Unit if we can't ask questions? It's a joke."

Kyle rose, sighing. "No point in asking why, Roberto. It just is. You know that."

"I don't suppose logic was ever the point of the exercise."

"In my opinion logic was singularly lacking in Detroit, and it doesn't appear to have much to do with what goes on in Washington. If you insist on things making sense, you'll drive yourself crazy. Take what you can get and be satisfied."

Katherine said, "So what did you think of the dolphins?"

Kyle said, "The Russian bears were far more fun. The blue team's goalie was pretty good, but I could have missed the whole thing and lived just as long. We probably should've had a cold beer someplace out of this fucking sun."

35

Mayor Hernandez, Chief Dersham, Captain Fowler, and media advisor Ron Torberg settled into plush, red-leather armchairs arranged around the coffee table in Hernandez's office. The mayor's secretary had left an ice bucket, glasses, and two bottles of Pinch.

Here they could sip their Scotch and consider their strategy in private. They could swear and fart and use all the sports metaphors they wanted. No secretaries. No tapes. No stupid nonsense they later might have reason to regret. In situations like this, deniability was mandatory.

The meeting would not likely last long. Hernandez had a reputation of getting directly to the point. He wanted clear, straightforward answers.

Ron Torberg, who had the least official power, poured the whiskey.

They sipped their whiskeys and, like the mayor, read the two summaries. Fowler had reduced the nuts and bolts of his investigation into the dog-food murders to less than a page. Chief Dersham's report on the Jah Ben Jah unrest ran a full two pages.

Hernandez, studying Fowler's report, said, "There's no possible mistakes, Don. This is certain?"

"That's it, Mr. Mayor. The *Herald* had it right. No mistaken identity. Topper was one of my men. Luis Fernandez was with the Drug Enforcement Administration."

The slender, civilized Donald Fowler was currently a media star, with the currency of fame to spend. The importance of this was not to be underestimated. The public didn't like its heroes to be unnecessarily fucked with; consequently Fowler had a choice spot in the *droshka*, several safe seats in front of Dersham.

Hernandez began reading Dersham's report on the Jah Ben Jah business.

Because Fowler had his eyes on Dersham's job, his conduct in critical meetings was so good-cop pure, bordering on Boy-Scoutish, that Hernandez sometimes wanted to puke.

Hernandez looked up from the report and cleared his throat. Whether or not the others had finished their reading didn't matter. He was the mayor, and he had. "Well, let's do it. George, what do we do about Jah Ben Jah?"

"We stay the proper course. This guy was selling dope big-time and screwing a string of twelve- and thirteen-year-olds. We can't be casual about that without risking an incredible backlash. This is a Roman Catholic city, not Africa. Also, there shouldn't be any doubt as to the outcome of the trial. The district attorney has the fucker pinned."

"Ron?"

Torberg said, "The dogs bark, but the caravan moves on. They'll grow weary of the drama. Besides, basketball season's coming up."

They all laughed.

"It'll cool. Television viewers get bored with demonstrations every night."

Dersham said, "Also, the rule is never feed an animal at the supper table. If you do, you'll never again have a meal in peace."

Hernandez sighed. "Captain Fowler, you say here you have two suspects in the dog-food murders, yet you don't name them. That omission is for reasons of security, I take it."

Fowler said, "One problem is that we don't know for certain that the same person committed all the murders. In fact, it's possible a different murderer was responsible for the last two deaths."

"A copycat?"

"The two suspects unnamed in my report were both friends of the dead officers. Both play the marimba. One is a pilot who is a link to Guillermo Banda-Conchesa."

Hernandez slumped. "I take it the most likely motive is the corruption investigation."

"Unfortunately, it appears that way, Mr. Mayor. I don't think you can come to any other conclusion."

"Fuck!" Chief Dersham poured himself another drink. The last thing he needed was for the dog-food killings to be connected to the festering sore of 73 cops suspected of being bad.

Hernandez said, "So what action do you recommend?"

Fowler said, "The pilot might have done it. His drug dealer friend—my second unnamed suspect—might have done it. They may have worked together. I don't know. All I can do is watch them at a distance and see what comes up. If we're lucky, we can collar someone within a few days. If not . . ." He didn't finish the sentence.

"Ron?"

"We have to give them something on this one," Torberg said. After his Jah Ben Jah Day performance, Torberg's position was the least secure of those in the mayor's office. "The trick is to rally public opinion on our side, Mr. Mayor. These were brave police officers who gave their lives so that we may all have a better community, and we'll leave no stone unturned in our search for the s.o.b. who killed them and mutilated their bodies. This is outrageous. We won't put up with it. Et cetera."

"I see." Hernandez looked at Dersham and Fowler. "I'm to peddle horseshit while you two try to give us deliverance. Is that the consensus?" He clenched his jaw. "Jesus!"

Chief Dersham was unembarrassed about knocking off a second drink. He poured himself a quick third.

36

Mima Martinez didn't think sailing was what it was cracked up to be in the classy magazines, but would never admit this to her neighbors. For one thing, in Miami, the sun blasted straight onto your skin at tropical, point-blank range; plus it bounced off the water. The double hit of both direct and reflected ultraviolet rays was just murderous; hours on the water seemed like weeks.

Despite bandannas and the most expensive chemicals and sunglasses on the market, Mima almost always returned feeling like a grilled hot dog: exhausted, with a headache, torched skin, and fried eyeballs. Such a wonderful time. Mima knew of women her age who had skin like old footballs from spending too much time lying around on the bow of a boat.

She would have preferred to roar out and zoom back, but sailboats were clearly classier than powerboats. It was okay to have a powerboat, but to have a top-of-the-line, high-speed cigarette boat was to remind passersby of the source of much Cocoplum money, and so was in bad taste. Cocoplum residents who played the marimba preferred strangers to think they had other sources of income. If you owned a cigarette boat, for Christ's sake, you docked it somewhere else.

Mima had forked out a quarter of a million bucks for her Swan 36 racing sloop, *Windsong*. She liked the idea of owning an elegant sailboat, evidence she too could afford to be stiffed by a snooty yacht broker, but not all the *mierda* that went with it.

God, how Mima hated the drill attendant to sailing: the tedious business of checking everything out; the chore of securing gear; the stupid knots; futzing with the sails; the stowing of food and drink; having to learn the stupid lingo and rules.

Looking as casual and Natalie Wood as possible, Mima liked to be up top going and coming. When you had it, you showed it; the masochistic necessity of actually sailing the damn thing was the price she paid for this pleasure.

Eduardo had sneered at the broker's suggestion of a roller-furling headsail, and insisted on racing rig: tall mast, triple spreaders, full spinnaker gear, rod rigging, and double-grooved headstays. He wanted to be able to change jibs without going bareheaded. He wanted wind. Speed.

And the fun-loving Eduardo was not above drenching his mother with a healthy scoop of the Atlantic by bringing the boat sharply around while she clung, white-knuckled, to the windward side. Mima loathed having sticky saltwater all over everything, especially in her hair and eyes, *ahhhhhhhhhh!*

Mima loved her daughter and understood that Lourdes wasn't deliberately being bad or naughty in falling in love with Roberto Guzmán. But Lourdes's infatuation was inopportune, at best. And unfortunately, the same thing could happen to Marta, and they all knew it.

The day Mima chose for the necessary family meeting turned out to be very nearly windless, which was a disappointment for Eduardo, who hated to slide sedately along like an old lady. If he was going to sail, dammit, he wanted wind.

Also, Eduardo ordinarily took a big-titted piece along for a quick grope forward. The very idea of going for a ride on a boat like *Windsong* juiced their *conchas*. He once tried to shock Mima and his sisters by taking along not one, but two succulent young things. The family took it in stride. Mima later told him that he must have inherited his stamina from his grandfather; she couldn't imagine that his father's genes had anything to do with it.

But Mima changed the routine on this trip. Serious family business was to be discussed. No gropes for Eduardo.

Windsong had an 18-inch-wide dish antenna, which meant Eduardo could watch television. No wind, no groping, so Eduardo made do with the Cubs and Pirates on the bridge deck while his mother took her obligatory nap below and his sisters sunned their *tetas*.

Mima wasn't sleeping. She stayed below, as the boat left the dock hating what she had to do.

Mima had good and lovely daughters, and they had worked hard on behalf of the family. Lourdes no less than Marta hustled marimbeiros, and the take from Lourdes's scores had beaten Marta's for the last two years. Lourdes, while shy and more reserved, had an intuitive feel for a mark with a genuine bundle, even Mima had to admit. Marta, more enthusiastic and energetic, was sometimes suckered by big talkers.

But Lourdes did not understand the expression "too soon old, too late smart."

The Martinez family had to stay together or they were doomed to live ordinary, boring lives. For Mima, there was no question of going back to saving food coupons or buying clothes off the rack and having to walk around looking like everybody else.

She couldn't imagine her son or daughters wanting to go back either. They had developed a taste for the good life. A craving. And why shouldn't they? Life was to be lived. It was too late for going back. They had no choice but to proceed forward.

As the head of the family, Mima had responsibilities.

Diesel throbbing, Eduardo piloted *Windsong* to Biscayne Bay in silence, save for the Cubs game. All he had to worry about was minding his helm to avoid incoming boats on his port and the green channel markers to starboard. But his mind didn't seem to be completely on the Cubs as he idled the boat through the canal.

Marta pretended to be engrossed in a romance novel, and Lourdes was dozing in the sun.

When they reached open water, Eduardo headed the boat into the wind and killed the engine. Marta reluctantly interrupted her novel and went to help her brother hoist the working jib in the listless, fitful wind. Eduardo passed on raising the number-one Genoa. This was unusual for him; his heart was ordinarily bent on capturing as much wind as possible.

As Lourdes made a halfhearted attempt to help, she suddenly stopped, as though she had thought of something. She paled. She looked at her sister, reading her face.

Marta glanced quickly down, avoiding Lourdes's eyes.

Lourdes looked at her brother, then back at her sister. "What's going on here, Marta? Can you tell me what's happening?"

"Lourdes, I . . ." Marta bit her lip. "Do you think we need more sail, or is this enough, Eduardo?"

Wingsong slid along in a half-assed broad reach, with the traveler slightly to leeward. The boom, out over the rail, bounced fitfully up and down as the pissant swells rocked the boat gently, spilling wind from the sheets.

"Eduardo?"

From below, a blender whirred.

Eduardo pretended to be distracted by the blender. He considered setting a spinnaker, but that would have required two other crew to keep it drawing in the light air, and nobody was in the mood for trimming sails. He thought, screw the spinnaker. Bullshit breeze, no matter how he looked at it.

He trimmed the sails as best he could in the flukey wind and started to lock the wheel, then thought the hell with it. He dropped the sails and raised the Bimini over the cockpit so he could have a little shade. He turned his attention to the Cubs.

Mima called topside: "Marta, can you help me with the drinks, please?" Mima was a responsible Cuban mother; the Martinez women did not drink alcohol or do drugs when they were together—although they all liked an occasional cocktail when they were away from the family. Mango smoothies were the custom on their outings on *Windsong*; Eduardo drank what he pleased, preferring margaritas when he sailed.

Marta, grateful for the call, scrambled quickly below.

Mima called up, "Sat on the rim of your margarita, Eduardo?"

"Yes, Mima," Eduardo called back.

There was an edge of disappointment in Mima's voice. "Okay."

Lourdes, studying her brother, lowered her voice. "You always have salt on the rim, always. Tell me, Eduardo."

"Tell you what?"

"What's going on?"

Eduardo did his best to look confused by the question. "What's going on, Lourdes, is that Mima and Marta are bringing the drinks up."

"Making your margarita has always been my job, Eduardo. I don't think Mima's ever made a margarita in her life."

From below, Mima was upset. "*Qué mierda!* Is it okay if we make it without the salt, Eduardo?"

"Sure, Mima," Eduardo called down.

Lourdes lowered her voice. "See? It's a wonder she doesn't chop her finger off in the blender. Eduardo, did Mima find out about Roberto?"

Eduardo, not taking his eyes off the Cubs, said, "Roberto who?" But he couldn't lie to his sister. He clenched his jaw and stared at the deck. He nodded yes.

"You were there when I met Roberto at Oysterman's. You and Marta knew how I felt about him when I slipped out of Club Passions. You ran straight to Mima, didn't you? Told her everything. Lourdes is in lu-uv, Lourdes is in lu-uv. Chanting like six-year-olds."

Eduardo answered with silence.

"Why, Eduardo?" Lourdes's voice trembled. "And so what has Mima decided? Tell me, Eduardo. You owe it to me. You owe me big."

He looked away, not feeling proud of himself.

"Not good?"

"Oh, you know, Lourdes."

"No, I don't know."

Brother to sister, a saddened Eduardo answered with his eyes.

Mima and Marta emerged from below, Marta with a tray of drinks.

Mima, pretending not to notice the stricken look on Lourdes's face, passed around the smoothies and Eduardo's margarita, and they moved to the port side of the cockpit, under the shade of the Bimini. "I couldn't get the hang of putting salt on the stupid rim. But salt's not good for you anyway, Eduardo. Give you high blood pressure."

Lourdes took her mango smoothie and quickly turned her back.

Mima glanced at Eduardo.

He nodded his head yes, Lourdes knew.

"What did you tell her, Eduardo?"

"She's not stupid, Mima."

Lourdes shuddered. Her shoulders began to bob.

Mima said, "Lourdes, we have to think of the family. You mustn't forget that."

Lourdes's body shook with a run of shudders, but she shut them off. Then they started again, and she began crying.

Mima reached to comfort her, but Lourdes yanked away and stood with her back to her family, crying.

Mima said, "Honey, what you don't understand is that we considered all possibilities. We even thought of dealing him into the family. I wouldn't have objected. A son-in-law might be fun, and Eduardo could certainly use the help. Isn't that right, Eduardo?"

"I sure could, Mima."

Lourdes, still crying, said, "Well, why didn't you, Mima? All the money the four of us take in. One more lousy share. Would it have hurt so much?"

"Honey, I asked Don Fowler to check him out. Just in case. Lourdes, Roberto Guzmán is an agent for the Organized Crime Unit of the FBI. He just cannot be allowed to learn about our family. It was just bad luck. You met a guy who is just not for you. Can't be. If he really had been a marimbeiro, maybe it would have been different."

Lourdes's body shook. She could not stop crying. "So, what . . . what now? Ma . . . Ma . . . Ma-rimba? Not Marimba, Mima. Not *ebo*. Please."

"We don't have any choice, Lourdes. We have Marimba's appetite to consider."

Lourdes slumped to the deck and looked at her mother, tears streaming from her eyes. "Please, Mima. Please. There has to be some other way. There has to be."

"Ogun protects us with Marimba, Lourdes. Ogun makes us invisible. *Vida para vida.* You know what Marimba craves. He has to be fed. You know that."

"Mima, I beg you . . ."

"Either you or Marta will have to invite Roberto home."

Lourdes sobbed. "Oh, Mima."

"You or your sister, Lourdes. What'll it be?"

"Not Marta, Mima."

"Decide, Lourdes. Right now. There's no sense making a production out of this. Emotion will get us nowhere. We have to act decisively, in accordance with Ogun's *ashe*, and get on with our lives. You'll find another Roberto. I'll ask Eleggua. I'll toast him some corn and yams."

"Eleggua!" Lourdes said scornfully.

Marta said, "Who scores the marimbeiros with real bucks, Lourdes? You, not me. You can have anybody you want, pick him."

Eduardo said, "Marta and I will be your matchmakers, Lourdes. Tell us exactly what you want in a man, and we'll find you one. Guaranteed. Right, Marta?"

"Right!"

"As long as he isn't an FBI agent," Mima said.

"Excluding FBI agents."

Marta said, "We'll go at it systematically. Whatever you want."

Mima said, "We'll see what Eleggua has to say. I'll give him smoked possum. Señor Rodriguez can get it for me."

Lourdes said, "Don't ask me to do something like this, Mima. It's not right. Please."

"Then Marta it is. She'll figure out a way."

Lourdes said quickly, "No, Mima. I'll do it."

"It has to be done, Lourdes."

"This is for me to do, Mima, not my sister."

"Done, then. You and Eduardo can work out the details."

Lourdes bolted for the companionway and went below, and wailed all the way forward to the V-berth. There, she began weeping in earnest.

There would be no more ritual sunning of the tits by Lourdes and Marta today.

The wind died; *Windsong* lay becalmed, rocking gently.

"*Qué viento más mierda. Coño!*" Eduardo started the engine and aimed for the entrance to the canal into Cocoplum. He turned the Cubs up full blast.

The announcer said, "Up and in. He set him up. You watch: this next pitch will be a fastball down and out, and the batter will have a hard time getting to it."

The crowd roared.

"See there! Struck him out. A perfect pitch. Right on the corner."

Mima and Marta remained up top, but there was no escaping Lourdes's despair.

Slowly, the crying began to get on Mima's nerves. Roberto

Guzmán was an FBI agent. Just what did Lourdes expect them to do? Try to buy him out and add bribery to the list of charges? They all felt crappy about it to begin with, but enough was enough. If Lourdes had followed the rules when she was at Oysterman's, none of this would have happened. She was there to work. One of their marks was present, and she ignored him. Eduardo had watched the whole thing.

Lourdes had brought it on herself, and now was trying to make everybody else feel shitty. Forcing them all to listen to her wails.

Mima tried praying to St. Peter for relief, but her daughter wept on.

By the time they got back to the dock, Mima was furious at Lourdes for continuing to pile up emotional IOUs with her relentless, pitiable sobbing.

Santa Barbara *vendita*! Mima could hardly stand it. Here she was, doing her best as a single mother to keep the family together, which was in the best interest of everybody. The future of the country was based on families staying the course and sticking together, even the President said so. As head of the Martinez family, she had taken responsibility in the matter of Roberto Guzmán, knowing her decision would not be popular.

This was the treatment she got from Lourdes. No consideration or respect for her mother, none at all. They had to have Marimba's protection. Ogun made it clear what he required at *ebo*. She didn't have any choice. Lourdes knew that as well as she did.

It occurred to Mima that such grieving as this could render Lourdes unpredictable and therefore dangerous . . . but no. Mima knew that after Lourdes had time to calm down and think over the alternative, she would agree that their obligation to Ogun would have to be fulfilled.

James Burlane and Roberto Guzmán had *warapo*—that is, sugar-cane juice—smoothies at El Palacio de los Jugos at 57th and Flager, then headed south at Eighth Street and 57th to El Pueblo to have lunch.

There must have been an accident on 57th, but they were lucky to make their spot before the traffic stopped completely.

El Pueblo, Guzmán's favorite spot, was a Cuban mom-and-pop diner located between the Bottom's Up nude bar and The Pasta Factory Restauant. It was one of scores of Cuban mom-and-pop–type diners Burlane had seen scattered throughout the city.

Guzmán loved Cuban food and was proud of it; Burlane didn't think his enthusiasm was extravagant. In Burlane's opinion, when it came to Cuban food, no amount of praise was hyperbole. It was a change from Asian food, true, but Burlane thought he was capable of being objective.

He did think the fuss over Cuban bread was perhaps a bit much. It was said by Cubans that their bread, baked in long loaves, had to be eaten the day it was baked. Yesterday's bread was *muy duro*—too tough.

El Pueblo had a special each day; the specials were rotated, and today's was written on the wall followed by an English translation: *rabo encendido* (oxtail): The other specials, not available today, were *vaca frita* (shredded beef); *fricasé de pollo* (chicken fricassee); *masas de puerco frito* (fried pork chunks); *carne con papa* (beef with potatoes). All came with *tostónes*—fried plantains—plus black beans and rice. A dozen stools, a half-dozen chairs, and what Roberto Guzmán regarded as five-star food; that was El Pueblo.

"We Cubans are big eaters, Khartoum. We like our food. That's why our women have those *culqs* of theirs."

The babble of Spanish among customers, waitresses, and cook was lively and animated. Burlane's favorite among the specials was *vaca frita*, plus a tall glass of cold *jugo de melón*—watermelon juice. The watermelon juice was so good it was decadent.

"*Rabo encendido!* This'll be real good, Khartoum. They cook the oxtails in red wine and tomato sauce seasoned with garlic, and throw in some green olives for good measure. This is almost as good as my mother's."

"And *jugo de melón*."

"Can't do without that at El Pueblo. All right!" Guzmán rubbed his hands together with glee. "This is gonna to be good, Khartoum. *Rabo encendido* the way it's supposed to be cooked. Guaranteed. This lady back here at the stove, she cooks food the old-fashioned way. She doesn't leave stuff out." Guzmán glanced at the street.

His eyes suddenly got wide.

Burlane turned and looked at the traffic. There, stuck in the traffic and the heat, top down on her 560 SL Mercedes convertible, was Lourdes Martinez.

Burlane, watching Lourdes, said, "Cuban coffee when we're finished, don't you think, Roberto?"

"Gotta have Cuban coffee."

Burlane checked the license number of the Mercedes. "Say, isn't that your friend Lourdes?"

"I . . . yes."

"It looks like she traded her bumblebee Yugo for something more stylish. What does one of those things run, eighty-five thousand bucks? Something like that."

"Something like that." Guzmán clenched his teeth.

"Hey, relax, Roberto. I thought you two were tight."

"I did too."

"So take it easy. The Mercedes probably belongs to her uncle or somebody. You two have been going out together, right?"

"Oh, yeah. We've been doing something every day, just about. But she always comes to my place to meet me. I took her down to the keys, and we went sailing. We spent a great afternoon at Penrods. Last night we had a great dinner, Maine lobster scooped live out of a tank."

"So what's the problem?"

"Remember when we bumped into her that night at Tropics, and I told you I was going to get her phone number?"

"I remember."

"Well, she wouldn't give it to me."

"She wouldn't? Why not?"

"She said she almost flunked out of school last term, and her mother freaked out. The University of Miami costs a bunch. She said no more boyfriends until Lourdes gets her grades straightened out. Lourdes didn't want her mother picking up the telephone with me on the other end."

"I see. Nothing wrong with that. And it accounts for her coming to your place for a date."

"A Mercedes!"

"And she's been calling you, right?"

"Oh, yeah. Every day. She's been a sweetheart. But she's alway driven that Yugo." Guzmán called to the waitress in Spanish. To Burlane, he said, "Listen, I think I better see what's going on here."

Burlane said, "Be cool, Roberto. There's probably a perfectly reasonable explanation. Maybe it's her brother's. Didn't you say she had a brother?"

"Eduardo."

"There you go. Why should she drive a Yugo when she can borrow her brother's Mercedes? Trace the license number. That'll tell you who owns it."

"She never mentioned any Mercedes to me. Not once. Dammit, I don't want to know later. I want to know now."

"Okay. I'm going to kick back and enjoy my *rabo encendido* while you're out there fighting that traffic in the heat."

"I'll see you later, Khartoum."

"Good luck."

Burlane watched Roberto get into his BMW, his eye on the Mercedes.

Burlane enjoyed his oxtail while Guzmán waited it out in his car. It was nearly ten minutes before the traffic started moving again, and Guzmán, waiting for a chance, pushed his BMW into the lane several cars behind Lourdes.

38

James Burlane had never set eyes on a meaner-looking dog than the Doberman pinscher that prowled the yard around the house wherein dwelled one Lourdes Maria Martinez, 20, registered owner of a Mercedes-Benz 560 SL convertible.

The Doberman was huge, lean as Lucifer. Muscles bulged like ebony ropes on its shoulders and flanks. The yard got enough light from a streetlamp that Burlane could see the animal clearly enough. What an animal! This was very nearly a surreal dog!

But he wanted a better look. He parked the Cherokee at the side of the curb across the canal from the Martinez house.

The dog, no doubt sensing it was being watched, struck an arrogant, defiant pose.

Its cut ears were as sharp as honed spikes.

Its malevolent yellow-brown eyes caught the light as it stared straight at Burlane.

Its nostrils flared.

It bared startling white canine fangs.

Burlane, glad that he was inside a vehicle, retrieved his binoculars from the rear of the Cherokee. He focused on the dog and brought it close up.

The dog's satanic eyes remained pinned straight on him. Its muscles tensed.

As though it knew Burlane was watching close up, it showed more teeth.

There was no fence around the peninsula. A dog like that could easily swim ashore. How in the hell?

Then Burlane saw that the dog had a substantial collar. He understood. The collar contained an electronic zapper. The dog was kept in check by a perimeter wire buried underground.

Burlane had seen enough Dobermans in his time to know that the animal in his glasses was truly an outsized specimen. As he studied the dog, a white Rolls-Royce slowed at the entrance of the residue. He knew that car.

He switched quickly to the driver, whose identity Ara Schott had learned from the license number on her Rolls-Royce. The woman with whom Captain Fowler had had the tête-à-tête in Fort Lauderdale, one Carmela Martinez, 45.

Ms. Martinez drove slowly up the narrow base of the peninsula, then stopped at a wrought-iron fence, the gates of which slid silently open upon her electronic command.

The Doberman raced to meet her, but skidded to a stop before the open gate. The electronic barrier was obviously under the road as well as along the perimeter of the peninsula.

Once through the gate, she stopped her Rolls and got out as the gate closed behind her.

Calling the dog's name, she tossed a bright red ball across the lawn, and the eager, athletic dog went racing in pursuit. The Doberman snatched the bounding ball before it came to rest. It returned the ball to her, accelerating with astonishing quickness.

The dog danced and bounded at her feet. Its tongue flopped. It was eager for another run.

Burlane was too far away to hear the dog's name, but he was curious. He slipped between the front seats of the Cherokee and got his parabolic mike out of one of his boxes of gear.

He went back to the front seat and snapped the mike into place on top of his binoculars. He slipped on a set of headphones and clipped a thin wire lead from the headphones into the parabolic.

He focused the binoculars on the woman.

She threw the ball again. "Go get it, boy. Atta boy."

The dog brought it back.

Burlane heard her clearly. She said, "You like to run after the ball, eh, Marimba? Run after the bouncing ball. Use those muscles and long legs of yours. Here, big guy. One more time. Get it, boy. Go for it. Run. Run."

Marimba! The dog's name was Marimba.

She threw the ball again. "That's it, you beautiful boy. Run, run. Watch the pretty red ball. Watch it bounce. Bring it back. Bring it back. Run, run, Marimba."

Just then a British-racing-green Jaguar pulled up to the gate, driven by a dark-haired girl in sunglasses. Burlane dialed Ara Schott on his cellular phone and asked him to run a check on the Jaguar's license number.

39

Over the years, James Burlane had learned to be patient when he was on a surveillance. There was no way to speed things up. This was not the movies. There was no script to change. No editor to cut the boredom.

The way Burlane passed the time depended largely on climate. He either read or engaged in his private passion, which was self-taught, amateur zoology/anthropology. He liked to observe and analyze animals of all species, whether they were at work or play: a flock of pigeons foraging in a bountiful gutter; a pair of ladybugs gnawing on leaves; Homo sapiens playing basketball on a cement slab.

A portable library of naturalist field guides—covering plants, birds, fish, mammals, marsupials, reptiles, and insects—was a mandatory part of Burlane's travel kit, only slightly less important than gas and oil for the Cherokee and the gear necessary to communicate safely with Ara Schott.

In Chicago, Philadelphia, or other northern cities, people were out and about and there was too much traffic on the sidewalks to risk using his fancy Bausch & Lomb binoculars or parabolic to eavesdrop on people in their high-rise living cells. Burlane was forced to read.

Burlane had enough privacy to use his equipment here, but there was no high-rise humans to observe. People didn't walk in the tropical heat and humidity; they drove in air-conditioned cars.

Burlane, munching his Granny Smith apple, finished the last article in the *Discovery* magazine and flopped it onto the rear seat.

Schott said the Jaguar that had followed Carmela home was registered to Marta Martinez, 18. The Jag had some months earlier been confiscated from a drug dealer in San Diego, California. The Drug Enforcement Administration had turned it over to its Miami agents for use in undercover investigations.

Schott's Dade Metro source made an educated guess that the DEA's Luis Fernandez had disposed of the vehicle in the course of an investigation. The source did not have access to the eyes-only internal memorandum that dealt with Fernandez's activities. What Schott was after was likely among Fernandez's notes and reports, currently in the hands of the Dade Metro detectives investigating his murder.

The source told Schott that if he wanted to see the Fernandez file, he'd have to ask Captain Donald Fowler.

Luis the consumed.

Luis. Marta. Carmela. Fowler. Guzmán.

Mmmmmmmmm.

The leaves of the trees rustled. A breeze. Burlane, hoping to scoop up some fresh air, opened the front door of the Cherokee. A stream of ants flowed up the gutter in a bustling file, coming and going from a colony established in a crack in the cement curb.

Burlane retrieved his binoculars.

He bit his lip in excitement as he watched a solo worker ant struggle with a seed three times its own size. It got the seed up to the stem of a fallen leaf, and could go no farther.

Up, up, the ant pushed.

The seed tumbled back, back.

Up, up.

Back, back.

The ant's comrades, bearing more manageable seeds, passed him on both sides. It never occurred to the ant to go around the leaf; like his companions, he was a straight-ahead insect. The approved way had always been forward; push forward with determination and discipline, and they would endure and survive.

The ant tumbled back.

It struck Burlane that a city gutter was not an especially hostile or debilitating environment for ants. They carried on, forming their elaborate colonies as they had for millions of years. Burlane had read that rhesus monkeys raised in captivity exhibited all manner of neurotic and self-destructive behavior that was absent in monkeys in the wild. When they were set free, they straightened up.

Burlane wondered: were not cities and civilization forms of cages to a species that had spent all but 100,000 of its million-year history as cooperative predators living in small bands? Hunter-gatherers. Then, *ka-bam, pow!* Agriculture and cities.

Why would anybody be surprised that the marimba had appeared in a species evolved and genetically programmed for life in the Kalahari Desert but forced to live in Detroit or New York or Miami Beach?

Guzmán's phone rang. Burlane perked up. Maybe something this time. He put the binoculars down and turned the volume up on the receiver.

"Hello, Roberto?" A score. Lourdes Martinez. Burlane recognized her voice.

Guzmán said, "Hey, what're you up, hon?"

"No classes today, so I took off with a couple of my girlfriends. We went to the Grove and hung out."

"Oh?"

There was a telltale hint of wounded lover in Guzmán's voice. However he might have wanted to conceal it, he failed.

Lourdes hesitated. "Oh, Roberto!"

It was difficult for Burlane to translate the beautifully ambiguous tone of her voice. Was it a remonstration? Disappointment? Burlane wasn't sure. If Guzmán was, he had a better ear than Burlane.

Lourdes Martinez dated agent Guzmán.

Carmela Martinez, Lourdes's mother, slipped Captain Donald Fowler a briefcase at lunch in Fort Lauderdale.

Those facts had to be related.

Burlane thought: Guzmán, even if you are crooked, remember you're a cop, for Christ's sake. Think, man. Use your brains, not your *pinga*.

Burlane didn't want to miss what Lourdes had to say. He adjusted the receiver again. She'd obviously been caught. How would she handle it?

She said, "Ah, you saw me out and about in my car, I bet."

"Not your Yugo. Your Mercedes 560 SL convertible." The master Latin lover was in love, and it showed from the unmistakable edge of hurt to his voice.

Lourdes laughed merrily. She was a charmer. "Oh, calm down, Roberto. This is a case where bad news brings good news."

"And the bad news is?" Guzmán sounded glum.

"I fibbed to you a little bit."

"Fibbed?" He was willing to be open-minded.

Burlane thought: Think, Roberto. Follow your own advice. It's bad form to let her lead you around by the *pinga*.

"Just a little, Roberto. I don't want you to be unhappy with me. I want you to promise not to be unhappy. I hate it that this awful mix-up had to happen, and I can't stand for you to be unhappy. Please, please, promise."

Guzmán sighed audibly. Whew! Everything was okay. There was an explanation, after all. He said, "I'm okay, I promise."

"Cross your heart."

"Cross my heart, Lourdes."

"Oh, thank you, Roberto. I knew you wouldn't let me down."

"And the fib was?"

"That I got bum grades at the University of Miami, and so my mother wouldn't let me date anybody until I got them up. I really do go there. That is, I take a course there now and then. I get good enough grades, Bs mostly, a C once in a while." She hesitated.

"Let's have the rest of it."

"Well, Roberto, you know those Gulf State car washes you see everywhere? My father owned forty-percent interest in those before he died. My mother sold the stock, and my uncle reinvested it for her in real estate. He knew what he was doing."

"Big bucks, I take it."

"You have to understand, Roberto, Mima's all the time worried that my sister Marta or I will marry some jerk after our money. She bought us the Yugo specifically so people wouldn't know. If we find someone we like, we have to be extra careful. Hence the fib. I did it for us, Roberto. Are you still sore? Don't be sore, Roberto. I think I'd go crazy if you were sore at me. Roberto?"

"Yes, Lourdes."

"*Te amo*, Roberto."

"I love you too, Lourdes."

"Then you're not sore."

Guzmán laughed. "How could I be sore about something like that?"

"Tell me again you love me."

"I do love you, Lourdes. I truly do."

"Mima knows all about you, Roberto. I told her how sweet and good to me you are. She's had time enough to get over her paranoia and wants to meet you. She says bring you on over. Oh, Roberto, I know she must sound awful and everything, but she loves us. It's her way of protecting us. You have to give her a chance."

"My mind is open. Really, it is."

"She's fun when you get to know her, Roberto. Would you like to meet her? Say you'd like to meet her."

"Of course I'd like to meet her."

"Then it's done. No use waiting around. You need some reassurance, I can see that. What if I drive over in my Mercedes and take you home to meet Mother?"

"No Yugo?" Guzmán laughed.

"No, I'll bring the Mercedes. Show it off a little. I think she's got a pork roast on, Roberto. You like roast pork, don't you? Plenty of chopped onions."

"*Mi placer*. Sure!" Guzmán said. "Lay those onions on me."

"Mima's black beans are just wonderful, you'll see, Roberto. Roberto, I'm so very, very happy I can't stand it."

"Me too, Lourdes." Guzmán gave her a kiss over the telephone.

Lourdes kissed him back. "One for you too. I'll be by in about ten minutes. I'll bring us some champagne. Mima loves champagne. Do you like champagne, Roberto? Oh, please, Roberto."

"I love champagne," Guzmán said.

"Oh, good! I'm happy everything is turning out for us, Roberto. It's been horrible for me ever since I met you. Having to sneak around. I can't tell you how much I've worried that something like this would happen. But it's behind us now. Say it's behind us and everything is okay. We look to the future. Say it."

"It's behind us and everything's okay, Lourdes. We look to the future. I love you still. I swear."

"Oh, good! I'll pick up a couple of bottles of Cristal. As you'll find out, Mima's a lot of fun when she drinks champagne. I'll see you in a few minutes, then."

"I can't wait, you little darling."

"*Te amo*, Roberto." She gave him a telephone kiss and hung up.

In the Cherokee, Burlane opened a can of Dr. Pepper—Cristal for proletarians—and took a swig; Mima and Lourdes didn't look like car-wash barons to Burlane. And he was confident they didn't have the patience to wait for investments to mature. They liked paint that dried fast.

It was entirely possible that Guzmán was just a clever FBI agent attempting to penetrate the Martinez family. It was also possible that the master Latin lover had choked in the clutch and fallen in love with the wrong girl. From the sound of Guzmán's voice, Burlane thought it must surely be the latter.

Burlane started the Cherokee and headed for Cocoplum and the house with the Doberman pinscher.

40

W hat?" Katherine Donovan sounded groggy, but she understood what Burlane had said all right. "Sid? What on earth?"

"You sound sleepy."

"I've been taking a nap, yes," she said. "What did you call me?"

"Special Agent Donovan." Burlane said this is as hohum a manner as possible.

"What in heavens are you talking about?"

"The connections looped back on themselves, which made the situation confusing."

"What connections?"

"Well, see, here I am, hanging out with FBI Special Agent Roberto Guzmán, wondering just how crooked he is, when I learn that his DEA amigo Luis Fernandez and a Dade Metro undercover cop were among the poor bastards who were butchered and used for dog food. But of course you know about that."

"I do? Roberto? Crooked?"

"He bought pure coke from me and cut it ten percent before he turned it in. Anyway, off we go to Oysterman's looking for Luis, and there you are, asking me cop questions. It was your sister that threw me off. You really *were* looking for your sister; that's what had me puzzled."

"I see."

"Later, we go to Scandinavia to meet a marimba player and behold, there's Donald Fowler. When Roberto spots you, he hustles me out of the place. That night you fly off to the Bahamas with Fowler."

"My, my. You have been busy."

"I'm betting you're looking for your sister on the side. It's the only thing that makes sense."

"Before we go any further, would you mind telling me your real name and who *you're* working for?"

"Sid Khartoum, soldier of fortune, late of Rangoon, Calcutta, and other exotic places."

"Uh-huh."

"By the way, Roberto's friend Jaime Guerrero launders his nick. In fact, Guerrero owns the house and apartment the government leases so Roberto can live like a proper marimbeiro. The taxpayers foot the bill so Roberto and Jaime can screw coke whores, including, once, your sister. Roberto's got it on tape." Burlane waited.

Katherine sighed. "What else?"

"The day after you went to the Bahamas with Fowler, I followed him to a restaurant in Fort Lauderdale. He had a tête-à-tête with a woman who drives a white Rolls-Royce, and she slipped him a briefcase under the table."

"Figures."

"I'm of the opinion that Roberto may have inadvertently gotten his wienie tangled in a terrible zipper."

"I see. Why is that?"

"Because he's fallen in love with Lourdes Martinez, a daughter of the woman with the Rolls. Luis Fernandez very likely gave a confiscated government Jaguar to her younger sister before he was fed to somebody's dog. Why do you suppose Luis did that?"

"Checking out the family?"

"That'd be my guess."

"Maybe Roberto's doing the same thing—investigating this family. What's the surname again?"

"Martinez. Did he mention it to you? If you are his

colleague, you'd know about something like that, wouldn't you?"

"Oh, crap. No, he didn't mention it to me."

"I can tell you with confidence that the great Latin Lover has loose noodles over sweet Lourdes. What's worse, a few minutes ago, he hopped into her Mercedes 560 SL convertible and rode off to Cocoplum to meet mom. I've got them on tape if you want to listen to their telephone conversation."

"On the take. Hot-damn special agent. Busting all those players and all the while on the take himself. I've been wondering about all the money he flashes around. Dammit to hell anyway, Sid!"

"I suppose we should try to help him out." Burlane waited. When Katherine said nothing, he said, "By the way, he never figured out you were Helen's sister, and I never told him."

"You saw the tape. That's why you knew about Helen."

"That's right."

"It's all this money, Sid. All this money floating around."

"Big money. Little people."

Helen sighed. "Yes, I suppose we should see what we can do to save his damnable hide."

Cocoplum's curving streets and cul-de-sacs were fine for admiring the monuments of conspicuous consumption, but the residents themselves garaged their cars. In the name of security and the vague, unstated notion that neatness is somehow associated with social class, they preferred tidy, that is, empty, streets.

Visitors might drive by to gawk and envy as they pleased, as long as they kept moving.

It was certainly no place to hang out in a dirty Cherokee; to pacify the more anal residents of Cocoplum, Burlane ran his vehicle through an automated car wash on his way to pick up Katherine Donovan.

They drove for a while in silence; then Katherine said, "So, I was right from the beginning. You're a cop."

"Adventurer."

"Bullpuckey."

In Cocoplum, Burlane quickly found Palmetta Street and slowed as he approached the Martinez residence on the right.

Ahead and across the street an RV with New York license plates was parked.

Burlane opened the glove compartment and snatched a road map. "We'll pair up with the visitors. Part of the same party, for all anybody knows. We've got a map for a prop."

"Last week a man flew down from Washington telling us to lay off Donald Fowler. He told us Fowler was working on a special assignment the government didn't want compromised."

Burlane glanced back at the Martinez house. "You mean, doesn't want to be made public. Don't you just love euphemisms, Katherine? Look there, in the yard. I see he's out and about again."

"Ooooh. What a dog!"

"Isn't he something?"

"I don't think I've ever seen a Doberman that large."

Burlane leaned over the seat and retrieved his binoculars, which he gave to Katherine. "Take a closer look. I've got a parabolic if you want to listen in. By the way, his name's Marimba."

41

The first thing that caught Roberto Guzmán's eye as he was swept through the green and black marble portico of the Martinez mansion were the three-legged, blackened iron pots on each side of the door. Three pots to the left of the door, four to the right.

Guzmán, his arm around Lourdes, was introduced to Mima Martinez while cheery sister Marta bounded about pouring everyone Cristal champagne in elegantly slender champagne glasses.

After brother Eduardo shook Guzmán's hand, he went outside and began retrieving the blackened, eight-inch pots. He put them on an elegant white marble table that was the centerpiece of the white room where the family had gathered. The pots contained crudely fashioned iron sledges, hammers, picks, pikes, spades, hoes, rakes, and even a miniature anvil.

The pouring of ritual champagne for the new couple was a joyous occasion for Roberto and the Martinezes, and they all held their glasses high, laughing and joking.

Then the genial Eduardo, whom Guzmán assumed would be his brother-in-law, raised his glass in a toast to the future of the handsome couple. They all had a sip of celebratory bubbly.

Guzmán, holding his glass for a refill, wondered what the pots and tools were all about. "Say, these are interesting, Eduardo. Some kind of folk art, I take it."

Eduardo said, "They're handmade, yes. They were made in Cuba by my great uncle."

"They look like *soperas* with little tools."

"*Soperas, sí.* Only we don't use them for soup. They're used to hold the blood at *ebo*."

"*Ebo?*"

"A sacrifice for an *orisha*."

"Ah, *orishas.* You're talking about Santería, then?"

"Ordinarily an *orisha's* holy stones are put in the bottom of a *sopera*, but Ogun requires iron tools rather than stones."

"Hey, that's something. Blood for the saints and all that. Okay to pick one up?"

"Sure. Hold it and feel the coolness of Ogun."

Guzmán picked up a pot containing an iron pick and a shovel. He weighed it in the palm of his hand. It felt cool. "Which one is Ogun?"

Mima, who had been listening to the conversation, said, "A warrior. Ogun is the *orisha* who protects this household, Roberto."

"I see." Guzmán, spooked by Mima's eyes, quickly returned the pot to the table.

Lourdes giggled. "Oh, you're so cute, Roberto." She ran her hand up under her collar, and gave him the sweetest kiss that Roberto Guzmán ever had. She ran her fingers gently through his hair, and let her soft little hand rest lightly on the nape of his neck.

Guzmán forgot all about the pots and tools. He wished her hand would linger there forever.

Hijo de puta! Roberto Guzmán woke up on the floor, his wrists handcuffed behind his back and secured to the chain between his ankles. Thus bound, he could go nowhere.

He lay still for a moment, drifting in a mental fog, listening to the voices above him.

He heard Mima mention something about Eduardo "cleaning him out." Did she mean Guzmán? Clean him out?

He remembered the iron *soperas* and the crude little tools. Santería. The pots held blood for the saints.

Guzmán felt a shoe give him a nudge in the shoulder. Eduardo said, "Come on, wake up. Hey, hey!"

Guzmán, still foggy, shook his head. "Give me a minute." As his head cleared, he felt Eduardo detach his handcuffed wrists from the leg chain. With Eduardo's help, he sat up.

Eduardo said, "Hold it there for a couple of minutes before you try to stand up."

"*Coño!*"

"You remember Lourdes's hand on the back of your neck?"

Guzmán blinked.

"She put what the docs call a transdermal patch on your neck. Fentanyl is the name of the drug. Knocked you right out. Lot better than the old-fashioned Mickey Finn."

A patch on his neck? Chains? Guzmán had to think, but it was difficult. His vision cleared, for a moment.

Where was Lourdes?

There they were. Mima, Lourdes, and her sister. All dressed up. Were they going somewhere?

Guzmán said, "Where you going?"

Mima Martinez and her two daughters swept out of the door and were gone.

Eduardo said, "They're going shopping. They love to shop." He helped Guzmán to his feet, and although his prisoner was nearly too groggy to walk, took him to the toilet, where he freed his ankles and wrists.

"Okay, strip. Off with everything."

Guzmán, disoriented, dizzy still, saw that Eduardo was armed with a silenced .45 automatic.

"Hands behind your back."

Guzmán did as he was told. Eduardo again handcuffed his writs, then pushed him back onto the toilet. He replaced the manacles on Guzmán's ankles and looped and secured the chain around the base of the toilet.

Eduardo opened the door of a medicine closet and took out an amber bottle. He slopped a dose of clear fluid into a water glass and held it up to Guzmán's lips. "Drink this."

"What is it?"

"It won't hurt you. Drink it."

"No. What's it for?"

"It won't hurt you or knock you out or anything. I can hold your nose if I have to. It's up to you."

Guzmán drank it.

Eduardo said, "I'll leave the door open a crack and turn up the tube so you can listen to the Cubs."

"What's that stuff you gave me?"

"Phenolphtalein."

"Huh?"

•   "Spelled p-h-e-n-o-l-p-h-t-h-a-l-e-i-n. Some word, eh? All those consonants run together. You'll be feeling the effects momentarily."

Guzmán, wondering what the hell phenolphthalein was, did feel something, a twinge of pain in his lower bowels. His mind had cleared to the point where he could actually defend himself, but here he was, chained naked to a toilet. He could relieve himself, and that was it. Anything else and he was screwed. *Mierda!*

Lourdes was off to shop with mom and sis while boyfriend and brother enjoyed the Cubs and got to know one another. Man-to-man stuff.

Another twinge of pain.

Guzmán was stunned. His mind reeled. What the fuck had he stepped into?

Two little zings in his lower abdomen.

Guzmán had ridden from Coral Gables to Cocoplum marveling at how wonderful Lourdes was. She flirted with him the whole way with those incredible brown eyes of hers. It was inconceivable that she was doing this to him. Out of the question.

She was in love with him. There was no mistaking something like that. Guzmán knew it for a fact. She was.

But how? How could she do this?

Or was she merely biding her time, waiting for an opportunity to help him? He didn't know. If only she'd given him some sign or signal. Something. Anything.

A stab of pain. Another.

He thought back to the beginning. If Lourdes had come on to him at Oysterman's, it would have been different. But she had not. He was the one, not her. He had picked her out of the crowd and gone for her big-time. And in the end, she had whipped it on him, reducing him to a damned fool, convincing him that what he really wanted was a son, her son, to teach how to ride a bicycle. *Qué estúpido.*

And baseball. She said their son could go to baseball games

with his Uncle Eduardo, who loved the game. *Esto no puede ser. Ayudame, Dios!*

His guts were suddenly gurgling and twisting. One zap of pain after another.

What the fuck?

Cramps. Ay! *Coño!* The *cabrón* had given him a laxative. His insides were turning to fluid.

In the next room, the television announcer said, "And now the Reds'll move that infield in, yep, here they come. They want to nip the runner at the plate. 'Course that means if Ryno gets good wood on the ball, he can blast it right by 'em."

"Is the tube loud enough, Roberto? Can you hear what's going on?"

A wrenching twist of pain. Ay! Guzmán found himself saying, "The Reds're moving the infield in to cut off the plate."

"Got Ryno at bat. You feeling okay now? Head cleared and everything?"

Guzmán's innards were in a roar. Grimacing, he pushed hard on his abdomen to fight the twisting pain. "You gave me a laxative."

Eduardo laughed. "You don't have to worry about making it to the can. The fentanyl patch might make you sick. If you have to puke, just let fly."

A minute later, Eduardo appeared at the door and ripped off a wad of toilet paper and gave it to Guzmán. "You'll be needing this."

So this was the genial, baseball-loving Uncle Eduardo who, in Roberto and Lourdes's fantasies, was supposed to take their son to ball games. This was the Eduardo who would buy his little nephew a Coke and hot dog with too much mustard. His sister Lourdes's cute little tyke. Every kid ought to have an Uncle Eduardo.

His bowels emptied with a rush and the pain was gone, and he set about the awkward task of cleaning himself with his wrists handcuffed behind his back. He yelled, *"Me caco en su madre, hijo de puta!"*

Eduardo was too engrossed in the Cubs to be bothered with taking offense.

Guzmán wondered why in the hell Eduardo didn't call upon the *orishas* to do something about the Cubs' lousy pitching.

* * *

The door of the refrigerator closed. Glass clinked. In proper baseball-fan fashion, Eduardo was getting himself a beer.

Back on the couch, Eduardo belched loudly. "Sandberg can't hit righties for shit. That's his only weakness. That, and the guy's personally uptight. He can't hang. You ever notice that?"

"Where'd they go shopping?"

The crowd roared. "All right, it's out of there. What?"

The announcer shouted, "Holy cow! Ryne Sandberg caught a high fastball and hitched a ride with the wind."

Eduardo said, "I take it all back, Ryno. Every bit of it. What'd you say?"

"I said, where'd your mother and sisters go shopping?"

"*Botánica*."

"What?"

"They went to a *botánica* in Hialeah. They gotta get some crap for tonight. Sandberg really creamed that one, shit! Cubs up four, two. Okay!"

Guzmán, thinking about Eduardo's beer, suddenly had to urinate, and so did. When he finished, he felt uncomfortable because he couldn't shake his cock. A quick flip of his *pinga* was automatic after taking a leak. Feeling foolish, he wiggled his butt back and forth on the seat. *Coño*. He was grateful he hadn't had to vomit. "What're they buying at a *botánica*?"

"Now if the Cubs don't blow their lead like they did Sunday . . . Mima had to get some stuff for her dog. You may have seen him when you came in. Doberman. Big, mean-looking fucker. Collar around his neck."

"Her dog?" Lourdes had mentioned a dog when they arrived, saying it was inside.

"Mima has to get special crap for him. Big feed tonight. *Ebo* for Ogun. You know women."

The announcer said, "And here comes The Hawk, Andre Dawson, his eye on that wonderful wind."

"What big feed?"

"Say again?"

Guzmán suddenly didn't want to hear the menu. "What's the Doberman's name?"

"Marimba."

"Say what? Marimba?"

"Ogun's idea, Mima says."

Ogun named the dog? *Hijo puta!*

"Ogun requires food made sacred by sacrifice, although it's the dog who does the actual eating. I'm cool. I go along. *Qué importa?*"

"Ay, Dios! Why'd you give me the laxative? I want to know."

"If you're that anxious . . ."

"I'm that anxious."

"It's because there's nothing worse than having to butcher a corpse with crap in its bowels. *Yaauugghhh!*"

"What?"

"Farm boys grow up learning about stuff like that. I had to learn the hard way. I've found I can save myself a whole lot of grief by tying Ogun's offering to the toilet and cleaning him out in advance. Phenolphthalein is the most efficient laxative I've found yet."

"*Mierda!*"

"That's what it amounts to in the end. Before I cut you up, I have to bleed you, so we can fill the iron *soperas* with blood. Seven pots. That's a lot of blood. Ogun likes his *ebo* blood hot and human." Eduardo paused, then added: "It has to be fresh, though. No microwaving."

oberto Guzmán told himself to relax. Worrying wouldn't do him any good. The best way to help Lourdes was to anticipate what she was up to. What was she planning? What should he do to help her?

How many hours had he been there? Two? Three? He wondered what time it was.

Then, suddenly, mother and two daughters were home, babbling and laughing; they made straight for the mirrors.

Mima said, "Sorry we took so long, Eduardo, but we decided to shop for some clothes."

Marta said, "Lourdes was feeling down. We thought some new clothes would perk her up. Show Eduardo what you got."

Guzmán heard Lourdes going into her bedroom. In a few minutes she was out again. "Well, Eduardo, what do you think?"

Eduardo whistled. "Ooooooh, sexy! Let's see what it looks like. Go ahead, model it for us, sis. Walk around a little."

"You like it, really?"

"All right!"

Mima said, "Twelve hundred bucks. We told her no way she was going to wear clothes like this if she married some wage-slave cop. Doesn't she look hot? Show us your jacket too, Lourdes. Go ahead. Wait'll you see this, Eduardo. An eight-hundred-dollar pop."

"Okay, Lourdes! Eduardo said. "Shows off that form of yours. I like the detail work."

Marta said, "Eduardo's not kidding, Lourdes. It's you. It really is."

Mima said, "Clothes like this cost, hon. If you want clothes like this, you have to keep your wits about you. You have to bear in mind, Roberto Guzmán can't afford your bubble gum."

Couldn't afford her what? From the toilet, Guzmán shouted: *"Puta mierda!"*

Mima, furious, screamed, *"Callate la boca, maricón!"*

Eduardo said, "Oh shit, forgot the door. Sorry, Mima."

Guzmán listened to Eduardo's footsteps coming fast.

Eduardo said, "Can't take you anywhere," and slammed the door shut.

Listening to the Martinez family chatter while Lourdes preened in front of the mirror, Guzmán realized what this was all about. Mima wanted the best. So did Eduardo and Marta. Lourdes too. Guzmán wanted the best. Everybody wanted the best. Nothing but the best. Larger. Flashier. More expensive.

Appetite. It was all about appetite. A craving for a larger share of the trough. Guzmán was no different, he had to admit. He didn't want to be a cop if he couldn't play the marimba. Shove uniforms and neckties. He didn't want to be ordinary. Screw that. As long as he was cool, content to nick a little here and there, his scam was risk free. Just lay lines and fuck blondes and take pictures of pussies sprawled all over his pad.

What could be better?

Sid Khartoum had said his ambition was to lead an examined life to the fullest extent possible. Khartoum said he couldn't imagine anybody on his deathbed remembering having owned a new car.

Well, that was bullshit. Guzmán remembered his BMW quite clearly, thank you. He wished he was in it, rolling down the causeway to Key West, this crap behind him. He'd have a big-titted blonde by his side and a vibrator and his camera in the glove compartment. They'd stop at a roadside seafood joint and have key lime pie—touristy, he supposed, a cliché, but delicious.

The BMW was replaced by a montage of images and

memories: Luis Fernandez; Sid Khartoum; the night he met Lourdes at Oysterman's; he and Lourdes in Manatee; Eduardo; a Doberman named Marimba.

Mima was a santera with a hungry dog. *Que la salga un cancer en el culo.*

Wait a minute. All this worrying was stupid. Lourdes was biding her time, going along with the family until the time was right to rescue him. Had to be.

Suddenly Guzmán understood. He'd passed the threshold of faith. He believed in Lourdes's love with all his heart and mind and soul. She. Her. He worshiped all pronouns referring to Lourdes. He loved Her completely and without reservation. He adored her.

Lourdes would never let him down. She was his salvation. She would come through; that was the promise of their love.

Guzmán concentrated for all he was worth. *Dearest, sweetest, Lourdes, I believe in You. I love You more than myself. Please, please, don't let me down.*

Help me, Lourdes.

Spare me.

After Lourdes saved him, in gratitude for his deliverance, Guzmán vowed to sell it all—his house, his apartment building, everything—and anonymously donate the money to cocaine treatment programs.

He'd get rid of his BMW and buy himself something sensible. He'd give away his Italian love seat. His art. His antique chess sets. Screw this life. Even the blonde pussies were becoming boring.

He'd resign from the FBI. Tell the pooh-bahs in charge that he was tired of this life. He'd pinned a lot of big-time marimbeiros for them, heavy-duty players, and was in the process of tracing the contacts of one of Banda-Conchesa's pilots; they'd never suspect that he'd been doing a little business on his own. Even if they did figure him out, no big deal. To avoid the humiliation of admitting that they'd been had, they'd quietly let him go.

Guzmán felt relieved and released. Freed.

He thought of Sid Khartoum cooking weeds in his wok. He'd let Khartoum off the hook so the silly bastard could instruct him on the philosophy of simple living. He'd learn to cook and eat weeds like Khartoum.

Wait a second.

Mercy?

From Lourdes? That mercenary, money-hungry little bitch of the western world?

Give up his hot tub and Jacuzzi?

Guzmán giggled, yanking at his bonds. What a dumb fuck he was. *Coño!*

Lourdes was supposed to spare him?

She was to give him deliverance?

Salvation?

What shit was that? He was sane, then a nut case, then sane again.

Escorias!

He tried not to think of what he had been fed. Tried to block it from his mind.

Guzmán wanted food that comforted. He remembered his mother's black beans and rice and her roast pork with chopped onions. She marinated the pork in garlic and lemon and orange juice all night before she roasted it, surely food for the gods.

Sitting there naked, tied to a toilet, he could taste the roast pork. He savored an imaginary bite, held it in his mouth, and it was so, goooooood. *Mmmmmmmmmmmm.*

43

In the dying sunlight, the Doberman paced to and fro on the lawn outside the Martinez house.

Katherine Donovan watched the dog through James Burlane's binoculars. "I don't think he likes people hanging around." She gave them to Burlane.

Burlane focused on the dog. The Doberman stared straight back, teeth bared. "There's nothing between him and us except his fear of getting zapped. Here, take another look at those eyes of his." He handed her the glasses.

"Ah, I see what you mean, Sid. If the urge to sink those teeth into something ever overcame the fear of the shock . . ."

"He's showing a lot of teeth. Shall we mike him and see if he's talking to us?"

Katherine smiled. "Sure."

Burlane gave her the parabolic and retrieved the amplifier from one of the air-conditioner safes. He punched the power button as Katherine focused the parabolic on the dog.

Grrrrrrrrrrr!

"Oh, he is pissed!" Katherine said. "A growler, not a barker."

Burlane grinned. "He's a watchdog. He's earning his keep. It'd be in bad form to have a barker in Cocoplum."

"Barkers are in bad form wherever they are."

Their initial anxiety at sitting parked behind the RV disappeared as the minutes passed and no curious gentleman or lady of Cocoplum came tap, tap, tapping at the Cherokee's doors or windows.

A white Miami squad car with blue stripes cruised by at five-thirty. The cop behind the wheel slowed the Caprice Classic but apparently saw nothing wrong with a puzzled couple studying a map on the front seat.

Then it was dark and they waited.

Eduardo Martinez, dressed in white except for a red sash around his waist—and bearing white shirt, pants, shoes, and socks—appeared at Guzmán's toilet cell at 11 o'clock.

He flopped the white outfit onto the sink. "The *orisha* is straighforward and pure at *ebo*, so we all wear white in his honor. My mother and sisters will wear green and black beads for Ogun. I'll wrap a green and black sash around my waist. We're all virgins at dying, so you'll wear all white."

"I was looking forward to a sash of some kind. A touch of color." Guzmán couldn't tell whether Eduardo was stoned or in a trance.

Eduardo brought a chair in by the john door and sat down, spraddle-legged. "All this got started with blood, which is what Ogun should be getting, according to his *ashe*. But rooster or dog blood, not human blood. Then Ogun said he wanted to try human flesh for his *ebo*. Just once to see what it tasted like. It was a violation of Ogun's *ashe*, but Mima went ahead. Whatever Ogun wanted, Ogun got. Ogun loved it! Now he has Marimba addicted to it—all the time, not just for *ebo*. And the family has to keep him fed."

"Addicted to human flesh? The Doberman?"

"He's gotten to where he can't do without it. He likes the *pinga* and *cojónes* the best, but he's partial to the liver, too. And little goodies like the ears. When he eats the toes it sounds like he's munching popcorn."

"*Coño!*"

"Yes, human flesh. He just craves it. Getting so he turns up his nose at beef. We even tried bringing him beef within minutes of the animal being slaughtered, but no go."

"Santero *maricón!*"

"If he goes too long without it, you should see him out there, pacing. Goes nuts. Can't live without it, to hear Mima tell."

"You killed Topper MacRae and Luis Fernandez to feed your goddamn dog? *Mierda!*"

Eduardo looked chagrined. Reluctantly, he nodded yes. "And ten others. All marimbeiros; no other cops that we know of. Either nobody's found any of the bones that I threw away, or those that have been found haven't been identified. I tell Mima we're going to have to back off, but there's no talking to her."

"*Sadisto hijo de puta!*"

"All I have to do is flash enough hundred-dollar bills, and the blonde *conchas* spread their legs. You've been playing the marimba, you know how that works. So, if I have to feed the damn dog, I'll find a way to feed him."

"Me. You'll feed him me."

"Sure you. Why not?"

"*Me caco en ti, y tu familia. Hijo de la gran puta!*"

Eduardo laughed. "When the freezer's getting low, and we have a victim on hand, Marimba gets it fresh as *ebo* to Ogun. The rest of the time we have to thaw it out for him. I got the best butcher's gear on the market, meat axes, a saw that zips right through bone—everything I need. Fancy freezer. Now, I've even got a machine that grinds the bones up into a meal that we can use in the garden or flush down the toilet. No more kids finding skulls on the Tamiami."

Guzmán paled.

"If you hadn't been a cop, we might have worked you into the action. We talked about that when we first found out. We really did."

Guzmán clenched his jaw.

"I ask you, what am I going to do? What would you do if you were me?" Eduardo weighed the white shirt with his hand. "I tell you what, Roberto. I don't like a target to jump around on me, even at point-blank range, so I'll leave your feet tied and at least one hand cuffed while you put on the shirt, and both hands cuffed when you put on the pants. Fair enough?"

Eduardo disappeared a half hour before midnight and came back again in a few minutes, his silenced automatic in hand. "Well, it's almost time, amigo. Comes to all of us. How're you doing?"

Guzmán said, "I like sitting around on toilets. I could have used a double-header though, and maybe a cold beer."

"Sitting here on the toilet with nothing to do but whistle and let farts. Air from both ends, eh? Probably had a lot to think about. By the way, Roberto, we perform the sacrifice outside, under the moonlight. The family has to accept risk."

"Part of the ceremony."

"The ceremony of eating. *La gran comida*. Also, Ogun requires us to give you at least the illusion that you have a chance of escaping."

"The illusion?"

"It's theoretically possible for you to escape, but not likely. We haven't had a player yet who didn't think he was going to make it. Everybody seems to think he's the exception. Marimba's teeth are there, but not for them. It won't happen to them."

"But you are going to give me a chance."

"None of this is any big deal if you think about it, Roberto. We've had human sacrifices for tens of thousands of years, only now we disguise the names of the victims and the forms of execution."

Guzmán took a deep breath and let it out slowly.

"You give me a hint of shit between now and the opportunity we're offering for you to beat the dog, and I'll shoot you, bam, no problem. With this silencer nobody out there'll hear a thing."

"*Qué sacrificio.*"

"If you're quick and smart and agile enough, who knows?" Eduardo paused, watching Guzmán.

Guzmán licked his lips.

"If I shoot you now, I have to clean the blood out of the bathroom. It's bad enough having to butcher you after the dog does his thing."

"*Mierda!*"

"I bet you're figuring there's even a chance Lourdes will come to your rescue. Her heart's delight, or a handbag forever full of hundred-dollar bills? Which one will she take? That's the bet before the house, bottom line."

"*Maricón!*"

"I bet you've been telling yourself maybe Lourdes is just biding her time, waiting for a chance to help you and take her vows of poverty as a cop's wife. Pop out of bed every morning to fry you eggs for breakfast. Fry 'em just the way you like 'em, yolks just right and everything. Anything for Roberto."

Guzmán shifted on the toilet seat.

"The gift is more powerful if we have a live sacrifice. That way, the blood is hot and fresh, just the way Marimba likes."

44

Burlane and Katherine watched the Martinez residence and waited. The lights were on. Above, wisps of clouds slid by the full moon—more than enough, light for Burlane's binoculars. One hour passed. Two. Three.

A few minutes before midnight, Mima and Marta, in white dresses, set up a marimba on the lawn in the shadows of the eaves.

At midnight, they began playing. Mima played the low register. Marta took the high. Their mallets scarcely touched the keys. Their notes did not intrude. They settled in, easy, rhythmic, *simpática con la noche*. Cool, mellow notes, finely struck, floated lazily through the humid night. Gentle runs and laid-back riffs.

"What do you think, Sid, Santería, with those white dresses?"

"That'd be my bet. You wanna mike them?"

Katherine focused the parabolic; Burlane readjusted the receiver.

A young man dressed in white strolled onto the expanse of lawn bearing a large cardboard box from which he removed, one at a time, seven white roosters. He set each surprised bird gently onto the grass. His chore done, he returned to the house.

The roosters, with wrinkly skinned, big-beaked, Bertrand Russell faces, seemed bewildered by their sudden freedom. They walked tensely about, inquisitive eyes wide, heads jerking. One of them made a lonesome, somewhat tentative call, *bwaaaak, bwaaaak, bwaaaak,* then shut up as though suddenly realizing the gravity of the situation.

Eduardo Martinez had taken the all-white Guzmán to an eight-foot-by-eight-foot white anteroom. A door of steel bars separated the anteroom from the interior of the house. Everything was white, even the bars. Guzmán's legs and hands were free, but his only escape led to the dog outside. He massaged his wrists, trying to assess his situation.

Eduardo, cradling a silenced rifle in the crook of his arm, slid a key under the bars and took a seat on a bar stool. "You can go ahead and unlock the door, Roberto. Open it a crack. I want you to hear the music. But if you run before I tell you, I'll have to shoot you in the leg, and then you won't stand a chance."

"Got it." Guzmán did as he was told. Outside, a marimba was being played.

Eduardo said, "It's beautiful, isn't it? So lyric. So soothing. The word *mellow* describes it. Even better, *murmur.* Mellow and murmur are marimba. That's Mima and Marta, by the way. Aren't they good?"

Guzmán said nothing.

"Lourdes is receiving Ogun for the first time. She's been studying his *ashe* for six years, but this is her first time to give him *ebo*. Both she and Marimba will be vessels for Ogun. When they're filled with him, I'll tell you when to run for it. Go ahead, open the door."

Guzmán opened the door. The night air felt warm and good.

"They're summoning Ogun with the music. When the dog hears that music, he knows it's time for *ebo*, and he slowly fills with Ogun."

Guzmán stepped into the doorway. "Lourdes?" he called softly. He let his eyes adjust to the light. A breeze stirred, sweet across his face. "There's no dog out here."

"Just roosters. Ogun's *ashe* ordinarily demands dogs or roosters for his *ebo*."

"*Ay, Dios!* Why didn't you get dogs too?"

"It's one or the other, dogs or roosters, but not both. The chickens are easier to run down after it's all over. Mima stews them with noodles."

"*Mierda!*"

The roosters, with grave chicken-steps, slowly spread out from the center of the lawn.

"Marimba used to love roosters. Loved their blood. Just craved it. But now . . ." Eduardo's voice trailed off. He sucked air between his two front teeth.

"*Donde está tu perrito maricón?*"

Eduardo said, "You'll think faggot dog. We went out and bought ourselves a spring-loaded starting gate like they use for the greyhounds at Hialeah. The gate's a couple yards to your right. Marimba knows what's going on. By now the music's got him all worked up, and he's one with Ogun."

Guzmán glanced to his right, chewing his lip, listening. *Nada.* "*El perrito no tiene lengua, es mudo?*"

"He's not mute. He just likes to wait in silence."

"*Carajo!*"

"When he's released, he goes full tilt. You'll hear his paws digging in behind you, but by the time you hear them, you're history. Look, here comes Lourdes."

Indeed, Lourdes, in a white cotton dress and wearing green and black beads, put a dish containing a white candle in the middle of the lawn, and lit the candle. She rose and, to the mellow marimba music, she began a slow, ritual dance around the candle. She raised her feet high and lowered them slowly, as she hacked at the air with angry fists. In her right fist, she grasped a small white plastic something.

"Those are machetes she's swinging. That's a remote in her hand there. The music will tell us when both Lourdes and Marimba are filled with Ogun."

"So Lourdes gets to punch me out."

"I think she does like you, dude. She didn't want her sister or her mother tapping the button, or me. Right now, she's inviting the *orisha* Ogun to mount her and ride. Ogun is a warrior and defender so she entices him with this dance in which she slays enemies of his *ashe*. If the *orisha* descends, she will travel with him to Ile-Ife. Watch her dance, Roberto. She's saying, *see what a mighty warrior I am, Ogun. Come be one with me.*"

Lourdes danced slowly around the flickering candle, slashing and hacking enemies of Ogun's *ashe* with dramatic ritual slashes of her imagined machetes.

She looked straight at Guzmán.

Did Lourdes see him? Was this a performance for her family? Was she secretly on his side?

Guzmán couldn't tell.

Had she already given him a signal that he was too stupid to understand? Was there something he wasn't getting? Was that it?

She looked right at him, right through him. He had no idea whatsoever. None.

Ayudame, Dios!

"I can't find the dog. He must still be inside." Burlane edged the muzzle of his .22 special sniper's rifle just above the window.

His eyes swept the grounds, looking for the dog. Where the hell was the dog?

"Sid, listen! The music is changing."

The marimba players had begun jamming in earnest.

"Okay, partner. Hear that music? Lourdes is filled with Ogun. Remember, she can send him in after you if she wants. Go on, run for it."

Guzmán took another cautious step just outside the open door, adrenaline pumping. He suddenly sprinted for the water, ran to the left of Lourdes and her remote. Ran hard as he could, head up, arms pumping.

Roosters scattered, flapping clipped wings.

He heard nothing behind him.

Twenty feet to go.

No dog.

Fifteen.

Ten.

Lourdes hadn't tapped the button. She couldn't. Couldn't tap it. Wasn't in her.

He was going to make it.

Yessss!

*   *   *

Burlane and Katherine watched Guzmán run.
Nothing.
Katherine said, "He's out of there!"

Behind Guzmán, a loud slam.
Marimba's feet.
Lourdes! *Puta!*

Near the edge of the lawn, the charging Doberman pushed off its massive haunches and seized Guzmán by the throat with its powerful jaws and twisted, laying its weight into the strike.
Guzmán's neck snapped.
The dog yanked several times, ripping veins, arteries, sinew, and muscle.
Finally, Guzmán's head popped free.
Eduardo Martinez, carrying a white plastic bucket, sprinted from the door and grabbed the feet of the jerking, shuddering body. He cupped the stump of Guzman's neck with the bucket, and, without looking up, dragged the corpse rapidly toward the open door. Guzmán's feet, locked in death throes, bucked and hopped, churned and kicked, but Eduardo held on, struggling to capture all the blood in the bucket.
Behind him, with savage rips of its jaws, the Doberman stripped the skin and nose and ears from Guzmán's face and skull.
Burlane pulled down on the Doberman's bobbing head as the dog choked down what was left of the neck at the base of Guzmán's skull and jabbed his powerful snout inside the cranial cavity . . . and fired.
The dog howled and twisted, falling across the underground wire, accepting the electrical zap without letting go of Guzmán's head. Then he was in the water. Gone into the darkness.

THREE

HELEN'S SONG

45

James Burlane took another sip of Irish coffee. "He was eating Roberto's head. I didn't want to hit Roberto. Stupid emotion! Roberto was history. The doctor hasn't been born who could have sewn his head back on. I can't believe I was such a fucking fool!"

Katherine Donovan said, "We want the family, not the dog, Sid."

"I choked. There's no other word for it."

"You used a silencer. There's no way they could know what got into the dog. It just yowled and was gone."

"It's out there roaming around in Cocoplum, for Christ's sake. With Roberto Guzmán's skull for a bone. I should have Ramboed my way in there and taken care of the son of a bitch." Burlane signaled the bartender for another cup of Irish coffee.

"We'd be crazy to spook the Martinezes until we find out the nature of their relationship with Donald Fowler. Fowler's protected by someone in Washington. For all we know, he's privy to everything both of us are doing."

"How could Fowler know what I'm doing?"

"Oh, come on. He's probably the guy who had your pad torched. Have you thought of that?"

"I was looking for the man, when I should have been thinking of the dog. I'm losing my stuff. Shit!"

"The dog was on him quicker than a blink. Good luck trying to drop him that fast. William F. Cody, maybe, or Audie Murphy. But Sid Khartoum?" She shook her head.

"We had the Luis Fernandez connection. We did. Luis was a victim of the dog-food murderer. I saw the dog earlier. Mean mother. I should have been more careful, face it. Marimba. She was calling it Marimba."

On the tube above the bar, a pretty woman said, "Tonight, a killer dog stalks Cocoplum. Stay tuned for a WPLG Channel Ten special news bulletin."

"Oh, shit," Burlane said.

They waited through station identification and several minutes of commercials, after which a handsome man with a sincere, concerned voice said, "Tonight a tragedy of major proportions is taking place in posh Cocoplum. A large, male Doberman pinscher remains at large after having attacked, killed, and in two cases partially eaten, three visitors to the fashionable suburb.

"Police say the dog did not display behavior typical of rabies, but the final word on that won't come until it's captured or destroyed. Until then, people living in Cocoplum and surrounding communities are urged to stay indoors. For more, we take you to Janet Burford, live with the Dade Metro Police in Cocoplum."

Pretty Janet, standing by a police van, blonde hair whipping from the wash of a helicopter *whack, whack, whacking* overhead, shouted dramatically at the camera. "Things are pretty wild here in Cocoplum as you might imagine, Earl. The police are withholding the names of the victims pending notification of their relatives, but as near as I can piece together, the killings took place over a forty-minute period during which many visitors were emerging from Friday-night dinner parties with Cocoplum friends.

"The first victim, we're told, was the fashion-model wife of a Miami commodities broker. The woman had just stepped out the front door of a Cocoplum house when the dog leaped from the shadows and decapitated her.

"Several minutes later, the dog struck again, three blocks away, this time killing and eating the genitals of a banker prominent in a recent money-laundering probe.

Pretty Janet checked her notes. "In the final incident, the dog devoured the face, throat, and much of the upper torso of the girlfriend of a Miami-area real estate developer as her stunned friends watched through a picture window.

"The police have blocked off the streets leading into the area and, as you can see, the sky is filled with helicopters sweeping the fashionable district with high-powered search-lights. Police are telling residents to please stay inside their homes until this dog is brought to bay."

Sincere, concerned Earl said, "Are there any Dobermans known to live in the area, Janet?"

"Yes, there is one and possibly more, but there was nobody home when police checked, and the animal's owners are gone, apparently for the weekend."

"They're still checking that one out, then."

"Yes, they are, Earl. I believe it may have been completed, but we haven't been given any names. Chief George Dersham arrived to personally take charge of the search, but so far we've not been able to talk to him. Earl, Captain Donald Fowler has agreed to answer a few questions. Captain Fowler learned about the tragedy at home on one of our first bulletins." She moved next to Fowler. "Captain, what can you tell us about the status of the search at this point?"

Fowler looked grave. "First, I would remind your viewers that this is Chief Dersham's operation, not mine. I can tell you with assurance that the chief is doing everything possible to locate the animal. By the way, the dog you referred to a moment ago, the Martinez dog, has been located and cleared. The family had gone to the Keys, and they took their dog with them."

"Have you located any others?"

"I believe there are reports of at least two more Dobermans in the area, and we're checking those out. We ask anyone having information that might help us to please call. I can't stress enough the importance of following Chief Dersham's request that residents of Cocoplum or the areas immediately surrounding it should stay inside. And folks outside of the area should stay out. This is a killer animal with a thirst for human blood, and none of us have any way of knowing which way he'll turn next."

"Can you tell us if this episode has any connection with the dog-food murders of Miami-area drug dealers?"

"That's a question that comes to mind. Right now, we don't know enough to even guess at the answer. It's always possible, but we won't know for sure until we've captured or destroyed the animal and have an opportunity to match its teeth with markings on the remains of the people killed tonight. Also, although the dog didn't display the classic symptoms, it's far too early to rule out rabies."

"Which assumption are you proceeding on, Captain Fowler?"

"I'm not proceeding on any assumption. This is Chief Dersham's responsibility. He's in charge, not me. All I can do is give you an educated opinion. But I truly don't think we have the luxury of operating on any sort of assumption. All we know is that a Doberman pinscher with a thirst for human blood is on the loose. It's our duty to stop it from killing more and to see to the safety and well-being of people who live in the area. We'll do our very best to do just that, as quickly and efficiently as possible."

"We have to return to our studios now. Good luck, Captain Fowler."

Fowler looked grim. "Thank you, Ms. Burford. I assure you, we need all the luck and prayers that we can possibly get. This is a terrible thing that has happened."

She faced the camera. "The question here in Cocoplum: is the crazed Doberman roaming somewhere in this posh residential area a rabid animal, or does he just like to eat people?"

Earl said, "Can you give us some idea of what it feels like to be out there? It must be pretty unsettling knowing that dog could burst from the shadows and be on you before you knew what happened."

Ms. Burford said, "Unsettling hardly describes it, Earl. It's downright spooky is what it is. The mobile police command established here in Cocoplum has taken on all the appearances of a military unit preparing for combat. You'll note how the people behind me are either sitting in their vehicles or gathered under streetlights with their weapons at the ready. Helicopters are in the air, searchlights sweeping the yards and streets. In the distance we can see specially trained riot police with shotguns beginning a cautious sweep through the neighborhood. They're protecting themselves as best they can with riot helmets, face shields, and bulletproof vests. And Chief George Dersham, Miami's designated General Schwartzkopf for the night, is on the spot, in command of the action."

On the monitor, the grim-faced policemen moved warily under a streetlight. Behind them, the grand Cocoplum houses were alive with lights, word having been passed by phone from neighbor to neighbor. The camera's telephoto lens picked up anxious faces peering out from upstairs windows.

The policeman moved past impressive portico after handsome portico. This one made of imported Italian marble. That one fashioned from pastel-yellow-and-green stones imported from Ecuador. A third from a raspberry-colored stone quarried in Alaska.

"These police officers are on the front line. They enter the territory of dread, a zone of murderous intent, not knowing when, without warning, the murderous dog might leap from the blackness, straight for their throats. For WPLG Channel Ten, this is Janet Burford in Cocoplum, where things are most certainly going bump in the middle of this sultry Miami night."

46

Until they knew the full story of Donald Fowler's relationship to the Martinez family, Burlane and Katherine had to stay away from their usual haunts and digs.

At three A.M., with police units still sweeping Cocoplum in search of the killer dog, they had eggs and sausage and grits in an all-night diner, Danny's, on the edge of Coral Gables, then headed south on U.S. One. Burlane parked his Cherokee under a coconut palm at the edge of a beach on Key Biscayne in southeast Miami.

He unfastened the fake air conditioners from the floor and stacked them in the front seat with the rest of his crap. He then flattened the rear seat, leaving room for him and Katherine to stretch out and sleep, covered by a single, light cotton blanket that was part of the vehicle's traveling kit.

Burlane knew he needed all the sleep he could get, but he was doubtful of the prospects in these circumstances. Next to him, Katherine's warm form was companionable and comforting, but they were both too tired and keyed up for anything sexual.

He lay there, replaying the possibilities in his mind.

As Miami's showpiece drug buster, Donald Fowler was

rather like a battlefield general. He likely was privy to the big picture, that is, where the DEA, the FBI, and the other alphabet battalions had deployed their soldiers and fifth columnists in South Florida. In order to coordinate their activities with the Dade Metro Police Department, he likely knew their targets in general terms. But it was unlikely, unless he had a legitimate reason to ask, that he knew the details of all their investigations or even the identities of all their agents.

He hadn't known about Katherine, or he wouldn't have flown her to the Bahamas.

The pretty television reporter, Janet Burford, had been riding an adrenaline rush as she reported the news from the mad-dog front. War was fun. That the alphabet soldiers in the war on drugs wore civvies instead of uniforms was beside the point. An army was an army. War was war. Soldiers were soldiers. Combat was combat. The object of the drill was in all cases the same: a megahit of adrenaline, The Rush.

Burlane was not so casual as to forget the midnight bomber who had torched his pad. The attempted torching had given somebody a kick, but then fun and profit were as comfortable together as gin and vermouth.

Who had done that? Who? A crooked cop working for Donald Fowler?

When Burlane finally got serious about getting some sleep, he saw the ravenous black dog ripping Guzmán's face from his skull. He saw the ebony head bobbing hungrily up and down.

He opened his eyes again. He could feel Katherine breathing.

He closed them. The dog. Eating.

He opened them. "Are you awake?" he asked. He knew she was.

"Yes."

"I can't sleep. All I can see is that dog choking down what was left of Roberto's head."

"Count beds. Imagine the earliest bed you can remember sleeping in. A bed from your childhood. Then take them one bed at a time. See each bed in your mind's eye. Remember how warm and cozy and comfortable it was. Remember going to sleep in it. Each bed. Try it. Go back. Concentrate on the details."

"Is that what you're doing? Counting beds?"

"Yes. Or you can pick one special bed and concentrate on

it; sometimes that'll work just as well. Go back and slip into that one bed and see and feel that world. Pursue the memory until you fall asleep."

Burlane closed his eyes. He saw the man dragging Guzmán's headless corpse by the feet.

He pushed the corpse from his mind.

He saw an eight-foot-by-four-foot shack with a corrugated tin roof and tar-paper siding. The shack, which had once been a chicken coop, was insulated with yellowed newspapers; the corners were festooned with cobwebs. The 40-watt light bulb on the low ceiling was turned on and off with an old string, dirty from use, that hung above the foot of the bed.

He saw the blood squirting from the stump of Guzmán's neck. Loops of crimson, shooting out.

He forced the blood from his mind.

He returned to the inside of the shack. He saw blankets piled high over a folding metal cot. There was an aged electric heater on the cracked linoleum floor beside the cot. At the edge of the heater, a jagged divot in the linoleum looked like a running buffalo. Outside, a north wind blew hard and cold from across the river in Washington.

He followed the wind as it rushed over rocks left bare by Chinese miners sluicing for powder gold, and whistled through leafless willows, and raced past a barbed-wire fence, and snaked across frozen cowpies and an irrigation ditch and another fence, to hammer and shake at the tar-paper shack.

He saw the dog eating Guzmán.

He saw the bed. He put his hand on the bed. The surface appeared literally frozen. He turned on the space heater. The brittle rubber blades started up: *ka-ka-ka-whump, ka-ka-ka-whump.* The wire slowly turned orange.

Little Jimmy Burlane took a deep breath and stripped his clothes off in a frenzy. Dressed in T-shirt and jockey shorts, he yanked the filthy string, dousing the light. Stiffening from the cold, he dove beneath the flannel sheets. *Brrrrrrrr!* Shit! He clenched his chattering jaws to ride out the cold, knowing from experience that the insulating heap of blankets would do its job in due time.

He got warmer and warmer until his spot was womblike, all comfy and cozy. The weight of the blankets embraced him, but the zone of warmth afforded by body heat was limited. Jimmy had to lie still; if he flipped or flopped, left or right, he entered the territory of *yyyyaaaagggghhhh!* Ice cold! *Aaaahhhh, sssshhhhiiiitttt!*

The eating dog crowded its way back. Burlane fought it off.

He returned to the tar-paper shack in the wind.

He waited for the warmth to close in and hold and comfort and keep him.

Coyotes yipped and yelped in the willows by the river. The heater wires glowed orange; the rubber blades went *ka-ka-ka-whump, ka-ka-ka-whump, ka-ka-ka-whump!* The wind hammered against the shack: *wh-wh-wh-wh, wh-wh-wh-wh.*

Listening to this symphony of winter, little Jimmy Burlane, warm and comfy in his womb of blankets, wondered: Did the coyotes on the river yip and yap because they hated the north wind and were cold, or because they were hungry, or because they were somehow born to howl in the night? Or did they like the wind? Was that possible?

As was his habit, Burlane woke with the rising of the sun.

Beside him, Katherine said, "El Sid arises to face the Moors."

Burlane rubbed his eyes. "What time is it?"

"Six-thirty."

"I suppose you're already milked the cows and changed the irrigation-water."

"I've only been awake a couple of minutes. I want some coffee. Did you think about a past bed last night?"

"Yes, I did."

"What did you remember?"

Burlane said, "I remembered coyotes howling in a cold north wind in the dead of winter."

They pulled into La Palma on Eighth Street and ordered Cuban *café con leche* with Cuban toast.

Miami television stations had locked onto the drama of the killer Doberman at large in Cocoplum. It was the story of the day, and reporters and cameramen from the national media had descended, having flown from New York in the early morning hours.

Cocoplum residents, with the aid of automatic door openers, were able to come and go from their houses, but the police, swarming the area with shotguns and tracking hounds, were unable to find the killer dog.

Then one of the reporters was interviewing Mima Martinez, elegantly dressed, looking serene and in control. A handsome Doberman lay against her left foot, either asleep or being extra cool.

Burlane and Katherine both stopped talking and listened . . .

. . . as Mima Martinez explained how her family had gone to their cabin in Key West for the weekend and taken their dog Mari with them.

Mima said, "Mari just loves the Keys. Don't you, Mari? We were asleep when we got the call from Miami asking where was Mari? Well, you were right there with us, weren't you, honey?" She nuzzled Mari's neck, but the dog, indifferent, paid no attention. Mima said, "One bad Doberman can give all Dobermans a bad reputation. It isn't fair, is it, Mari? No, no, no. Poor baby." The dog ignored her.

Burlane said, "You know, I don't think that's the dog we saw last night."

"This one's far smaller, and a female, I'll bet. Different dog."

The anchor hustled his viewers from the unctuous Mima to an interview with the beleaguered Chief George Dersham.

Chief Dersham did not like having to justify his leadership or prove his competence, which had always been forcefully touted and casually accepted in Miami as a matter of civic pride. No city wanted to believe it had an average chief of police.

In this nightmare of nightmares, a mad dog loose in Cocoplum, Dersham was called upon—with a repetition that in his opinion bordered on the obsessive—to answer the Big Question. All televised Moments of Crisis featured at least one ordinarily unanswerable Big Question. The Cocoplum Big Question, asked flat-out as well as in numerous concealed and malevolently treacherous, oblique forms, all of which were as land mines to Dersham's tenure as chief, was this:

Why in hell—with all the resources at its disposal up to and including the National Guard—were the Dade Metro Police unable to capture a dog that had killed and partly eaten five people? The police were responsible for community safety, weren't they? This dog was eating people. Consuming the genitals of its male victims. What the hell was going on?

Since George Dersham was the man in charge, wasn't he responsible? He was the chief. Wasn't it his fault? Fault meant someone was guilty of something and had to pay.

As determined and cool and professional as Clint Eastwood with an assault rifle, the reporters aimed their microphones and cameras at Dersham, full-automatic fault weapons, and fired terrible bursts of career-wounding fault bullets: *Fault-fault-fault-fault; fault-fault-fault-fault!* On top of that he had to sidestep incoming rounds of guilt mortars. Allegations of guilt exploded all around him: *Guilt! Guilt! Guilt!*

The loose dog was a gaping hole added to the festering wounds of crooked cops and unhappy defenders of Jah Ben Jah. The more Dersham found himself on the defensive, dodging fault bullets and guilt rounds with all the skill he could muster, the more he was hit—openly bleeding unacknowledged defeat—and the more the reporters bore down on him.

And if some grinning chickenshit chose to, just for the hell of it, he or she could lob in the fact of Dersham's big-titted mistress, a hand grenade of moral turpitude. A chief of police was entitled to some perks. The public understood that. But a big-titted redhead was not among them. If they could, just for the jolly hell of it, the envious reporters, wee tiny little people with shiny teeth and bullshit smiles, would lay the outrageousness of her boobs on him smack across the face, one tit at a time, *ka-whop! ka-whop!* And that'd be it.

The station cut from Chief Dersham to a commercial break.

"Poor Dersham," Katherine said. "Sid, don't you think Fowler was an amazing cop to have found the Martinezes so quickly in Key West, if that's where they were supposed to be? He shows up in the middle of the action to bail them out, then disappears as quickly as he can."

Burlane said, "You know Fowler a little. Suppose he wanted to go hide out and watch the show in private. But he doesn't want to go far because he's got the Martinezes to worry about. Where does he go?"

"He goes to his little hideaway at the south end of Biscayne Bay."

"Oh?"

"There are dozens of tiny islands down there, some hardly more than an acre in size. They're everywhere. Fowler has a place on one of those islands. He took me there on our second date."

The waitress arrived with their breakfast. Burlane looked forward to some Cuban coffee and toast made from long, crusty loaves of Cuban bread. He said, "If we rented a boat, do you suppose you could find that place again?"

47

Years earlier, Company instructors at Camp Peary, teaching James Burlane and other apprentice spooks the art of surviving in the secret world, had stressed the critical importance of Mr. Murphy's famous doctrine. Whatever could go wrong almost certainly would.

When you were in the field, Murphy was your only comfort. The instructors drilled their students on the crucial, often lifesaving importance of having duplicates, backups, fallbacks, and just-in-cases for every delay, fuck-up, oopsie, and oh shit! imaginable and then some. Be prepared. Be prepared. Be prepared. They were Boy Scouts run amok.

Burlane was taught that this attitude was at the heart of what it meant to be a professional. A boxer who didn't want to get knocked out kept his hands up. A baseball player who wanted to get a hit kept his eye on the ball. A spy who would survive was paranoid; he at all times, and in every circumstances, protected himself and whatever secrets or other goodies were the object of the mission.

In deference to Murphy's wisdom, Burlane brought waterproof plastic containers for his audio and video gear and tapes. He stashed these in a weighted bag of brown plastic netting; this bag fit into a slightly larger bag of the same plastic netting, only bright yellow. If Burlane had time to stash them in a given location—at the end of pier X or under buoy Y—he would use the brown bag alone. However, if he had to dump the tapes in the broad expanse of Biscayne Bay, the yellow would make them easier to retrieve.

Also, in case Burlane and Katherine wanted to go ashore for a closer look—or flee the fishing boat anytime they chose— he took his flippers and scuba gear.

James Burlane stuffed his pants pockets with Sheridan Harnar's expense-account benjies—a big-time marimbeiro, rich and so deserving of respect—and drove first to Crook & Crook on 27th Avenue and U.S. One where he bought Katherine a pair of flippers and scuba gear of her own, plus a saltwater rod and reel. He bought her a good Penn reel and a carbon-graphite composition rod; it was Harnar's money, and Burlane didn't have time to search for bargains. Finally, he bought himself a Coast Guard chart of Biscayne Bay.

He then proceeded to The Captain's Tavern, a superb fish market on 96th Street, where he bought a whole grouper, two yellowtails, and several snappers, which he knew could be caught at night. These he iced down in a portable ice chest.

Finally, his bets covered, he drove to the Biscayne Bay Yacht Club on South Bayshore Drive.

He wanted a fast, flat-bottomed boat so Fowler couldn't chase him over shallow water. He rented an 18-foot fishing boat with a 115-horsepower Suzuki outboard and a Johnson electric trolling motor for slow, quiet running. He would have preferred a black boat, but Florida fishermen were given to light, heat-reflecting colors, white mostly, and Burlane settled for a pale blue.

Despite the authority of his impressive roll of cash, it took nearly two hours of palavering, filling out insurance forms, surrendering benjies for onerous deposits, and being shown how everything worked before Burlane and Katherine were able to load the boat with their gear.

Burlane cast off at five-thirty P.M., piloting the boat south down Biscayne Bay. Coral Gables was on his starboard; the skyline of downtown Miami and the white concrete of Rickenbacker Causeway were to his stern.

On his port: Key Biscayne, where Richard Nixon, in his

pre-Watergate salad days, used to hole up with his wheeler-dealer pal Bebe Rebozo. The island, although well developed, was lush with tropical undergrowth, and Burlane could see only glimpses of white exteriors and red-tiled roofs.

After a half hour, they were among scores of small mangrove islands separated—in some cases—by twisting, narrow channels. All of the islands were overgrown by brush, but wealthy Miamians had cleared a few of the larger ones for partying retreats.

Burlane, from his fishing outings with Luis Fernandez and Roberto Guzmán, was familiar with the larger routes among the islands. But Fernandez had known what he was doing. The idea of threading the confusion of islands closer to shore with darkness settling was daunting.

They entered a maze of brushy outcroppings. Katherine scanned the shore with binoculars, looking for Fowler's hideaway, and Burlane traced their progress on the chart of Biscayne Bay.

He slowed the boat to an idle, then killed the engine, and they floated momentarily as he switched to the electric trolling motor for silent running. They continued, sliding nearly soundlessly through the dying light. The sky turned orange, then red, then purple.

Then darkness was upon them, and the islands were glimmering, eerie ghosts on both sides.

"Give it up?" Burlane said.

"No, no, we're just started. It's out here somewhere. If we just go slow and chart our way."

Burlane, his eyes adjusting to the darkness, peered through the gloom, which was at once eerie and beautiful. The engine whirred softly. Finally . . .

"Yes!"

"Got it?"

"Ahead and to our left. See it?"

Burlane saw it. He cut the engine. They floated. She studied the shore with the night binoculars. Burlane could see a lighted one-story house, but no detail. The water lapped gently against the side of the hull. The islands trilled with orchestras of crickets.

She said, "Fowler and another man are there. And the Martinez woman. The mother. We can tape and mike everything from here as long as nobody rousts us."

"At least we don't have to deal with barking dogs."

"It's all glass and patio on the water side. He's got alarms around that place you wouldn't believe."

Burlane said, "You think we'd better do it from here?"

"Far better, even though they can see us if we can see them."

"There's plenty of light for the camera and no sweat at all for the parabolic. I'll keep it close to the brush where the shadows are best." Burlane punched the anchor winch. The mushroom-shaped metal slipped *ker-sploop* into the water.

Fowler, Mima Martinez, and the third man moved to the patio for drinks and settled in around a white, glass-topped metal table. They'd brought out to one side, a television set tuned into the evening news on WPLG.

Burlane and Katherine assembled their gear on the boat's flat bottom. Burlane hooked the parabolic microphone to the sound recorder. He screwed the mike onto a tripod made of fold-out aluminum tubes. Finally, he mounted his infrared video camera on a second aluminum tripod.

He took a quick peak through the binoculars at the bungalow. "Mmmmmmmmmmm."

"Do you know him?"

"Know who? Fowler?"

Katherine gave him a look. Of course she meant the third man, a gentleman with a black mustache and salt-and-pepper hair.

Burlane scratched his head, thinking.

"They're watching the evening news."

He said, "How about you? Do you know him?"

"Yes. I know him," she said.

"By what name?"

"Adrian Kyle. Moved laterally from the Detroit Police. He was the guy who came down to give me the hook when I started checking out Fowler. And you know him by what name.

"Another name."

"Chickenshit. I showed mine. Your turn."

"You have to remember that chickenshit makes the grass grow green. You want to work the mike?"

Katherine, annoyed, aimed the parabolic on the three figures.

Burlane focused the video camera on the figures. With the

patio lights and the camera's infrared lens, he could see them well enough. The tape would be dim, true, but Burlane wasn't going for an Academy Award; his subjects' features would be clear enough to recognize, and that was all that mattered.

Watching the patio, Katherine said, "Not a hair out of place there. Mr. I'm-in-Charge." She adjusted the parabolic.

Burlane said, "An anal retentive."

"Walter Matthau's an anal retentive compared to you, Sid."

Burlane said, "A spiffy dominant, and he just loves it. You can tell by his body language. 'My name is Marimbeiro, king of kings/ Look on my Confar suit, ye Mighty, and despair!'"

Katherine Donovan turned up the volume of the receiver so they could both listen to whatever it was that drew together, in solemn, covert rendezvous, Captain Donald Fowler, Mima Martinez, and the man who had forced her and Roberto Guzmán to sit in the withering heat through an entire game of water polo played by dolphins.

48

As Captain Donald Fowler switched from WPLG to WSVN Channel 7 to see if he could pick up the dog story there, Adrian Kyle held his drink up to the light, admiring it. Fowler had a wonderful little hideaway. He had gone art deco all the way. Even his cocktail glasses were art deco, clear with vertical, pastel-green stripes.

Kyle said, "Dog-food murders and a killer dog on the loose are big news under any circumstances, and the world is getting smaller. You have to understand, Don, living in Colombia is not like being on the the moon. Banda-Conchesa watches CNN in Medellín. When people are in a fit up here in Los Estados Unidos, he knows about it. Enough that he's fallen in love with Lynn Russell's lips."

"He's what?"

"He loves that voice of hers. A mellow rumbling, he says. He especially likes to watch her mouth move when she reports the news. It's her lips. Her lips are the thing. She's got these big, full lips. Different parts of her lips go this way and that. He says the sound produced by the English language don't do justice to her lips."

Mima blinked. "Really?"

"Yes. Down there in Colombia, infatuated with a television reporter in Atlanta. It's like she's got a soccer team in one set of lips, he says. He says she knows she's got sensational lips too, the way she swabs on the color. She could really have her way with him if she only knew. Name her price."

Mima briefly touched her own lips with the tips of her fingers. "I don't watch the news. I don't understand. Lynn who?"

"Lynn Russell in Atlanta. Watch her on CNN sometime. You'll see what I mean."

Fowler said, "We'll switch to CNN when the local news is finished."

Kyle took a drink, raising his glass with a gesture that said he was finished with chitchat and Lynn Russell's lips. "Señor Banda-Conchesa wants reassurance that you can give the public a solution to the dogfood killings once Dersham goes under. We can't have you tarred with it at the beginning of your tenure as chief."

Fowler said nothing.

"Under the circumstances, I'm sure you can understand his anxiety. He wants you to act decisively and successfully."

"Show my stuff as Dersham's potential replacement."

"You have to give the public a satisfactory tit to calm things down. If you don't, Mayor Hernandez will look elsewhere for his chief. He'll have to, in order to protect his own hide."

Fowler seemed calm enough. "I've been thinking about all that, of course. The solution to the dog is simple, if you think about it."

"Simple?" Kyle narrowed one eye and cocked his head. "How?"

"Roberto Guzmán was an FBI agent. Although it wasn't his case, he had a hunch about the dogfood killer. He captured the murderer's dog. We know this because he checked in to say he was taking the dog to police kennels. It escaped and turned on him."

Kyle stroked his mustache, thinking. He liked it. "I see. Then bounded off to chow down on rich folks in Cocoplum."

"Hungry as hell. But we don't know the identity of the pervert who was killing people to feed him, because Guzmán never had a chance to file his report."

Kyle said, "And when they finally shoot the dog, the teeth

will match the marks on Guzmán's skull, physical evidence to match your story."

Fowler said, "Match them perfectly."

Mima said, "They'll never catch Marimba." The local news was over. She switched the set to CNN, the sound still off.

"Sure they will."

She shrugged. "Suit yourself." A woman was reporting the news. Mima looked puzzled. "Those lips don't look like any big deal to me."

Fowler said, "Mima, for Christ's sake pay attention. We've got a serious problem to deal with. Besides, that's not Lynn Russell."

Mima said, "Oh." She was disappointed. She wanted to see the woman with the lips.

Kyle said, "Also, you have to keep your distance from the Martinezes, and the Martinezes need to straighten up their act." He gave Mima a quick look to make sure she understood the point. "Too much is at stake here, Don. Conchesa will pick up the tab for the initial fix, but eventually the money for this will have to come out of your hides. Yours and Mima's here. You're the ones who fucked up."

Mima was not contrite. She did not take *mierda* from anyone, no matter if he was speaking for Guillermo Banda-Conchesa. She stamped her foot angrily and bunched her face at Kyle. "Look at all the marimba players we delivered. Look at the arrests and headlines. Not one of them was a Conchesa player. Only your competition."

She narrowed her eyes and waggled her finger in Fowler's face. "With our help, you personally demonstrated that the war on drugs is working. We made you a national hero. Profiled on '60 minutes.' If it hadn't been for us."

Fowler was sick of having '60 Minutes' thrown up in his face, and it showed. Big fucking deal. It was as though being on that one jackass program had somehow made him immortal. It didn't make a damn whatever else he did. '60 Minutes.' '60 Minutes.' '60 Minutes." That's all he ever heard. Would there ever be an end to it? Shit!

But Mima, oblivious to Fowler's body language, continued without dismay: "*Cabrón!* You should be glad Marimba got loose. If this doesn't push the old *pendejo* George Dersham over the edge, nothing else will. He's ready to go, and we all know it. Have you seen him on television? Have you? And you're Mr.

Supercop, his most likely successor. What more do you want, for God's sake?"

Kyle, letting her have her run, took a sip of his drink.

She said, "Tell Señor Banda-Conchesa the Martinez family can still deliver."

"Señor Conchesa will have to think about it."

"Think about it? *No jodas!*"

Kyle held his hand up in surrender. "Okay, okay."

Fowler said, "Mima's right in a sick sort of way, you have to give her that. If the dog doesn't push Dersham over, nothing will."

Kyle said, "When Sid Khartoum pops his head up again, I want him properly snuffed, Captain Fowler. Please, no botch-ups this time. And no corpse. The same with Agent Katherine Donovan, who has been hanging out with him."

"Agent who?"

Kyle removed a photograph from the inside pocket of his power suit and gave it to Fowler. "This woman."

Fowler looked at the photograph. His mouth dropped. He paled. "I . . ."

"Yes. From the Organized Crime Unit. She was going right after you. Picked you up in that sweat factory and allowed you to whisk her off to the Bahamas."

"I didn't know. I had no idea. You have to believe me. I . . ."

"She's Roberto Guzmán's colleague. If it hadn't been for me flying down here to intervene, no telling what she might have found out."

"She's with the FBI?"

"I pulled her off, so don't worry. But who knows what she found out?" Raising one eyebrow, he looked at Mima. "And the family. Who knows what she may have found out about the family?"

Mima looked startled.

"Special Agent Donovan has to be snuffed. We have no choice. You understand that?"

Fowler nodded, yes. He understood.

Mima glared at Fowler. The advantage was momentarily in her favor, and she was not about to overlook it. "FBI agent? You men. *Templar y joder*: That's all you ever think about. *Coño.* After a while anybody with any brains would learn something. But not you. Mr. Hot Damn Cop. You think through your *pinga* like every male. Only you choose FBI agent! *Carajo!* You complain about Marimba? Look at you!" Her face was hard, and she was nearly shouting.

Kyle said, "Now, now, Mima. Just keep calm."

Mima looked indignant. "Keep calm? You expect me to keep calm? Well, I'm not going to. Besides, nobody can hear us out here." She checked her hair with the palm of her hand, pouting. "You lecture me about Marimba and how I'm supposed to be risking everything. And all the time you've been sleeping with an FBI agent. Flying her to the Bahamas. *Come mierda!* And you want me to stay calm?"

"Slept. Past tense." Fowler said. "She learned nothing of value."

Kyle said, "Just get rid of her, Captain Fowler. And Khartoum."

Another woman had assumed CNN's anchor chair in Atlanta. Mima, pursing her mouth, perked up. "Tell me, is this the one? Is this the one with the lips?"

On the fishing boat, James Burlane was jubilant. "Guillermo Pena de la Banda-Conchesa is in love with Lynn Russell's lips. He's down there in Medellín watching her every day. Pining his macho heart away. Isn't that wonderful? Life truly is filled with the splendid and the wonderful, Katherine. It's truly to enjoy."

"You didn't answer me before, Sid. Who is that guy?"

"Listen to the bugs. It's party time for night bugs. I had this friend in Hong Kong who once got into a fight on a tennis court at night with bugs zooming everywhere and—"

"I don't care whether you've personally laid eyes on him or not, you know, dammit. Out with it."

"Mmmmmmm."

"What does mmmmmmm mean?"

"It means yes, I know who he is."

Katherine waited. "Come on."

Burlane smirked. "How do I know I can trust you?"

Katherine rolled her eyes in disgust. "Oh, bullshit. Out with it. Who the hell is he?"

On the patio, Donald Fowler said, "I don't want anyone to turn or look, but there's a fishing boat sitting at the edge of the island across the way."

The man with the good-looking salt-and-pepper hair licked his lips. "What? A fishing boat?"

"One of those flat-bottomed numbers. I just now saw it. Don't turn around. Don't look. Don't."

"I don't suppose there's any chance they're just fishing."

Fowler said, "Did either of you see when it anchored there?"

"What? A boat? Mima Martinez turned to stare into the darkness. *"Carajo!"*

"Aw shit, Mima!" Captain Donald Fowler grabbed his cellular telephone and began punching numbers.

49

Had to happen, I suppose." Burlane abandoned the video camera. He yanked open the lid to the forward hatch where the white nylon anchor rope lay coiled. Turning quickly, he began hauling in the anchor, hand over hand. "We got everything we need anyway, and probably then some."

Katherine set about getting the binoculars, parabolic mike, and video gear stored in their plastic containers. "A legal smoking gun, do you think?"

"If this doesn't count as a smoking gun, I don't know what the hell will. We'll have to pitch the gear." He pulled the dripping anchor from the water and flopped it into the hatch.

He hurried to the helm and tapped the starter button. The 115-horsepower Suzuki *ker-bur-bur-burbled* to life.

As Katherine folded a tripod, Burlane pushed the accelerator lever forward—*burr-ooohhhmmmbbb!* And they were off in the direction they had come.

Burlane said, "When we get out of these islands and into open water, Fowler can have a police boat pull us in if he wants, right?"

"Yes, he can."

Burlane turned hard port down a brushy channel and took

the first available opening starboard. He doused the engine. "Before we do that, tell me what you think. It's your hide too."

"Fowler can flush us out of here with a police helicopter, but I'm not sure they can come into water this shallow without calling in special boats."

"How long would that take, do you think?"

"Forty or fifty minutes, maybe. I don't have any idea." Katherine snapped shut the latch that sealed the video camera's plastic case. The gear was ready for the water.

Burlane let the boat float. They listened to the water lapping against the hull.

Burlane said, "Should we use the trolling motor for a while and see what happens?"

"Let's try it."

"Dump our gear here, then? Jettison the tapes later, if we have to."

"As good a plan as any."

"Impeccable logic. Smart woman."

"What if I'd said run for it?"

He grinned. "I'd have overruled you. My boat. My rules." He studied the chart. "Okay, let's do it. We'll hold onto the tapes a little longer. No sense risking losing them if we don't have to."

He pitched the video camera. Katherine followed with the parabolic, and in seconds *plop, plummp, ker-spplassh,* his gear was in the water.

"You want to chart our progress while I watch for branches' and debris?"

"Sure," she said.

Burlane gave her the chart and ballpoint pen. He started the electric trolling motor. "We've got two hours on each battery if we need them. He slowed at an opening to port. "Turn here?"

"Looks as good as any to me." She marked the turn on the chart.

"We'll see if we can't sneak out of here like Apaches in a John Wayne movie."

Using the half-moon for light—and with the trolling motor humming smoothly—Burlane piloted the boat gently and all but silently through the trilling of crickets and gloom of darkness, shrouds of mangrove islands on both sides. Katherine marked their progress on the chart.

In a half hour, they heard the faint, distant *wh-wh-whooping* of helicopter blades.

Burlane pushed the boat tightly against an overhang of brush and killed the motor.

The helicopter had two searchlights mounted on its skids.

Burlane said, "Looks like they've done this before."

"I'd bet on it. In fact, I'll bet they're able to pick up our engine heat. No expense spared in the war on drugs."

"We'll see what happens. I've got the Suzuki. We can still run for it if we have to. We need to think about ditching the tapes."

Katherine studied the chart.

The chopping of helicopter blades grew louder.

She showed him the chart. "We're here."

The helicopter turned. It *was* getting louder, and it *was* coming their way.

Burlane said, "We know where we are. We can come back."

Katherine retrieved the weighted brown plastic bag from the yellow and stowed the yellow in the tackle-and-gear box in front of the helm.

Burlane started the Suzuki. "They might already have a fix on us. We'll give 'em a few yards for insurance." He gunned the engine and built as much speed as possible in the dim light and with overhanging branches on each side. He passed another channel. "How about here? One more island to the west."

"We can find it." Katherine pitched the weighted bag of audio- and videotapes into the water.

Burlane headed starboard at the entrance to another channel, then port, then starboard again, as the helicopter closed on them.

He killed the engine.

The helicopter was suddenly above them, and two blinding spotlights pinned them in an incredible blaze of blue-white light.

A firm male voice from a loudspeaker called down: "This is the Metro Dade Police Department. Follow us to open water, please. Stay in the center of the boat. Keep your hands out of your pockets and visible at all times. Keep all items aboard. Do not throw anything overboard. We will be watching from above. Proceed."

Burlane, squinting from the light, did as he was told.

Katherine, shading her eyes with her hand, said, "What do you think, Sid? These guys legit? Cops as opposed to outright pirates?"

"They're probably legit cops who've been told we may be drug smugglers. But it's conceivable we are just fishermen who anchored off Fowler's place. First, Fowler wants to know who we are. Then he can decide what to do about us."

"You think he'll have us checked out on the open water?"

"That's what I'd do. He'd be foolish to have the police board us anywhere near his hideaway. He knows the rules of fuck-up. If he hadn't paid attention to Mr. Murphy, he wouldn't have risen to captain."

Burlane allowed the helicopter to guide him out of the confusion of mangrove islands into the open water of lower Biscayne Bay, where, as he and Katherine suspected, a Dade Metro patrol boat waited.

As they closed to twenty yards, the helicopter with the blinding light still hovering above them, a man on the boat gave them their instructions over a loudspeaker. "This is the Dade Metro Police. Cut your engines, please, and drop your anchor. We will be coming aboard for a routine inspection. When you finish with the anchor, return to the center of the boat and keep your hands visible at all times."

Burlane, still squinting from the light, cut the engine. "See there, Katherine, routine inspection. Nothing at all to worry about."

"Entirely routine," she said.

"The man said so."

"Sure, sure."

Burlane dug the anchor out of the box on the bow, and tossed it overboard.

Seconds later the 25-foot-long patrol boat came alongside the fishing boat, its engine burbling at a loping idle. The pilot cut the engine, and the boat floated alongside.

The boat contained six uniformed officers: One manned the helm; two, with shotguns at the ready, kept an eye on Burlane and Katherine; the obvious head dude and two assistants stood poised to board—one officer with a flashlight and clipboard, the second with a flashlight and shotgun.

The helicopter rose to give them some relief from the

clatter and wash of its blades, but still kept the fishing boat well lit.

The head dude said, "My name is Officer Wallach. That thicket of islands back there is a favorite rendezvous for drug runners. When a boat's reported in there at night, we have to check it out. This is routine only. What were you doing in there?"

"We did a little diving earlier on and on the way back into the bay we turned into the islands to do a little fishing. Looked like there should be fish hanging around all that brush."

"Not many people fish in there at night. Any luck?"

"A few snappers, a couple of yellowtails, and a grouper." Burlane opened the ice box in front of the helm so Wallach could see.

Wallach leaned over and glanced at the fish. "Ahh, nice ones. Good for you. I'd like to see your identification and licenses. Take them out of your wallet, please. I'll need yours too, ma'am."

Burlane and Katherine did as they were told.

Wallach smiled. He studied their driver's and fishing licenses. "We'll have these back to you in just a minute." He gave the licenses to the aide with the clip-board, who took them back to the patrol boat. "We'd like to take a look around now, Mr. Khartoum, if you don't mind."

Burlane smiled. "Sure, help yourself. Anything we can do to help catch drug smugglers."

Wallach motioned to his two assistants, and they began giving the fishing boat a cursory going-over, thumping here and there for hollow spots.

Wallach said, "We're sorry for the inconvenience, but we have to check out all boats that meet our search criteria. You understand."

"Hey, like I say, no problem," Burlane said. "It was exciting, what with the helicopter and the lights and every-thing. Shotguns at the ready. 'Miami Vice.'"

Wallach wasn't sure whether the genial Burlane was hav-ing fun with him or not. "I can't imagine you'd catch much in those islands at night anyway, Mr. Khartoum. If I were you and wanted to fish at night, I'd tow my boat down to the Keys and anchor in a channel between the piers of the causeway. You have to do it when the tide's right, but there you'll catch some fish. Guaranteed."

"Thanks for the tip."

"Check with the people at Whale Harbour at Islamorada. They'll tell you about the tides. The tide has to be right."

The deputy checking the boat was finished. "Nothing, that I can find," he said.

The deputy with the clipboard was finished with the check of their licenses. "They're clear."

"We'll be going now," Wallach said. "We apologize for the inconvenience."

"It's been fun," Burlane said.

"Ms. Donovan." Officer Wallach gave Katherine a tip of his hand and followed his assistants, back onto the patrol boat. The pilot started the engine, and they were off with a burble and a roar. As they disappeared, the helicopter followed suit, darting up and away without ado.

Burlane and Katherine watched the running lights of both boat and helicopter grow smaller and smaller.

James Burlane started the engine on the fishing boat and, pushing as hard as he could for speed, headed for shore.

"Look there, Sid."

Another chopper was on its way towards them at high speed.

"Better get our gear strapped on."

Katherine grabbed scuba tanks and masks. "He got right on it, didn't he?"

"He sure as hell did." Burlane turned so Katherine could slip an oxygen tank over his shoulders. He helped her with her tank, then quickly slipped on a pair of flippers.

He pulled out the throttle of the engine as far as it would go and locked it in place with a twist of his wrist.

Katherine, sitting on the starboard side, met Burlane's eyes briefly, then pushed off backwards into the water.

Burlane did the same on the port.

They surfaced and watched the helicopter pursue the empty boat.

A thin flame shot from the belly of the helicopter toward Biscayne Bay.

The boat exploded.

In the water, Burlane and Katherine, treading water side by side, watched the boat sink quickly.

The chopper circled, looking for evidence of survivors.

Burlane and Katherine turned butts up and headed for the bottom. They swam northwest, working their fins leisurely in the nighttime darkness of Biscayne Bay.

50

The news was on television and on the front page of the *Miami Herald* as Burlane took a stroll for his final meeting with Schott: Mayor Paul Hernandez, under simultaneous pressure from discontented blacks, crooked cops in the Metro Dade Police Department, and a man-eating dog still on the loose, had accepted the resignation of Chief George Dersham, and named Captain Donald Fowler as interim chief.

Hernandez said a thorough national search would be held for Dersham's replacement, but in the mayor's opinion it would be nearly impossible to find someone better than Fowler, a man with a national reputation for his integrity and success in the war on drugs.

Chief Donald Fowler! Guillermo Pena de la Banda-Conchesa's man, in charge of the Dade Metro Police Department.

Boy oh boy, did James Burlane ever have a sockful of goodies for Sheridan Harnar. It would be like Christmas for him. Burlane would just reach down there and pull 'em out, one wonderful surprise after another.

And Burlane, who had truly wanted to please Senator

Graciela Boulanger, knew the chairperson would appreciate his success too—after she recovered from the shock.

Burlane and Schott had agreed to meet at the News Café, the sight of their first meeting in Miami Beach. Their contract nearing an end, Schott could now return to his stone cottage in Montgomery County, Maryland, and his history books.

Burlane stopped for a bottle of Coors in the bar of the Edison Hotel, across the street from the Ocean Front Auditorium at 10th Street. A modest undertaking, the auditorium was flanked on the right by a twelve-foot-tall tower giving passersby the date and time, courtesy of the city of Miami Beach. The tower did not give the relative humidity, which wasn't featured in any tour brochure, either; it was the humidity, not the temperature, that made tropical weather so trying.

On the far side of this beachside park, trails led up a small rise where ground cover held back the blowing sand.

He walked across the park at the edge of the sand. As he turned his back against the wind, he saw that he was standing a few feet from a blonde slumped up against a palm tree. She was in her early to mid-20s and wore an imitation leopard-skin outfit designed for aerobic exercise. It was pulled tight against, her crotch, revealing her hips and buns, and even from a distance Burlane could see that most of her breasts was casually exposed.

A casualty of crack cocaine. For sale to passersby. Burlane knew it wasn't hip for her to be hanging out under the palm trees. Legal statutes of the city of Miami Beach required more discreet carnal transactions.

Wait a second. Burlane was momentarily stunned by the shock of unexpected recognition.

Was that Helen Donovan?

Above her, a young Hispanic talked, gesturing with his hands.

Burlane set off down the trail, past the girl and the Hispanic.

Yes, it was Helen. Her sister had already returned to Washington. What could Burlane do? Kidnap her?

Helen's blue eyes looked glazed. Her displayed tits looked more pathetic than sensual or desirable.

As Burlane passed them, the Hispanic told Helen he had to go.

Helen said, "Say, you couldn't spare fifty cents, could you?"

"Naw, I'm broke," the Hispanic said. He didn't want any part of a filthy derelict. He'd seen crackheads before, and this one was in her final stages. He cruised past Burlane, walking at a brisk pace.

Burlane stopped and looked back. The money he had in his wallet was supposed to be for expenses. It was Harnar's money, not his. He called, "Hey, where you from?"

Helen focused on him, her eyes red. "Around here. Over there." She sensed he was business. She did her best to look interested. "Wherever. You want to party, mister? I'm a party animal. I'm real, real good at partying."

"You live where? In one of those apartments? In a house? What?"

"In a house." She pronounced it more like *hoose* than *howse*.

"Baltimore."

She looked surprised. "Hey! Pretty good."

"I've known it since East Baltimore Street was really East Baltimore Street."

"I bet you did."

"Saw Blaze Starr at the Gaity. But I suppose that was before your time. If I give you, say, a thousand bucks, would you give me your word to buy yourself an airplane ticket and go back to Baltimore? Don't talk to anyone. Just go."

Helen hesitated.

Burlane pulled out his wallet and peeled off ten benjies. "And see if you can't get that shit out of your system."

"Sure," she said. She took the money, staring at it in disbelief.

"It's not my money."

"I bet it's not."

Burlane turned and strode off, quickening his pace. He knew Helen was watching him.

Such casualties turned his mouth dry. The image of her eyes lingered. What was a lousy thousand bucks to Harnar? He probably expected Burlane to pad his expenses anyway. It was a long shot, Burlane knew. He figured the odds Helen would use Harnar's money to go to Baltimore were about one in ten thousand.

51

The apartment building in South Miami Beach, condemned by the city because of drug use, was locked and empty except for Helen Donovan, who had pried some two-by-sixes from a window with a hammer she had lifted from a hardware store.

Her only furniture was a lumpy Serta mattress, covered by yellow and brown, paisley-shaped semen and piss stains. She had found the mattress flopped over a garbage bin in the alley between the apartment buildings and had managed, with a struggle, to stuff it through the window. The mattress smelled of mildew on top of everything else, but Helen didn't care. She wanted privacy, and she had found it.

She had wanted to watch her Panasonic TV, prize of prizes, so she swiped and electrical extension cord and strung it through a broken window in the crack house next door. The cord was orange, and she assumed it wouldn't be long before somebody spotted it and pulled the plug.

The shoplifting had taken all afternoon, but she had covered a 20-block shuttle up Collins and back on Washington. Along the way she had lifted a bottle of Stolichnaya vodka plus nine Bartles and Jaymes wine coolers—three black cherries, two berries, two tropicals, one peach, and one original—plus some Eastern Family plastic cups so she could mix the vodka and the Bartles and Jaymes. For food, she swiped a bag each of Fritos, Nalley's barbecued potato chips, and peanuts with salty shells she liked to suck on, plus a jar of green olives stuffed with pimentos.

When she had assembled her food and drink, she had it all. Peace. Privacy. No cocks or outsized dildos or vibrators pumping in and out of her orifices. A good TV with a remote. It was party time. Time for old movies, succor for the lonely.

Her pussy was so sore she could hardly believe it. Her ass was bruised after having been spanked nearly raw three nights previously. Her pussy and her asshole were essentials to her survival. Like a brickmason's trowel and level, they were the tools with which she earned her living.

No holes, no money. No money, no crack.

When the purplish, dime-sized lesion appeared on the inside of her ankle, she knew what it was without being told. Kaposi's sarcoma.

She knew what it meant.

She unscrewed the cap of peach cooler and dumped some in a cup together with a dollop of vodka and took a sip. Ahhhhhh! She punched up *Macao* with Robert Mitchum and Jane Russell.

Mitchum and Russell, both drifters with a past, have washed up on the Portuguese colony, Mitchum to gamble and look mysterious, Russell to wear sexy dresses and sing torch songs. Mitchum has befriended William Bendix, a klutzy, apparently well-meaning nerd who is really a New York police detective pursuing the villain, an arrogant asshole who runs a casino. The villain thinks Mitchum is the cop, not Bendix, and he wants to hustle him out of town.

Sexy Mitchum lays this fantasy on beautiful Jane about how they should drop their pointless drifting and settle down on a banana plantation outside Singapore, or somewhere goofy and impossible, and sip rum and coconut juice. But Jane, who has been burned by bedroom eyes and cockeyed stories before, isn't buying it for a minute. No, no, no.

Helen thought Jane was a dumb shit for not responding to Mitchum's offer. Helen never had anything like Mitchum's offer. She had been fist-fucked, yes, and beaten, and had her tits tortured, but never once had she received an offer of kids and cold rums on a banana plantation.

Amid all the manure, the scriptwriter had given Russell the observation to Mitchum that "We're all the same when you come right down to it. We're all lonely, worried, sorry, and looking for something."

Helen thought it was a good line, B-movieish but true. It applied to her, certainly, but she had long ago forgotten what it was she was looking for. Once, she had dreamed of meeting her own Robert Mitchum, but had abandoned that fantasy as so much existential poop.

She lit her pipe and took a hit of crack, and momentarily floated. Thus inspired, she took the empty Bartles and Jaymes bottle to the bathroom and cracked it against the edge of the sink.

She threw the bottom of the bottle into the disconnected bathtub and took the broken neck back to her mattress. She opened a black cherry and spiked it, and grabbed a handful of Fritos.

Was it just bad luck that a Mitchum had never come her way? Maybe Helen wasn't Jane Russell, but she hadn't been bad before cocaine had taken her under.

On the tube, William Bendix enlists Mitchum's help in a ploy to lure the villain beyond the three-mile limit that is his legal protection. Mitchum's a good bad guy. Mitchum goes to the docks for a dangerous rendezvous with the bad guy, but when William Bendix tries to help, he takes a knife in the back. In his dying moments, he tells Mitchum that he's fixed it with the authorities. Mitchum can go home to New York if he wants.

Finally, Mitchum and Jane are in a boat. They've tricked the bad guy. He thinks they're taking him to Hong Kong, but they're really delivering him to the police waiting just over the three-mile limit—a line arbitrarily drawn on the water by The Dads.

Helen had given The Dads considerable thought. At whatever level she had encountered them—from uptight professors to Miami cops—the self-righteous bureaucratic Dads, all of whom she suspected of being firstborns, behaved predictably. They spent their entire lives as defenders of the orthodox and the traditional; in order to please their phantom mommies and daddies, they were determined to impose rules and limits and responsibility and discipline on everybody else.

They loved rank and order and were most dangerous when they formed police and military units.

The drug-war Dads went around spanking people with jail time. Spank, spank, spank. They didn't have time for The Moms, fluff-brained pussies who kept asking if all those masculine, allegedly essential rules made sense except to keep the marimba bucks churning.

In their effort to keep everything spiffy and proper, The Dads went so far as to demand loose search rules and piss checks, the equivalent of keeping the bathroom doors unlocked. Helen didn't understand how people could be so docile as to put up with such an outrage. Surely, a lock on the toilet door was one of life's basics.

Once, not so very long ago, Helen had been an aspiring fashion model. That was why she had gone to Miami. She had the face; everybody said so. And she had the body. She had everything.

And yet . . .

Munching on a peanut, she drew a neat line of blood across her left wrist with a piece of glass. She figured there was no hurry. She had thought about what it would be like for weeks and had adjusted to the idea that it would be messy. She had overcome the unsettling stages of anxiety and fear, and had arrived in a zone of calm and resolve.

Watching the blood well up, she gave her sore pussy a slight squeeze with her right hand, and took another hit on her crack pipe.

She drew a line of blood across her right wrist.

She stuck her tongue out and tasted a dab of warm, salty blood from her left wrist.

Very quickly Helen had blood all over her arms and hands. On her blouse. On her jeans. On the floor. On the envelope with her sister's name on the front. What a mess! Yuch!

She unscrewed the cap on the bottle of tropical and mixed it with a slug of vodka. She took a drink and ate a couple of green olives. The blood was just impossible. All over everything. Warm and slippery. She did another hit on her crack pipe. She held the smoke in her and felt the lethal rush.

Commercial time. The announcer said the conclusion to *Macao* would follow the break. Shit!

Would she make it through the commercial? At the critical

moment, a commercial interrupts the Hollywood ending. Money. Money. Money. Figured.

Helen had never seen the movie before, but more than anything she could remember, she wanted Robert Mitchum and Jane Russell to have their stupid banana plantation. A small pleasure at the end of her last meal, but it was all she asked. She didn't want to die in the middle of a commercial for a collection of taped popular songs of the 1950s and 1960s for $19.95, four bucks for shipping and handling, viewers to call the 900 number with their credit card ready.

She wanted music, yes, but not "Let There Be Drums." Owing to the marimba, which had consumed her, a profitable human snack—so much the better for being good looking and fuckable—she wanted nothing to do with percussion of any kind.

No more marimba for Helen. She wanted violins. She wanted to fade away with B-movie violins soaring.

She felt light-headed. Her hands and forearms and lap and thighs were slick with blood.

She held her wrists faceup on her thighs, watching the blood, and concentrated for all she was worth on making it through the commercial. The goddamn thing was taking forever. Would it never end?

She wanted Mitchum and Jane to throw in together and take off for their plantation. She thought: please, please, give them a chance, let them make it.

52

In James Burlane's opinion, C-SPAN—the cable-sponsored public-affairs channel that followed the action on the floors of the House and Senate and into committee hearings—was the best television channel in the United States.

C-SPAN left it to the viewer to make up their own minds, so it was probably the least-watched channel on television. The fair and patient C-SPAN hosts and interviewers, defending the values of intelligence and civility, patiently pursued the political grays along with the standard packaged opinions. Unfortunately, this patience produced few uncivilized confrontations and rare shouting. Neither were the hosts necessarily beautiful or handsome. The females had tits that were typical of their species, but they did not feature them. There were no Lynn Russell lips. Only education and ideas.

All this added up to *borrr-rrring* television.

Burlane's charge as a staff investigator included the responsibility of giving the Committee on Drug Policy whatever conclusions and recommendations he was able to draw from his experiences.

Burlane met privately with Senator Graciela Boulanger and told her what he had learned in Miami. As far as Senator

Boulanger was concerned, the manner of reporting his findings to the committee was entirely up to him. She agreed that a carefully administered dose of C-SPAN coverage was in order; good work ought, at least sometimes, to be rewarded.

But Burlane said if he himself made an appearance on C-SPAN, he risked destroying his ability to work undercover, and he would effectively be put out of business. Under the circumstances, could Ara Schott, CEO of Mixed Enterprises, fulfill his duty of reporting to the committee? Schott would require the help of FBI Special Agent Katherine Donovan.

Boulanger said yes, certainly. She told Burlane that two undercover DEA agents working in Los Angeles, and a good-looking Miami woman, Ms. Carmela Martinez, would testify at the closed-door meeting beginning at nine A.M. Ms. Martinez was said to have managed the longest-running and most successful sting in the history of the war on drugs.

Boulanger said the Metro Dade Police Department's newly appointed chief, Donald Fowler, was the scheduled star of the televised open session of the Senate Select Committee on Drug Policy.

53

James Burlane watched the C-SPAN action on Ara Schott's TV in his stone cottage in Montgomery County, Maryland. He'd bought himself a six-pack of Beck's beer and some smoked herring. The herring was salty and fishy and not good for him, but screw it, life was to enjoy.

The open session began at ten-thirty. The committee listened to the opinions of a former FBI agent, a criminologist from the University of California, Berkeley, and an assistant to the head of the DEA, the so-called drug czar.

At noon, Senator Boulanger announced that Metro Dade's Chief Donald Fowler would offer his testimony immediately after lunch, and adjourned the hearing for an hour.

C-SPAN switched to action on the House floor, where congressmen were debating the wisdom of allowing California farmers to use subsidized water to raise subsidized crops.

Burlane punched the sound off and popped up to make himself some egg foo yung and a nice pot of oolong tea. The previous evening he had cooked dinner in his wok for Ara and Katherine, during which they had planned today's strategy, and he had leftover beef stock. The gravy for the egg foo yung, made with honest stock, was superb.

He punched the sound on again when C-SPAN returned to the committee room. Senator Graciela Boulanger, Democrat of Montana, sat in the middle with her fellow Democrats on her left and the Republican minority on her right.

To the rear of Senator Boulanger and slightly to her left sat the committee's chief legal counsel, Sheridan Harnar. Harnar advised the committee on the legality of its inquiries and proposals and coordinated the depositions and appearances of witnesses.

Administration officials, bureaucrats, and various witnesses sat in a row behind the small witness table. When called, witnesses rose and took their place at the table. When finished, they returned to their previous seats, available for further questions, until the session was completed.

Behind the witnesses, visitors to the public hearings were accommodated by a slightly raised gallery of 80 seats.

The chairperson was calm and patient as the senators, bellies full, suppressing burps, straggled in and took their seats on the raised dais.

Chief Donald Fowler waited his turn beside the bald-headed, genial Adrian Kyle, a former Detroit cop recently appointed to the FBI's Organized Crime Unit, who was to follow Fowler in testifying.

As the senators whispered to their aides and shuffled through their notes, Fowler made himself aware of the locations of the red-lit Cyclop's eyes of C-SPAN's cameras.

Fowler had discussed his Senate testimony with Hernandez to make sure there would be no unexpected policy oopsies. With Hernandez looking on, Don Bundy, Hernandez's new media assistant, a former administrative assistant to the minority whip in the U.S. Senate, had briefed him on what to expect and how to behave.

Bundy had said the session would open with professed good intentions all around. Fowler would be be praised to the extreme. He in turn should praise the committee for its fairness and hard work, and tell them how grateful he was to be invited to give testimony on a subject of such great, if not critical, importance to the nation.

Bundy advised him to remember that congressional investigations had everything to do with politics and only a little to do with the truth. None of the committee members would want to come off as soft on drugs, so Fowler should tell them what they, that is, their constituents, wanted to hear: the war on drugs was working; taxpayer dollars were not being wasted.

In the interest of verisimilitude Fowler should stress that the drug traffic was a complicated problem, as everybody knew. And having said that, Bundy advised, he should tell the Democratic members what they and their constituents wanted to hear: that more money was needed for education and treatment programs. Then he should give the Republicans a little of what they wanted to hear: a declaration that cops, piss checks, and stiff jail sentences were essential. With persistence and dedication and enforcement budgets that meant something, the pox of drugs could eventually be excised.

However, Bundy added, Fowler's main chore was to be humble and sincere. To show that he was paying attention, he should nod gravely as each senator in turn expressed his or her fury at the drug trade. Bundy said Fowler should do this with clenched-teeth seriousness. It didn't make any difference how stupid, arrogant, dishonest, or insufferable the senators were as individuals, or how curious or incomprehensible their opinions, it should be yes sir, yes ma'am, all the way.

Watching them now, Fowler felt most of the committee members were beneath contempt. The unadorned truth was that if you mashed tens of thousands of unemployed blacks, purples, or anybody else butt-to-butt in a wretched slum, you either had to add tranquilizers to their drinking water or expect problems. Until that reality was somehow changed, the idea of forcibly eliminating the drug trade was so much warm poop.

Fowler wondered: Did any of these senators actually believe that you could offer a kid in the slums a couple of hundred bucks to deliver a package two blocks away, and that the kid—remembering Michael Jordan saying, 'Don't be stupid. Don't do drugs'—would sprint to the nearest telephone and punch up the cops? A patriotic little volunteer. Did they?

The kids in the street knew how markets worked as well as Trump knew loans and Bo knew baseball.

Senator Boulanger looked like she was getting ready to begin.

Fowler inhaled deeply and let his breath out slowly to steady his nerves.

Graciela Boulanger gaveled the committee to order. "It is my special privilege to introduce as our first guest this after-

noon one of the nation's most successful, honored and respected law enforcement officers, and the new chief of police in
Miami's Dade Metro Police Department . . ."

When the committee finished with Chief Donald Fowler's
testimony on the solid progress being made in the war on
drugs, Senator Boulanger announced a short recess to accom-
modate what she called "unusual circumstances."

"I have asked Mr. Adrian Kyle's permission to postpone
his testimony until later in the day, and he has graciously
consented. If you'll all just bear with me, I'll be back in a few
minutes. And I do apologize for this unexpected break."

Without another word, Boulanger rose, circled the end of
the dais, and glided past the witnesses. She was aware that
heads were turning, following her, as she walked up the
visitors' aisle and through the public entrance to the hearing
room.

She knew that senators did not casually mix with proletarians in public. She also knew that a chairperson did not leave
his or her exalted seat to assist witnesses. By overtly departing
from the dictates of Senate ritual, Boulanger raised the curiosity
of both C-SPAN viewers and members of the press watching
the hearing.

Of course, Boulanger's colleagues knew why she had
drawn attention to herself by leaving the room: she had
obviously struck political gold and wanted her participation to
be seen, noted, and remembered by C-SPAN viewers—and not
just those from Montana.

Boulanger knew her idea of sending a committee investigator to report on the marimba could be a turning point in her
career, and she was determined to make the most of it.

There would come a time when the Democrats would try
again to run a woman for vice president. Unlike Geraldine
Ferraro, Boulanger, a former Missoula newspaper editor, was
squeaky clean. She was a hard worker and respected; she was
a forceful speaker; and she had no questionable husband to
drag her down. Before she went to Washington, her spouse
sold rabbit mash and egg layer in his feed store; he'd cut and
baled alfalfa to earn the down payment.

Boulanger strode all the way to the Senate parking lot,
where she had reserved five spaces for Ara Schott, and where
Schott and Special Agent Katherine Donovan waited in Schott's

15-year-old Ford sedan. Parked next to them were four Dodge passenger vans—rented by Schott out of Mixed Enterprises' committee budget—out of which now piled a troop of 11 Boy Scouts and a troop of 11 Girl Scouts plus their leaders, two men and two women. All Scouts and Scoutmasters were in uniform, with merit badges on display.

Schott, wiping perspiration from his upper lip with the side of his forefinger, got out of the Ford when he saw Boulanger coming and opened both back doors and trunk. Special Agent Donovan popped out to help.

The Ford bulged with travel valises, each with the colors and logo of a major-league baseball team. Twenty-two teams from both leagues were represented.

One by one, Schott slung the bags from the car onto the cement, piling them high, like so much laundry.

Burlane had said that the public had long ago become calloused to impossible numbers, and in fact newspapers had long ago given up on the zeros. It was a $25-million appropriation here, a $2.3-billion tunnel there. A $1-trillion national deficit was a vast, surreal sum that nobody comprehended.

He quoted former Illinois Senator Everett M. Dirksen—a million here, a million there, it added up—but the only thing that would impress a viewer with a couple of 20-dollar bills in his wallet was actually seeing the cash. Setting eyes on it.

Boulanger agreed.

Further, he had suggested they rule out dollies or wheeled luggage carriers. He said a person could wheel gold or feathers on wheels and nobody would know the difference. He wanted people to appreciate the weight of the bags as they were lugged into the hearing room and to the witness table. Owing to their size, the Scouts would have to struggle a bit. More dramatic that way.

Boulanger stared, amazed, as Schott finished his chore. "How much do those weigh?"

"Close to fourteen pounds each, Senator."

Senator Boulanger turned to the Scouts. "Do you kids think you can each handle one of these? Go ahead, try one and see."

As their leaders grinned, the Scouts, giggling, each grabbed a valise. Yes, they could handle the weight. It was a struggle for a couple of smaller girls, but they were confident they could manage. Besides, if they got tired, one of the adults would carry their valise to the front door of the committee room. None of the Scouts wanted to be left out. They all felt honored to be chosen.

"You all understand what you're supposed to do?"

Heads bobbed. More giggles. They had been drilled by James Burlane. They understood.

Boulanger said, "I'm curious, Mr. Schott. What teams are missing?"

Schott smiled. "The Boston Red Sox, both New York teams and the Los Angeles Dodgers. James says he's tired of reading about the major market teams. If he'd had his druthers, he'd have given the Chicago White Sox several bags. That's owing to Nellie Fox, his childhood hero."

"I see. Fair enough. Okay, kids, each grab a bag and let's go. Line up single file, please. If you need help with your bag, just holler."

The merry Scouts did as they were told.

Senator Graciela Boulanger, rather like Mary Poppins— with Ara Schott, Special Agent Donovan, and the Scoutmasters bringing up the rear—led the file of Scouts out of the parking lot.

54

With a calm, resolute stride, Senator Graciela Boulanger led the procession into the hearing room. The 22 boys and girls had been thoroughly rehearsed by James Burlane on what they were supposed to do.

As Boulanger took her seat behind the dais, the first Scout, a boy on the plumpish side, unzipped his California Angels valise and, with as much vigor as he could muster, dumped a pile of loose one-hundred-dollar bills onto the witness table.

Then a Girl Scout, a brunette beauty in the making, gave a shy peek at the senators watching from the dais, and did the same with the contents of her Minnesota Twins bag.

Both visitors and senators watched in silence as, one by one, the scouts emptied the contents of their valises onto the table and retreated to the back of the room where their leaders waited. When their chore was completed and a mountain of money on the table spilled onto the floor, the Scoutmasters and their troops quietly settled into empty seats at the back of the room.

Boulanger broke the silence. "You may take your places, Ms. Donovan, Mr. Schott."

Ara Schott and Katherine Donovan took their assigned seats side by side behind the table.

As he sat, Schott couldn't resist taking a peek at the previous witness, Metro Dade Chief of Police Donald Fowler, who sat almost directly behind him. Fowler's face was a stolid, enigmatic mask.

Burlane had suggested that Schott give Fowler a little wink, but that wasn't Schott's way. Besides, this was a committee of the United States Senate. Serious business. Schott's mouth was dry, and he smelled like a goat from nervous sweat.

Behind Senator Boulanger's left shoulder, the committee's legal counsel, Sheridan Harnar, licked his lips.

Boulanger gaveled the committee to order and proceeded as if the pile of money did not exist.

"I apologize for the delay, and thank you, Mr. Kyle, for your patience. With your indulgence, we will now hear from two unscheduled witness, Special Agent Katherine Donovan of the FBI's Organized Crime Unit, and Ara Schott, former Chief of Counterintelligence at the CIA, and now CEO of Mixed Enterprises. It was a Mixed Enterprises agent, James Burlane, who went to Latin America and Miami as this committee's investigator.

"We'll all get time to read and digest Mr. Burlane's four-hundred-page report before we meet in executive session to ask him questions. Have I got this straight so far, Mr. Schott?"

"Yes, ma'am, you do."

"And can you tell us about the money on the table before you? I'm sure everybody's wondering."

"Yes, ma'am. Mr. Burlane saved all the money he made smuggling cocaine, and it is his wish that the committee and the public get to see, literally, the fruits of his adventures. The Scouts here today are from my neighborhood in Montgomery county. Mr. Burlane thought it would be an educational experience for them to participate and watch the democratic process in action."

"They are entirely welcome, Mr. Schott."

"If there are no objections, as payment to the Scouts for their help, Mr. Burlane proposes, at committee expense, to take them and their families to an Orioles double-header, followed by all the pizza they can handle."

Boulanger, suppressing a grin, glanced left and right at her colleagues. "There are no objections, Mr. Schott. So ordered."

"In accordance with the contract he signed with your counsel, Mr. Harnar, Mr. Burlane kept a strict accounting of his earnings and expenses. He made two twelve-hundred-kilo trips for some Bolivian gentlemen. He was paid two thousand dollars a kilo, a total of four-point-eight million dollars for both flights. He made four fifteen-hundred-kilo flights for the Colombian drug baron, Guillermo Banda-Conchesa, for which he was paid twenty-five hundred dollars a kilo, a total of fifteen million dollars. Each of the twenty-two travel bags emptied by the Scouts contained close to fourteen pounds of hundred-dollar bills, about nine hundred thousand dollars. That's a total of two-hundred-seventy-three-point-six pounds of bills worth nineteen-point-eight million dollars.

"I should mention that Mr. Burlane crashed his forty-year-old D-18 Twin Beech at an airstrip in Nicaragua. He regrets the loss, but Señor Conchesa generously replaced it with a brand new King-Air at no cost to the committee or the taxpayers."

Boulanger smiled. "As I understand it, Mr. Burlane would like to give his formal recommendations to the committee this afternoon, also in the form of a videotape, which he would like us to see before we read his full report. Is that correct?"

"Yes, ma'am."

"Are there any objections?" Senator Boulanger looked left and right.

The committee members had their eyes riveted to the money. Audiotapes had sent Richard Nixon packing from the White House. Boulanger's references to videotapes had them extra alert. To be able to see conspirators as well as hear them was extra deadly.

Nobody objected or raised a question, not even Senator Anders Gittes of Michigan, an airhead with a mouth that flapped like a shutter in a gusty wind.

Katherine Donovan peered over the mound of one-hundred-dollar bills as Graciela Boulanger signaled for floor attendants to begin rolling portable television monitors into the room so senators, witnesses, and spectators could share in the tape that would be shown on C-SPAN.

As the technicians did their thing, Boulanger—accepting a pile of papers from Counsel Harnar—killed time by reviewing the schedule of upcoming witnesses and sessions.

Katherine remembered that her sister Helen had been an

exceptionally happy but ridiculously bald baby. Baby Helen had loved it when the family went to a crab feed at a place where the management spread butcher paper on the tables and everybody tied stupid paper bibs around their throats. The crabs, fresh in from Chesapeake Bay, were piled high, and Katherine helped her parents pick the snow-white meat for Helen, who smashed it in her mouth with both hands. The dirtier and crazier jolly Helen's face became, the more the family loved it.

Katherine remembered family outings in Annapolis. She and her mother loved to cruise the shops that featured everything from homemade dolls to hand-carved duck decoys and watercolors, while their father adjourned to a bar with a television set tuned to whatever ball game was in season. Katherine's mother once took a photograph of baby Helen in the arms of a handsome midshipman from the Naval Academy in his spiffy white uniform. The midshipman had been pleased to pose for the picture. Happy little Helen, enjoying being in his arms, had just beamed.

A white uniform.

White as crab meat.

When Katherine was home from college at Northwestern University, the family took day trips. She remembered cruising Amish country outside Lancaster, Pennsylvania, one of their favorite outings. The wheels of the horse-drawn Amish carriages had literally worn ruts in the macadam highways. As the Wingates drove past Blue Balls, their father inevitably kept his women entertained with off-color remarks, with Helen punching him playfully on the shoulder for being so naughty.

Once, they stopped for a dinner prepared by black-clad Amish women to raise funds for the Bird-in-Hand volunteer fire department, and Helen, to everybody's amazement, was able to consume four pieces of shoofly pie.

And Katherine, already an FBI agent, remembered going to Helen's high school graduation. The happy, bald-headed baby had grown up to become a slender blonde beauty with a scholarship to Johns Hopkins University.

From Chesapeake crabs through shoofly pie to crack cocaine.

Katherine's mouth turned dry at the memory of her parents' eyes, so very sad and empty and uncomprehending as they buried their younger daughter. Her lips tightened at the thought of the disheartening majority of the senators in front of her who preferred comfortable goods and evils, blacks and whites, to the complicated grays of the truth.

The truth was that not all drugs were the same; their addictive qualities were different, as were the consequences of their addiction. The word *drug* meant everything and so almost nothing; *drug war* meant even less.

And for those drawn to the pure white of the pious and righteous, in which their opinions were always correct— unsullied by actually having to think—the moral fervor was nothing less than addicting.

Katherine wondered: Was righteousness more addicting than cocaine or heroin or the obscene pile of money on the table in front of her?

The monitors were in place and ready to go.

Boulanger interrupted Katherine's reverie. "These are the sound recordings and videotapes made by you and the committee's investigator, Mr. Burlane. Is that right, Ms. Donovan?"

Katherine, speaking over the pile of one-hundred-dollar bills, her voice firm, said, "Yes, ma'am. Ten days ago in Biscayne Bay. Mr. Burlane operated the video camera with infrared night vision, and I worked the parabolic recording microphone. Of course the quality of the videotape is not as good as you get with a regular camera with good light, but you should be able to identify the participants easily enough."

55

James Burlane, standing in from of Ara Schott's TV set with a bottle of Beck's in his left hand and a smoked herring in his right, wiggled in delight. He finished off the herring, chasing it with a hit of beer, and licked his fingers.

The camera panned the wide-eyed senators on the dais.

For Burlane, the most frustrating thing about watching the action on television was that only part of Sheridan Harnar's face—his ear, some salt-and-pepper hair, and part of his mustache and jaw—was visible when the cameras were on Senator Boulanger. Only when Harnar leaned to his right to confer with his aide, sitting directly behind Boulanger, could his entire face be seen.

The cameras taped the witnesses from the committee's point of view. When they focused on Ara or Katherine, Burlane could see Chief Fowler and Mima Martinez behind them.

The infrared videotape began with the legend BISCAYNE BAY, FLORIDA, JUNE 20 scrolling across the bottom. Three figures around an elegant table on a patio, drinks in hand: Donald Fowler, Mima Martinez, and the man with salt-and-pepper hair—the committee's legal counsel, Sheridan Harnar.

Burlane watched Harnar speak to an intent Fowler at Fowler's Biscayne Bay hideaway:

Harnar took a drink, raising his glass with a gesture that said he was finished with chitchat. He said to Fowler, "Señor Banda-Conchesa wants reassurance that you can give the public a solution to the dog-food killings once Dersham goes under. We can't have you tarred with it at the beginning of your tenure as chief."

Burlane wished he could see Harnar's reaction during the playing of the tape. Unlimited opportunity for treacherous action on behalf of the drug lords wasn't enough for him. No, no, no. The motherfucker had tried to have Burlane torched in ambush. In bed!

Well, shit like that pissed Burlane off most royally.

Mima stamped her foot angrily and bunched her face at Harnar. "Look at all the marimba players we delivered. Look at the arrests and headlines. Not one of them was a Conchesa player. Only your competition."

With Burlane's camera tight on Mima, a C-SPAN super scrolled across the bottom of the screen: CARMELA 'MIMA' MAR-TINEZ, A KEY FIGURE IN A DADE METRO POLICE STING, APPEARED BEFORE THE COMMITTEE IN CLOSED SESSION AS AN EXPERT WITNESS.

Burlane remembered fishing for yellowtail off the Florida Keys with Roberto Guzmán and Luis Fernandez, one a sleaze, one an honest cop. Staying honest wasn't easy, as they pointed out; it was difficult to ignore the goodies peeling off the chum ball.

Mima narrowed her eyes and waggled her finger in Fowler's face. "With our help, you personally demonstrated that the war on drugs is working. We made you a national hero. Profiled on '60 Minutes.' If it hadn't been for us."

And when public servants got to the succulent squid, nearly as white as Señor Conchesa's cocaine, there were those, inevitably, who could not resist.

Burlane went into the kitchen for another Beck's.

As he returned, Fowler explained to Harnar his plan for blaming the out-of-control Doberman pinscher on a screw-up by Roberto Guzmán. *Mima Martinez said, "They'll never catch Marimba. Never."*

C-SPAN returned to the committee room, and the camera cut from Harnar to Fowler to Mima Martinez. They sat in shock, ashen-faced.

Behind Ara and Katherine and the table piled high with

greenbacks, Chief Fowler looked left and right, then up at the ceiling.

Beside him, Mima Martinez stared at her lap.

Sheridan Harnar swallowed. Banda-Conchesa's man opened his mouth to say something, but what? He closed it. He too was suddenly fascinated by something in his lap.

Senator Graciela Boulanger banged her gavel hard, once, twice, three times, to settle the commotion in the hearing room. Ever since James Burlane had come to her with his revelation, she had been anticipating this moment, and she was not disappointed.

She had resolved to be cool and calm in her moment of triumph. This was a moment the viewing public truly needed to see, a genuine public servant in action, and she did not want to disappoint them or the boys and girls in the back of the room.

"Order, please. This committee is still in session." She banged her gavel again, gave it a hard whack. "We will have order. Those failing to comply will be escorted from the room. We have no votes scheduled for the floor this afternoon, and there being no other agent business, we will proceed as planned. We gave Mr. Burlane permission to present his recommendations to the committee in the form of a videotape, and we will honor our word."

Senator Anders Gittes, glancing at Harnar, said, "I . . ." He blinked, mouth at the ready, but brain uncertain.

Boulanger raised an eyebrow. "Do you have an objection, Mr. Gittes?"

Gittes glanced at his colleagues, who all wanted to know what other surprises Burlane had to offer. "No, ma'am. No objection."

Boulanger said, "The honorable gentleman from Michigan should know all of us are startled and enraged at this turn of events."

"Uh, yes," Gittes said.

"We now know the truth, at least, and in the coming days we should learn more details as to how it came to happen. For that, I think, we can all be thankful.

"With minor differences, Mr. Burlane says, the proposed solution offered in this videotape is precisely his recommendation to us. He did not show me the tape, which was made by public television. I'm seeing it for the first time along with the rest of you. May we now view the tape, please."

The tape, with INTERVIEW WITH GUILLERMO PENA DE LA BANDA-CONCHESA, MEDELLIN, COLUMBIA superimposed at the bottom, opened with Banda-Conchesa and a reporter sitting at a white table under a red, white, and green parasol. They were by the side of an enormous swimming pool that featured both three- and six-meter diving boards at one end.

Conchesa smiled. "Yes, you Yankees got the poor Gachas and Manuel Noriega. You had to invade Panama to get Noriega. Look at what all that cost you. Billions of dollars. The Colombian government allowed American troops to kill Colombians on their own soil and try Colombians in American courts—may all Colombians hang their heads in shame.

"And what did it accomplish, all that flexing of Yankee muscle? Nada, *señor. It accomplished* nada. *You Americans claim to believe in the marketplace. Let the market do it, you say. This is your political ideology. Here, you have created a black market for cocaine and complain bitterly about the results. Do the intelligent thing for once. Eliminate the black market, señor."*

56

It was nearly dusk when little Terry Newsome, seven, of Homestead, Florida, saw the big black dog standing in the lengthening shadows.

Was the dog watching him?

Terry liked dogs. He had a big black dog, too. Maybe not as big as this dog, but pretty big. That is, his family had a dog. His dad, actually. Sammy was half Labrador, half English pointer. The only parts of him that weren't black were his yellow eyes.

The Newsomes had bought Sammy out of a paper bag in a Bi-Mart parking lot and raised him since he was a puppy. The joke was, Sammy didn't know he wasn't human. Terry could ride him and pull his tail and do what he wanted, and Sammy never seemed to care. If Sammy was in a car and started squirming, everybody knew he had to take a leak. And he never took a leak in the house, either; he always waited until he was let outside.

When Terry's dad went somewhere in his pickup and didn't take Sammy, Sammy got sore and acted all put-upon.

Sammy's only really lousy habit when he found a dead animal and rolled around in the rotting corpse on his back.

Yuch! When he did that, Terry's dad got real, real irked. Terry got to drool pink dishwashing soap on Sammy's back while his dad, swearing always that the stench was enough to gag a maggot, hosed him off.

When Sammy was hungry and hadn't been fed, he sometimes paced, as this dog was doing now as it watched Terry.

Terry wondered if the dog was hungry. He trotted toward the dog with his hand outstretched. "Here, doggie, doggie, doggie. Here, boy. Are you hungry? Would you like to eat?"